Dietrich
the Kalteis
Deadbeat
Club

Dietrich Kalteis
the Deadbeat Club

ECW PRESS
TORONTO

TO ANDIE,
WHO ENCOURAGED ME TO WRITE
AND TAUGHT ME TO DREAM

. . . GANGBANG

THE HUMMER rolled off the Port Mann Bridge and took the Number One, turning onto East Hastings, into Bumpy Rosco's turf. Nav Pudi sat in back, hidden by the tinted glass, laughing at something Bij Kumar, the kid driving, said. The kid hadn't stopped talking since they drove up from the armpit of the city. Nav put it down to first-time jitters, remembering his own first time.

It was his sway that got the kid coming along, Nav thinking he was ready, sticking him behind the wheel of the Hummer H2, letting him drive, letting him get a taste. The other two were hard guys, Rajeev and Rosh Ramin. Guys he would stake his life on: Rajeev grinning from the passenger seat, Rosh clapping the kid on the back.

Going to take out one of Bumpy Rosco's meth labs — a case of tit for tat — the Indo Army coming for payback for the grow-op Rosco's people fragged a week ago: a pipe bomb tossed through a window left two of theirs dead, twenty grand of weed and equipment destroyed.

It was an old, rotting trailer by the tracks behind the grain terminal along the waterfront, drums and pallets stacked next to it, graffiti on the front and down the sides. The tipoff came from a junkie swearing it was there, saw it with his own eyes, betting his life for a fix.

"How many you think?" Bij asked.

"Should be empty," Nav said, knowing it wasn't. What was the point of payback if somebody didn't pay? He told the kid, "Guys just come and cook, you know. Mostly at night."

Bij nodded, driving past the PNE grounds, quiet this time of year, a couple of weeks before Christmas. A jolly Santa on a sign wishing everybody *Season's Greetings*. Not a holiday any of them celebrated, Bij saying, "Some fat fuck in a red suit comes down a chimney in my hood, he's getting popped for sure." The others grinning.

The knobby tires rumbled on the asphalt. Felt good being behind the wheel, the five-thousand-pound king of the road, Bij rhyming off the street names as they passed: Slocan, Penticton, Kamloops, Nanaimo. Eyes straight ahead.

Nav knew the kid's hands were wet on the wheel, the Ruger heavy under his jacket. Far cry from pitching for the Surrey Chiefs, best closer the team had ever seen, but not good enough to get him into the minors. Fuck that. Bij was moving on, wanting to get his tat, the scorpion they all had on their right hand, the tail curling around the wrist.

Nav told him to make a right up ahead. Rosh stuck a magazine in the Kalashnikov, checking it over, the half-crate of C13 grenades under his foot, green globes packed with C-4, asking Bij if he ever pitched one of these babies, put one right across the plate. It got Bij laughing, saying he wouldn't mind.

Coming up on Victoria, calling the street name, Bij slowed for the light, amber to red, Nav telling him not to beat it, keep it cool, repeating for him to hang a right. A female cyclist drew even, waiting for the light, Rosh and Rajeev checking her out.

It was a white Uprise bread truck on the opposite corner that got Nav's attention, the blue-and-green logo on the back, the four-ways flashing, the driver getting out, adjusting his cap and tapping the side with his hand, going around the back and lifting the rear door. A bread truck parked in front of a Scotiabank, across from a Petro-Can station, neither business carrying bread.

Nav caught it a second too late, pulling his pistol, yelling for the kid to make the turn. The back door of the bread truck rolled up, and a second man, older than the one in the cap, hopped down out of the back, raising an RPG to his shoulder, stepping into the street away from the truck, putting the Hummer in the crosshairs. The man smiled around a bagel he had in his mouth; the cyclist shouted something and tried to move.

Grabbing the door handle, Nav threw himself from the Hummer, the rocket striking the grill, blowing the truck off the pavement, lighting up East Hastings, the half case of C13 grenades adding to the blast. Last thing Nav remembered was an axle dropping in front of him, somebody yelling. Pain and the smell of skin and hair. Then nothing.

. . . MESSAGE IN A BOTTLE

THE ASIAN-LOOKING kid went by Airdog, kept the skateboard tucked under his arm, the stickers, scrapes and worn trucks showing on the bottom of the board. The hoodie read *Skate, Eat, Sleep, Repeat*, covering cargos worn low. Even with the rasta cap topping the Guy Fieri hair, the kid barely rose above the roof of Travis Rainey's ride, one of those big, square Chryslers. This one black with Lambo doors that opened like Dumbo ears.

"Up for some cheese rolling?" Airdog asked, smiling.

"Know a guy named Stevens?" Travis stepped out, a couple decades older and a foot taller than the kid, a solid frame inside an Eddie Bauer windbreaker. The bottle of Hop Head in his hand was half gone. Travis was never much of a drinker, but he loved a good breakfast brew.

"Grey? Yeah, sure, who doesn't?" Airdog said.

Travis let the kid size him up, silver hair over the ears done like wing tips like some gangster he'd seen on HBO. Drinking beer on a Sunday morning had the kid thinking American tourist.

"So where do I find him?" Travis put the bottle to his mouth, swallowing and turning his head for a look at the overflow lot. Empty except for a couple of backpackers gathering their stuff from the trunk of their car and heading toward the slopes.

Airdog was still checking him out. Travis catching him looking at the shoes that weren't cop-issue. Then through the Chrysler's tinted windows: no wife, no kids, no bike on a rack, no hiking gear in back, too square to be here to catch the Dudes over at the Boot. So he was either up here hunting mountain pussy or was one of the guys Grey had warned him about.

"If you're looking to score . . ." Airdog said.

Travis's mouth twisted into a smile. Tipping the bottle again, he leaned back against his door, not in a hurry now, saying, "You help me out with Stevens, I'd appreciate it?" He didn't know Grey Stevens to see him, just talked to him on the phone the one time, explaining his options, giving him a couple of days to think about it, told him he'd be coming to see him.

Airdog set the board down, one foot on it, and he peeled off his cap, hair spilling out. Shaking out a Baggie, he said, "What I got here's the Holy Grail, dude. Eight Miles High. Same as you'd get from Grey."

Travis looked at the dime bag, then back across the lot at the cluster of floodlights and security cameras mounted on the light standard the city put in last year. Far enough away from the cameras, quiet like you'd expect on a Sunday morning in the middle of August.

5

"Don't sweat it, dude. We're cool here," Airdog said, thinking he could handle this. "Got the donut boys trained to look the other way."

Polishing off the beer, Travis checked out the label on the bottle.

"So, how about it?" Airdog jiggled the bags. "Do you a double dime bag for say, twenty-five. Primo nug, man." Betting this crusty old dude wouldn't know kush from ditch weed.

"Want to talk to the guy who's got more than a dime bag in a hat," Travis said.

Word was Grey Stevens picked up where his uncle Rubin left off, running a string of grow houses, producing decent pot, running it through a couple of ex-bikers and a bunch of street-corner musicians, Stevens fronting as a bartender at some place called the Cellar. Didn't sound like much of a threat, this whole territory wide open since the Sabers MC went down to crown prosecutors. Bumpy Rosco sending Travis up here to secure new business before the Indo Army showed up. Bumpy's people mixing it up with the Indos over territory down in the city. Travis firing the rocket from the bread truck set things in motion, bodies stacking up for the last eight months.

Travis knew the ex-bikers that ran the weed for Grey Stevens and had already had a word with Benny Rivers and Ivan Glinka, the two of them knowing better than to stand in his way. Said they were making one last run, then they'd come over, work for the Roscos.

"What are we talking, an eighth, an ounce?" Airdog asked.

"Talking about all you got." Travis wasn't smiling now.

Stuffing the bag into his cap, Airdog slapped it back on his head. "For that, I got to make a call."

Travis waved a hand, meaning go ahead.

Taking a burner from a pocket, Airdog punched in Grey's number, getting a busy tone, then trying a different number, saying, "Yeah. Me. Got a dude here talking large." Waited, said yeah a couple more times. Turned back to Travis, saying, "My man wants to know —"

"Here . . ." Travis snatched the phone from the kid's hand, thinking he had Grey on the line, saying, "Got tired of waiting."

The voice on the phone said, "Who the fuck's this?"

Not Grey Stevens.

These guys weren't taking him serious. Travis said, "I'm the guy up here hitting the slopes." Flipping the bottle in his hand, he smashed it into the kid's face.

Airdog went down, didn't know what happened, his front teeth knocked out clean. Blood flowed from his mouth, his eyes round as plates. Touching a hand to his mouth, he looked at the blood.

"What the fuck's going on?" Mojo barked into the other end of the phone.

"Think you fuckheads call that a bonk." Travis kicked the skateboard away and planted a foot on Airdog's chest, kept him down.

"Listen, asshole, put the Dog back on right the fuck now."

Reaching under the jacket, Travis pulled the black P5 from his belt. Kneeling, he stuck the short barrel into Airdog's mouth, kept him from yelling, "gun," stuck it all the way to the tonsils, getting blood on the blued steel.

Gagging for air, Airdog wished Mojo would stop pissing this guy off. Banging the barrel around the kid's molars, Travis pulled it out, wiping blood on the hoodie that read *Skate, Eat, Sleep, Repeat*. "Tell Stevens I'm waiting." Disconnecting, he said to Airdog, "Next time you're out here, kid, you're selling for me. You got me?" He dropped the phone, pocketed the Walther, waiting for a nod, then he picked up the two teeth, holding them between his fingers, thinking they looked smaller than they should. "Hold your uppers like this, by the crown, see? Not by the root, and get them in milk or saline fast as you can."

Airdog bobbed his head, looking like he was going into shock.

"No water, got it? Get your ass to a dentist fast as you can. Any luck, he'll replant them."

Taking the teeth the way he was shown, Airdog said thanks, blood spilling from his mouth.

Climbing into the Chrysler, Travis pulled the Dumbo-ear door closed, rolled down the window and, on a last note, said, "Oh, and kid, you really think that yellow hair looks right? Think again." Then he drove a wide arc around the surveillance cams, past a sign posted at the entrance promising SmartPark meters were to be installed, the city turning this into a pay lot. Travis headed for the Village, arm out the window, the early sun feeling warm.

Man, this place had changed. Last time he was up had to be ten years ago, back when the Sabers controlled the dope trade, Grey Stevens's uncle growing for them, a guy who knew how to do it. Left the distribution end to someone else. And if Grey Stevens was smart, he'd do the same. Still had time.

Fishing out his own cell, Travis punched in a number, sounding pissed when he spoke. "Where the hell are you?" Not liking the answer, he said to hurry the fuck up and clicked off. Glancing at his watch, he figured he had time for a bite before the next piece of business.

. . . JUST A FUCKING CAR

Dara Addie was thinking it, smart enough not to say it, sticking her hand out the passenger window, black fingernails riding the air current, something she did as a kid in her mom's Olds. The guy behind the Camaro's wheel was around the age her dad had been when her parents split, hair gelled and combed back, narrow face, hawk nose, chest hair sprouting from the half-buttoned shirt, a GQ jacket, shiny like it had been varnished.

Nick Rosco wasn't the first guy to use a car like a dick extension. She got a flash of Mr. Walden, her tenth-grade lit teacher back at Britannia, flirting with her. Walden wore his shirt like that, half-buttoned, with his colored pens in the pocket, a comb-over, puffing out his chest like some bird doing its courtship ritual, asking her to stay after class for some one-on-one — tutoring, he called it — offering her a lift home in his Boss Mustang, horsepower and leather seats. Get some on his way home to the burbs, the wife and kids waiting. It didn't happen then, sure wasn't happening now. Dara, wagging her hand in the breeze, the skull ring on her finger.

So far, this guy Nick hadn't shut up about the car, roaring up the 99, miles of pines flashing by. Since they left the Drive two hours ago, he'd barely mentioned the job he wanted done. He was going on about the car being an ss, inferno orange with the special trim package, talked about high output and horses under the hood and whatever the fuck vvt was.

The Camaro purred along the Sea-to-Sky, Nick doing fifty over the limit going down the long cut, his hair giving off a hint of grapefruit scent. A leather hand on the wheel, holes around the knuckles, Foreigner blaring from the speakers, Nick letting her know they were *numero uno* in his book, the greatest rock band of all time — fuck the Beatles, fuck the Stones — pointing a leather finger in the air, throwing in a "bar none" and "end of story." Then singing along about a fever of a hundred and three.

Shoot me now. Dara tried to tune out him and his flaccid rock. Could ask him to change it, but it could get worse: 'N SYNC or Simply Red, shit her mother listened to. Probably seem rude to stick in her earbuds, click on her iPod, her hand swishing the air out the window.

The only other thing Nick talked about the whole way up was all the road construction still going on long after the Winter Olympics, dust blowing all over his new finish, saying if he got so much as one stone chip . . . Letting it hang.

Dara thinking, what do you expect, taking a job lead from Cam, her ex, who worked stock at the Urban Fare where she worked the cash. Likely pulled the ad off Craigslist, Cam always trying to get back with her.

Making the call, she agreed to the rendezvous at East

Side Mario's, Dara being dumb enough to let Nick interview her right at the table over cheese dip and boomers, asking if she had a license, asking to see it. Pretty stupid showing a stranger shit with her address on it. Like duh. But here they were on the drive to Whistler, Nick making the first run with her, showing her the ropes, hadn't even mentioned how much per hour.

"Not worried about getting a ticket?" she said, looking at the speedometer.

That got him going on a new tangent. The only ticket he ever got in his life was the time he beat a red. The fucking traffic camera at Marine and Taylor Way nailed him, some pig behind a desk sending the ticket along with the photo, his ex-wife opening the mail, seeing the shot of him beating the red, the chick on the passenger side not her. A tasty piece of evidence, her bottom-feeding lawyer called it. Sure, Nick could laugh about it now, having his privacy invaded like that, the bloodletting of a savage divorce, Nick keeping the lawyer's accident to himself, the Lincoln's brakes failing coming off the Ironworkers Bridge, the car skewered by the guardrail, the lawyer lucky to escape with minor injuries. Nothing the cops could prove, Nick and his ex coming to a settlement without further legal representation. Right before she left town.

Then he was back on about the Camaro, talking about rack-and-pinion this and close-ratio that, Dara letting her hand ride the breeze, thinking her nails could use a touch-up.

"Press this button, the bitch practically drives itself," he was saying, turning his head and checking her out. Hair the color of shoe polish, enough makeup for an ancient Egyptian, a silver stud on the side her nose. Could be more metal under the jeans; he couldn't tell. He bet there was. Bet he'd find out, too. Her skin was pale, the chick a bit on the boney side, small tits. But he liked the pouty lips painted stop-sign red. Had a fragile thing going. Point was, in spite of Travis Rainey and his old man telling him no, Nick was showing up with this chick, and she was going to mule for them, just like he wanted. Time for Travis and the old man to understand who was running this show.

"How much longer?" she asked, telling herself a job's a job. Whatever it was, it would get her out of her mother's basement suite. The two of them had been like oil and water since the old man split, getting worse all the time.

"You even hear a word I'm saying?"

She glanced at him, the breeze lifting her hand. "Yeah, but you still haven't said exactly what it is I'll be doing."

He lightened up. "Guess I been going on about the new ride, huh? Just picked her up; you know how it is, boys and their toys."

"Yeah, it's a cool ride," she said, "and I love the new leather smell, but . . ."

"Can smell it's Italian, right?"

"Sure."

"Waited three months for her. Special order."

"Cool."

"You're the first one on that seat."

First one what? This guy was creeping her out.

Reaching into the armrest compartment, he slipped on

aviator shades, the sun hiking to the tips of the treetops. Taking a vial of Binaca, he sprayed his tongue, his eyes watering from the hit of mint.

Watching him do it — the sniff of Binaca mixing with the Old Spice and grapefruit — she tried swinging the conversation back to the work, asking about benefits.

"What it is, you do this run every Friday. No punch clock, no shit like that. Just get in the car and drive, get it done. And don't ask questions."

"Yeah, you covered that. What you haven't said is how much or what it is I'm running."

"Two-fifty a week and all you do is drive. A box of restaurant supplies in your trunk. You pick up two envelopes. One you keep. Be waiting at the front desk of the Wilmott every week. Ask for Stan. Stay the night if you want. I keep a suite, bed's comfy and the place serves a decent continental breakfast. Then you bring me the other envelope. Other than that, keep your receipts, I pay the gas, you pay anything else. Pretty much all you got to know. Sweet deal, you ask me. And could lead to more, a lot more."

"This the car I'm driving?"

He looked over the top of the shades, like maybe she was kidding. "Asked you back at the Drive if you had wheels."

"Asked if I had a license," she said. "Showed it to you, remember?"

He held the look over the shades, his front wheels crossing the solid lines.

"Fuck! Watch out! Jesus!" Her hands clutched the dash.

The driver of the lumber truck rushing southbound blared his horn. A full load of logs chained on the back of the rig. Heart pounding along to the music, Dara heard Nick say something about this baby having airbags all the way around.

"Look, you got wheels or you don't?"

Dara was speed-thinking; she could pick up a beater for a lick and a promise through this guy Cam knew, pretty sure her Visa would handle it, pay it on the installment plan. "Yeah, I got wheels, not like this, but it'll get from A to B."

He told her to remember when it got white up here, meaning winter, the smokeys checked for snow tires; they'd turn her back if she didn't have them, something he'd learned the hard way.

"Yeah, no problem." She let go of the dash, her hand going back out the window, asking again what she'd be running.

"Told you, restaurant supplies. And what did I say about questions? Sweet gig is what it is. All you got to know, doll."

"When do you need to know by?"

Again the look over the glasses. "Thought we were past that back on the Drive. Look, kid, tell me right now, you want this or not, 'cause if you don't . . ." Nick was close to kicking her skinny ass out, let her thumb her way back to the city.

Two-fifty for a run once a week beat taking crap from the trophy wives passing through the cash at Urban Fare. Middle-aged bitches with their fake nails and boob jobs. "I'm in."

He nodded, looking at the road ahead.

Only thing she hadn't decided was whether to go lesbo or herpes when Nick tried putting his hands on her like she knew he would.

"Right move," Nick said, his face crinkling behind the shades. His cell rang, and he pulled it from inside his jacket, straightening in his leather seat, explaining to somebody on the other end why he wasn't there yet, blaming the fucking construction. Whoever was on the line wound him up, his lips becoming a tight line by the time he clicked off.

She pulled her hand inside and pressed the button, closing the window, asking, "So when do I start?"

"When I tell you."

"Drive, that's it, all I got to do?"

"That and don't ask questions."

After a few beats, "Who unloads the car? This guy Stan?"

He looked at her.

"Right. That was a question."

Sitting quiet till they passed the *Welcome to Whistler* sign, Nick downshifted, a smooth motion, recovered and smiled at her, his gloved hand moving past the shifter, patting her arm. "Guess I should say congrats." He rested his hand on the knob.

"Thanks."

"Gonna check in at the Wilmott, introduce you to Stan, unpack my bag. We can do some unwinding, then I got another guy I want you to meet."

"Another guy?"

Nick looked at her over the shades, downshifted and patted her arm again, Dara wanting to know when they were heading back.

A sci-fi woman's voice cut in over Foreigner singing about dirty white boys, the navigation system telling him to take the Village Gate Boulevard exit coming up on the right in fifty meters.

"Something you ought to know," Dara said, lifting the gloved hand off her arm, putting it back on the knob, thinking lesbo was the way to go.

. . . DUCKING IN

"Fucking asshole."

Dara said it loud enough for the tourist family at the entrance to the Summit to turn on the stone steps. Dad, mom and two kids looking at her. The doorman held the door, dressed up like a palace guard, minus the bearskin hat. He kept an eye on the skinny punk girl, shoeblack hair in spikes, nose stud, talking to herself. She kept walking, the doorman ushering the family through to their five-star stay, two hops towing in their Tommy Bahama luggage.

Welcome to Whistler, my ass. Everything about the place was stone and glass. Cold, without charm. Made her want to get on the next Greyhound and get back to the vibe of the Drive. Vancouver's Little Italy. Sort her shit out. Get a real job. Get her own place. Living in her mother's basement was driving her nuts, making her do crazy shit like take a job with a psycho like Nick, ride up here in his orange car.

Checking the rearviews of the angle-parked line of Audis, Beemers and Benzes, she caught her own reflection in the Northlands storefront, afraid Nick might sneak behind her, get even for punching his nuts.

Soon as he pulled into the Village, he got touchy-feely, put the leather hand on her leg, moving his lips toward hers, not buying her lesbo bit, said he wanted to get their working relationship off on the right foot, promising a bonus. Snatching his flip key from the ignition while the car was rolling, she gouged the hand grabbing her thigh. With the engine switched off, Nick was screaming, forced to fight the frozen steering, hand bleeding, stomping the spongy brakes, trying to avoid the curb.

Grabbing his Binaca while he clutched the wheel, she maced his face, then threw a fist to his nutsack, her skull ring leaving no doubt about her hands-off policy. Jumping out of the rolling car, screaming at him, she scraped a new racing stripe into the orange paint, then tossed his flip key down a sewer grate and hurried into the Village, this strange Disneyland North. Running till she felt safe. Asking the busker sitting outside playing his musical saw if the food was any good, Dara ducked into this place called Gretzky's.

Air thick with fryer oil, she took the last seat, a red vinyl swivel at the counter. The bookends on either side of her had *cop* written all over them, one tall with blond hair going grey, not bad-looking for an older guy. The fat one on her right might have been a jock back in high school, had the shoulders for it; the red plaid sport jacket cried school band, loud enough to be a crime scene in its own right. He glanced at her through orange-tinted glasses, shifting on his stool. His jacket hiked up, ass crack blooming above his pants, Dara thinking he could use a Brazilian.

Telling the waitress coffee, she settled her feet on the rail, watching the girl shuffle off down the counter.

Still feeling the sting of Nick's slap, she took a napkin, glanced around and started tearing bits from the corner. Three guys her own age with ball caps on backwards got up from a booth, goofing with each other, gathering their longboards, the one with the joint behind his ear taking the tab to the cash.

Travis Rainey entered and glanced around, shoving past the guys with the longboards, looking pissed. He took a booth by the window, as out of place as she felt, eyes colder than any winter, two-tone hair, silver over his ears, done to look like wings. Picking up a menu, he spread his elbows on the table and read the daily specials.

The coffee came, steam rising from the mug, Dara keeping an eye out for Nick, looking to the washroom sign, hoping for a back way out.

The cop on her left sipped down to the dregs. Making a face, Detective Lance Edwards pushed the mug away. Plaid was Jimmy Gallo, dipping a link sausage in his sunny-side eggs, cramming it into his mouth, working on a crossword on the back of the local rag. Eating low and loud. His fork was going like it was automated, shoving egg in after the sausage like he was stoking a boiler, his goatee doing nicely as a bib. Swiping the back of his hand across his mouth, he wrote in a word, let go a silent burp.

The place hadn't been busy when Lance and Jimmy came in fifteen minutes ago, but it was filling up fast, Gretzky's being a breakfast hot spot in spite of the fare. Lance took in the girl sitting between them, guessing her story. Her cheek looking red like it had been slapped. "Cream?" he asked her.

"What?"

"For your coffee." Jiggling the creamer, he noted the skull ring as she took it. Saw her looking at the guy that came in with the silver tips in his hair, sitting behind them at the booth.

"Yeah, thanks. Detective, right?"

Grinning that she made him, Lance said, "Not from around here, right?" The cop's way of placing people.

"Is anybody?" Dara poured cream, watching it swirl, expecting it to curdle, the coffee more grey than brown.

"You up for the cheese rolling?" Jimmy spoke around mashed sausage, not looking up from the crossword.

"Cheese rolling? That for real?"

"What they do," Jimmy said, swallowing, "they take eleven-pound wheels of cheese and roll them down a hill."

"Yeah right."

"I swear. Right over by Base II." Jimmy looked across the tinted shades, said, "Contestants chase them down, fastest one takes home the cheese."

She caught the hard nut in her peripheral, making her feel uneasy in spite of the bookends with badges. "Think you guys are pulling my leg."

"Why would we do that?" Jimmy pushed in the last bit of toast, dripping with egg, then wrote in a four-letter word for *twist*.

She tried her coffee, added more cream, tried it again, tossed in sugar, stirred it around.

"So if it's not the cheese, got to be here for the rock and roll, right?" Jimmy said, dabbing his napkin at the grease puddles at either side of his mouth, catching her looking at the guy in the booth again, then at the door. Jimmy may have been lazy, but he was more than a sharp dresser. This girl was running from something.

"Sure not the coffee." She set the mug down, getting up, signaling the waitress.

"Yeah, go figure anyone messing up a pot this bad," Lance said, eager to get going himself.

"You come in again, go for the key lime," Jimmy advised her, scratching out a word, writing in a new one.

"I'll keep it in mind." Dara rose and dug for change, asking if this town had a Greyhound stop.

Swinging by with the carafe, the waitress offered a top-up. Telling her no thanks, Dara caught the guy with the wings' reflection in the stainless carafe, looking her way. The waitress ripped Dara's tab off a pad, set it down, thanked her and topped up Jimmy's mug, then hustled away.

Jimmy beat Dara to it, sliding her tab to him, saying, "On me." He told her where the Greyhound stopped.

"Guess I should say thanks," Dara said, heading for the can, Jimmy watching her go, Lance taking out his ringing cell.

Drinking down half the city roast, Jimmy listened, wiping his fingers on the napkin, Lance taking the call from Ben Risker.

Hanging up, he filled Jimmy in, saying, "Kid got beat up over in Day Lot 4 — front teeth knocked out?"

"Yeah? How's that ours?"

"One of Stevens's roommates." Lance got up, looked over at the guy with the wings and moved for the door.

Lifting himself off the stool, Jimmy followed Lance past the cash, crumpling the girl's tab, tossing it at the trash bucket, sticking his hand in the little dish with the mints. His skin looked blue under the neon of the Molson sign as he walked out. One thing for sure, the assholes were here, and they were circling.

Last time he'd drink like that before he went to bed. Should have run over to Nesters on his last break and picked up a fresh supply of KD, had something decent to eat instead.

Light streamed through the venetians, the slats looking wooly from not being dusted since Tammy split. Grey Stevens groaned. His stomach bubbled, doing that alien gurgle-talk, threatening to send back the four-day-old mac and blue. The second pitcher of Gilligan's Island he'd mixed after his shift didn't help. Time to stop mixing cocktails by the pitcher, toking his brains out, then bingeing on leftovers every time something pissed him off at work.

Last night it was the asshole at the bar hitting on the minor drinking on a fake ID. A cute blonde with flat-ironed hair and freckles on a turned-up nose, the girl's body just coming into its own. The asshole at the bar looked like Tom Arnold, Grey catching him slipping something into the girl's Dram Slam when she went to the ladies', the drink popular after some rapper started singing about it. Splashing the glass in the sink, Grey told Tom's clone he needed to see him in his office, caught a fistful of collar and led the way to the men's room, the asshole on tiptoes, giving him attitude. The conference tag on his shirt said, *Hi, my name's Ted. I'm with Zero Waste*.

Ducking the clenched hand, Grey spun Ted around and ran him face-first into the Vortex hand dryer. Ted's glasses were history. Next swing, he was bouncing off the Durex condom machine, the knobs acting like little fists. Dropping to the floor, Ted stayed down, the angry red *V* of the Vortex logo stamped on his forehead. Reaching, getting a good hold, Grey ripped off the shirt pocket, got the name tag that said, *Hi, my name's Ted,* along with the Baggie with the roofies. He waited while Ted wadded TP, rolling it into a tampon, sticking it in a nostril, keeping pressure on it. Then Grey told him to get the fuck out, Ted's shirt looking like it belonged to David Banner after he hulked up.

Shaking the Baggie into the trash under the bar, Grey explained to the girl with the freckles that Ted had pressing business, had to get back to his conference. Setting her up with a fresh soft drink, he put her underaged ass in a taxi and told her to come back when her brains caught up to the rest of her, the girl giving him the finger.

Now Grey flipped away the covers, checked around for his jeans, feeling a long way from the times when Tammy hung the wash on the line out back, socks always matching and underwear folded in a drawer. That clean sunshine smell.

Like Tammy, Uncle Rubin was gone, and everything about the place felt past its expiry date. Everything except the real estate values. The place his uncle built back when Creekside was nothing more than a T-bar and a town dump, before the alpine bowls that offered all the leg burn any diehard could want. World class all the way, Olympic host city, right up there with places like Zermatt and Kitzbühel. And now city council was talking about casinos.

Grey stood to pocket some serious cash if he sold the place, but sentimentality weighed like an anchor, keeping him there running the business his uncle started over two decades ago. Learning to grow high-grade pot back when he attended the Waldorf School.

Now, tending bar several nights a week, making his tax return look legit, Grey was growing some of the best pot on the planet. He could retire by the time he hit his mid-thirties, leave the grow business to Pete and the guys downstairs. Take life easy. Snowboard the cold months, bike the hot ones. Do whatever he wanted.

It was Travis Rainey's call last Thursday that had him thinking about getting out even sooner. Rainey gave him a choice: grow for him or get forced out. His first instinct was to tell Rainey to fuck himself, then he did a little checking, finding out who this guy was.

What he found out, Rainey worked for Geovani "Bumpy" Rosco, a name on the Vancouver drug scene, a guy that didn't make idle threats. Expanding like Walmart, these guys were set on taking over Whistler. Simple as that.

Maybe it was time to get out. Grey thought about going someplace tropical, a place without memories or cops busting down the door or shit-heels making threats. Just babes and beach. Could open a little bar of his own. Learn to surf. Mexico maybe.

The kitchen table leg wobbled when he sat, cigarette burns dotting the old Formica top. Lighting the joint, he thought he had a Phillips in one of the drawers, wanting to tighten the screws holding the leg. He took a pull, looking at the greasy Moffat, the thing down to two working burners. His headache eased, the weed was Eight Miles High, their best strain yet, keeping him back from the edge of the memory swamp. Thoughts of his uncle and his ex and the way things used to be had a way of fucking up the whole day, something he wanted to avoid.

Before this Travis asshole called, making threats, Grey was thinking of fixing the place up, splashing a coat of paint on the walls. Change the bulbs on the main floor, half of them burned out, take care of the drain in the tub, Tammy's hair still clogging it. Taking another toke, holding it, letting it out easy and slow . . . he was thinking, fuck it.

In the front room, he switched on the old-school turntable, spinning a platter: Mungo Jerry, from his uncle's back-in-the-day collection. Found his jeans in a ball by the three-footer behind the couch, the plant growing like . . . well, a weed. Nice top cola without any spotting, no excessive bottom branching, Grey's idea of a houseplant. The high-intensity discharge lamp burning like the sun over it, adding five degrees to the August heat.

His Nikes were by the cocktail glass with an inch or so of Gilligan's Island left in it. Tugging on the jeans, he took the glass and sneakers into the bedroom. Giving a gargle, he swallowed the last of it. Waste not, want not. Chased it with another toke. Blasting the Nikes with the Odor Eaters can on top of the dresser, he stomped his feet into them.

From the front room Mungo Jerry was singing about the summertime and the weather being high and touching the sky . . . Yeah. His uncle's oldies had a way of improving his mood. His eyes met the guy in the dressing mirror. No idea where the gut came from. Must have gas or something. Fuck, what would he look like at forty? Just ten short years. Hardly blame Tammy for checking out and moving back to Rain City.

The split left him empty, Tammy ending up in a west side condo, two bedrooms with an ocean view and a claw-foot tub. Thinking she could be dating again killed him. No amount of Eight Miles High ever got her out of his head.

Knocking into the empty bowl of mac and blue (the blue being Gorgonzola), he kicked it out of his way and went into the can, dragging a disposable Bic across his stubble. The joint in his mouth had gone out.

He glanced out the window for signs of Pete's shit-brown El Camino. The road construction south of Pemberton likely slowed him down, the back of Pete's ride loaded with the harvest they cured last week. Then he remembered Pete was making a stop, handing off three bags to Rivers and Glinka, the two of them dealing it down in Squamish. Mojo, Airdog and Tuff Dub were waiting to bag up the rest in the suite downstairs, get it out to the buskers who worked the Village and the Creek, put word out on Facebook.

Mungo Jerry ripped up the front room with "Mother Fucker Boogie." Grey was bopping to it when the Gorgonzola belch sent him dashing for the porcelain. Not making it, he splashed white liquid across toilet and tiles, leaving him on all fours, moaning, feeling cool sweat across his back.

Doing a mac and blue encore, his stomach bilged itself, Grey retching bile right through "Daddie's Brew." When he was able, he pulled himself up on the sink, coming level with the window.

Holding onto the counter, he was thinking, who the fuck mixes Gilligan's Island with leftover mac and blue at two in the fucking morning, wakes a couple hours later and fires up a joint?

The sound of a car door shutting snapped his head up. Thinking it was Pete, he glanced to the window. Then another car door shut.

Fuck!

They were coming up the drive.

. . . CIRCLING THE DRAIN

The flash of something red passing the cedar boughs out front stopped him wiping his chin. Pete was a rail compared to the guy coming up the walk.

Detective Jimmy Gallo.

The service piece showed like a lump under the big man's blazer, red plaid like hunters wear, Jimmy's twist on the Mounties' Red Serge. Leisure pants and aviator shades with an orange tint. A powerful build with a tree-trunk neck, narrow eyes and a flattop hairstyle right out of the sixties.

The one coming from the driver's side was Detective Lance Edwards. Tall and fit in a Dennis Farina sort of way, minus the mustache. The salt-and-pepper hair hinting he was edging close to fifty.

Big-city dicks on loan from 312 Main, sent up here to get a handle on Whistler's rising drug trade. That's what they told Grey. Came by two days ago to warn him bigger fish were on the way, hoping he would supply them some dirt, telling him they were on the same side. Now here they were again: no backup, no vests, no battering ram, no sign of a warrant. But still, these guys weren't fundraising. Sure as hell weren't on the same side. Fuckers had to be getting their intel off Google, bent on getting their man, not stopping to ask what kind of self-respecting pot grower uses his own residence for growing.

That time the 5-0 showed up at the Brackendale house, they brought all their toys. Grey and Pete were there working the strain, didn't open the front door and had to duck out the back. The cops seized everything but couldn't make any charges stick.

Gallo and Edwards turned at the dead hydrangea and came up the steps, ringing the doorbell, at the same time Grey snatched his wallet off the dresser, moving through the kitchen, past the sink full of dishes. He tried the basement door.

Locked.

He tapped on it. Nothing. Mojo likely had female company and didn't want to be disturbed; Grey punched Mojo's number into his cell, damned thing going straight to voicemail. Shit. No way to warn him. Not sure how much weed the guys had downstairs.

He needed a diversion. Grabbing his jacket off a hook, he threw it on inside out, red lining facing out, the doorbell chiming again, followed by a knock. A cop's knock — loud — like they were coming in, like it or not.

Tiptoeing through the kitchen, he grabbed the house plant from behind the couch, forgetting to switch off the heat lamp, going to the mud room, shoving his phone in a pocket, grabbing a pair of safety goggles and his uncle's beaver cap with the earflaps from a shelf.

More knocking.

Inside the garage, he took his bike down off the rack, going out the back door. *Fuck!* Too late to do anything about the disc spinning on the platter, the damned turntable too prehistoric for auto shut-off. Mungo Jerry would be going round and round, fucking up the stylus.

Face behind the goggles, fur cap on his head, Grey tucked the pot plant under his arm. Steering the baby-blue Mongoose through the gap in the neighbor's hedge, he maneuvered around their backyard, missing most of the flowers. Ducking under the clothesline, he pedaled like mad down the driveway without a look back, swish-tailing onto Easy Street, steering with one hand on the bars, the other cradling the plant.

•

Jimmy and Lance looked at each other, then watched the freak in the fur hat and goggles pedal down the street, Jimmy calling for him to halt, coming down the steps, stopping ankle deep in the grass Grey never cut. Watching the guy pedal off, Jimmy caught the neighbour across the street standing in his bay window. A wiry bald guy with his hand inside his bathrobe and his dull eyes on the two cops. Block Watch sign on his lawn.

Delivering messages should have been kicked down to a uni, but up here in the boonies, if you wanted things done, you rolled up your sleeves: Staff Sergeant Ben Risker's own words. Jimmy Gallo watched Grey ride off in his chicken-shit disguise, the plant under his arm. Gallo said to his partner, "That what I think it is?"

Lance was watching the neighbour across the street, saying, "Guess we better find out." Flipping and catching the car keys, he walked toward the driver's side, pointing down at Jimmy's shoes, saying, "Not getting in my car like that." The dog shit squishing under Jimmy's shoe reminded Lance of his kid playing with the Play-Doh maker — his wife and kid were back in Vancouver.

Jimmy looked down, the lawn a minefield among the dandelion and thistle, Grey's green thumb reserved for the other kind of grass. "Fuck me." Stepping off one turd onto another, he tiptoed like he was doing *Swan Lake*, stomping his feet on the pavement to dislodge it. He looked around for something to scrape with. "See what it's come to?" Jimmy went on bitching about the department, saying how Lance had to use his personal ride. The two of them sent up here and being treated like . . . shit.

Lance got in. All they came to do was give Stevens a heads up, let him know his tenant, Jimmy "Airdog" Tan, took a beating this morning, had his front teeth knocked out, likely from the same guys Lance and Jimmy warned him about a few days ago. Broad daylight, in a parking lot. The way Lance saw it, Stevens and his partner Pete Melton had been lucky till now.

Intel told Lance that Risker and his county Mounties raided a grow house near Brackendale six months back, the tip coming from a wine-sopped snitch, his hand out for a reward. The spotter was sure Stevens and Melton were inside. Armed Mounties in helmets and vests took positions while Risker went to the door with the warrant in one hand, a ram in the other. Getting no answer, he crashed the door as his squad drew a bead. What they found was the back door hanging open. Neat rows of cannabis stood under grow lights, branches up like they were surrendering. No other arrests were made. Turned out Stevens and Melton worked with latex gloves, the forensic team unable to turn up a single fingerprint, nothing to tie them to the place.

Risker's subsequent search of their private residences turned up more nothing. Not a seed. Not a roach. Serial numbers on the equipment seized at the grow house gave up nothing, no credit-card record of purchases. No phone records. No emails. Nothing. These guys smarter than they looked.

The demand letter filed by the attorney for Stevens and Melton threatened legal action seeking punitive damages for defamation and harassment. The department and the Municipality of Whistler were put on notice, staring at police misconduct over illegal searches of the plaintiffs' personal properties. The warrant covered the grow house, not their personal residences; defense attorneys live for shit like that.

As far as Lance was concerned, Risker and his people deserved all the crap that would rain on them. They'd fucked up, but still, the tide was turning. Intel had the Roscos and the Indo Army taking a hard look at Whistler, both set to control the drug trade in the mountain playground, get in ahead of the casino gambling about to be rubber-stamped, meaning Stevens and Melton were on their way out, the big fish swimming in.

"Try to help the dumb fuck, and he runs," Jimmy said, sitting on the passenger seat, checking the bottom of his shoe, working a twig into his treads, flicking it out the door.

"Might be a lot of things, but dumb's not one of them,"

Lance said, filling him in. Grey's uncle moved his grow-ops indoors back when Sputniks orbited the Earth. All that time, local law never nailed him once. And the kid picked up where the uncle left off. Word from downtown was Rubin Stevens worked a long-ago deal with Ivan Glinka and the Rivers brothers, guys with ties to the Sabers Motorcycle Club, ruthless thugs with a liking for pick handles and burning shit. Stevens just grew the stuff, kept arm's length while the Rivers boys and Glinka brought the cash in Harley saddlebags, ran the weed down to Squamish by the vanloads, got chased more than once.

It was Johnny Cash Rivers that found a back way from his days of working as a land surveyor. The route connected Port Mellon to Squamish by a series of trails and forgotten logging roads, letting them run their weed under the radar. Never a hitch in fifteen years, till the day an undercover cop wiretapped the bikers holding church in Nanaimo, and the Crown stepped on the Sabers, making a dozen arrests and expropriating their clubhouse, causing the rest to patch over or run. Johnny Cash Rivers wasn't part of the club, but he was ratted out for a reduced sentence, nailed with enough weight, weed, coke and illegal firearms on his premises to get him three to five.

"And the uncle?" Jimmy asked.

"Cancer did what we couldn't," Lance said. "Think it was his lungs."

"Leaving young Stevens and Melton?"

"Yeah, and Benny Rivers and Glinka are still kicking around. Never arrested. And it's looking like our boy Stevens started dealing through local buskers."

"Street bums?"

"Licensed by the city, working their designated spots, selling dime bags to tourists, giving them a little entertainment, sending them on their way."

"Till the casinos come in?"

"Who knows," Lance said. Political head-scratching and posturing over decriminalization had been going since the Stone Age, nothing new there. But gaming meant hundreds of new jobs in Whistler, millions pumped through the slots and laid down on tables. A boost to the already bulging local economy, goods and services on steroids. Last thing anybody needed was for organized crime to step in. So, like a game of Mouse Trap, the marble pinged from the office of the premier, kicked down to the deputy commissioner, to the drug enforcement chief, an inspector, a sergeant major, dropping in a lieutenant's lap. Lance's lieutenant. A two-man investigation team was formed, and Lance and Jimmy were it, the last ones kicked.

"What we get for topping the loot's shit list," Jimmy said, working the twig.

"Yeah." Lance had been part of a botched wiretap case against crime boss Artie Poppa last year. It got him partnered with Jimmy Gallo, the laziest fuck to ever carry a badge, the two of them sent up here for thirty days to gather intel and give the loot enough to feed back up the chute.

Staff-sergeant Risker took care of booking them into a crummy two-room efficiency at the Beaver Lodge, five miles outside of town, mattresses like sacks of beans, a two-burner hot plate and a mini-fridge. Letting them know how the local law felt about their help. Towels that smelled like mildew. Place had a table out back where you could clean fish. The RCMP going all out. Made Lance feel better watching Jimmy scrape at his shoe with the willow twig. Pressing open the window, he said, "You done scrapin', what say we go catch this guy?"

Jimmy flung the twig on the fucked-up lawn, shutting the Laredo's door. Looking across at the guy in the bay window as Lance backed out, he said, "Could just send a unit, sweep the fucker up?"

"Want to make sure he understands this is real."

Lance was pissed they'd got turned down on the phone tap, the local judge saying they didn't have probable cause, Lance guessing it was the same judge that signed the search warrant on the Brackendale house, not wanting to fuck up twice.

"Sure'll feel good to bust his ass," Jimmy said, rolling up his window.

"Got him for dog shit, not cleaning up," Lance said, keeping a straight face.

"Wasn't a fucking yucca under his arm."

"True."

. . . OFF THE RADAR

THE OLD Wagoneer humped it, in and out of wheel ruts, bottoming on its skid plate. The fat tires spinning, stones pelting the undercarriage. Recent rains had deepened the ruts of the old logging road Johnny Cash Rivers discovered back when he worked that summer as a land surveyor.

It was barely passable this time, even for the hopped-up 4 × 4. Twice Benny and Ivan had to detour through heavy brush, chopping their way with hatchets, packing stones into holes, Benny donning waders and hooking up the winch while Ivan steered, keeping the wheels straight. Twice they forded swollen streams, water coming in, and winched the Jeep up clay banks.

The tires slid around, finding purchase, flinging muck and water onto Benny. In spite of the waders, his jeans and shirt were soaked, Ivan Glinka looking through the mud-streaked windshield, thinking it was pretty funny.

"How about I drive, you fucking push for a while?" Benny called, taking off the waders, throwing them in back, getting in, wiping his hands on his soaked pants, finding his boots on the floor.

Ivan pointed at the mud on Benny's face. "Missed a spot."

"Fuck you."

The back seat was packed with the garbage bags of Eight Miles High they picked up from Pete Melton in the parking lot of the Beaver Lodge.

"I'm having a taste," Benny said, wiping his cheek.

"Yeah, guess we earned it."

"We?" Benny dug his pipe from a pocket and reached across the seat, trying to get into one of the bags without ripping it wide open, cursing Pete for tying the knots too tight.

"What the fuck?"

Ivan's tone had Benny shifting back around in his seat. Up ahead a guy stood in the trail, hands behind his back. Middle of nowhere. The guy looked like he was sightseeing.

"What the fuck?" Benny repeated, looking at the East Indian guy looking at them.

"Lost hiker or something." Ivan reached past Benny and opened the glovebox, taking out his Colt.

"Hiking with no gear?" Benny asked.

"Maybe got a badge in his pocket." No way Ivan was going to end up in a cell like Johnny Cash Rivers. Looking around, Ivan put one in the chamber, telling Benny to go see what he wanted.

"Me again?"

"We both got to get muddy?"

Tucking the laces in his boots, Benny got out, left the door hanging open, his own piece tucked in back of his pants, Benny pretty fast at drawing it out. Careful where he stepped, he put on the smile, coming forward, asking, "Hey man, you lost or something?"

Nav Pudi watched this guy in the headband stepping around a mud hole, fifty feet between them, the other one with the blond hair watching from behind the wheel, engine idling. Danny DeWulf had been trailing the Wagoneer all the way from the Beaver Lodge. The Indos knew all about these two and their back road — and that Grey Stevens was supplying the pot. And they knew Travis Rainey was up here recruiting for Bumpy Rosco. Rainey being the one who fired that fucking rocket the end of last year.

"Hey, friend, you got flies in your ears? Asked you a question." Benny kept coming, one hand going behind his back. The last guy that didn't see things his way was found in Burns Bog nearly a year ago, duct-taped inside the trunk of his submerged Subaru, rotting for a week before some bird watcher looking for greater sandhill cranes spotted the bumper in the reeds.

Leaving the engine chugging, Ivan got out too, coming as far as the bumper, the Colt held low at his side, backing Benny's play.

"Road's closed," Nav said.

"That right?" Benny had his gun out, letting Nav have a look at it, stepping closer, thirty feet now, seeing the Indian guy's face was all scarred like a burn victim's, seeing the tattoo on the hand, knowing who he was. He pointed the gun, saying, "Suppose I reopen it?"

A guy as tall as Lurch stepped from behind a tree, a double Glock in his hands. The one stepping from the opposite side of the trail had an automatic pistol, shades over his eyes, hair slicked.

"Hey, okay," Benny said, backing up, the pistol at his side, "You say it's closed, it's closed. We'll just back the fuck out of here. How's that?" He was stepping backwards to the Wagoneer, Ivan getting back in and reaching the twelve-gauge behind his seat.

Lurch kept step with Benny, Benny trying to keep from slipping. The one with the auto pistol was closing in from his right. The one that looked like a burn victim hadn't moved, just stood watching. Benny would go for Lurch first, leave the other one for Ivan. He was nearly at the passenger door.

. . . A WHITE MEAT MAN

Sugar's was just off the Stroll, halfway down a lane, a Commerce Bank machine on the corner, a stone front pinched between a cigar shop called Up in Smoke and a Money Mart that never seemed open. Three parking spots and a nice magnolia in a glazed container out front. The graphics on Sugar's window showed a sexy mouth in red lipstick biting into an apple. Lots of juice. An open metal staircase next to the door led to a row of offices up above, a studio that offered portrait photography at discount prices and a place called Ice Air offering sightseeing and helo tours of the glaciers. Sugar's didn't say what it offered.

Travis stepped in, wiping his feet on the mat that read *Come on in and get wet*. Stepping to reception, he put his hands flat on the desk and took the place in. The serifs of the sign on the wall were silver, the words lit by pink bulbs. Mid-century chairs flanked a coffee table by the window; the place was supposed to look expensive.

The woman on the phone was clinging to forty, golden do with highlights done in a wave. Nicely built under the blouse coming off her shoulder, smelling like she came packed in rose petals.

Cradling the receiver, she gave him a full-on smile, flipping hair from her eyes. "Be just be a sec, hon." Cameron Diaz lips done in party pink, she smiled, blinking look-at-me lashes. She told whoever was on the line that it had been taken care of, said thanks a couple of times and set the receiver in the cradle. The light for the second line was lit.

"Surprised to find you open Sunday morning," Travis said.

"No rest for the wicked. Sundays are always busy. Now, how can I help?"

"Want to see Manny Pesco."

Holding up a finger, meaning just a sec, she said, "Sorry, hon, I just got to finish this." She swiveled to the file drawer behind her and tucked away a Duo-Tang, showing legs glossed in Body Bling. Nice muscle tone, a few extra pounds packed around her middle. Making a couple of clicks on her keyboard, she turned from the iMac, looking up at him, smiling at this hard-looking guy with his hair combed back. She liked the silver wings on the sides, the guy not hiding his age. Looked like he got his nails done in a salon. The hands still on her desk. Sure wasn't here looking for a date, so she took a stab, crinkling her nose, saying, "That a badge in your pocket?"

That got him smiling back, saying, "Second person today tried to figure me out."

"Not even close, huh?"

"Think you can do better than that."

"You're not looking for a date."

"Told you, I'm here to see Manny."

"And if I say he's not in?"

Holding the smile, Travis threw a thumb over his shoulder. "Car next to mine, one that's taking up two spaces, plate's got his name on it."

"So it does." She looked out and pursed her Diaz lips, still smiling, having fun with him, saying, "Be surprised how many we get — cops, I mean." She liked his way, this guy that didn't have a badge, this guy a little older.

"Yeah, well, the station's, what, two blocks that way?"

"They come by and park their Crown Vics right in the handicapped," she said, looking out at his big Chrysler taking up the spot. "Come in here with their attitude."

"And you think that's me?"

"Attitude, yeah maybe, but different."

"If I had to come in here frisking, sure I'd lose the attitude."

"Trouble is, they don't tip when they're frisking." Her eyes went to the phone, the light for line two still on, Manny likely fixing up a whole convention. Her finger found the buzzer under the desk, the one she was supposed to press if a guy like this came in. She didn't press it.

Line two's light went off. Both of them looking at it.

"Appreciate if you didn't hit the button, want it to be a surprise."

"Know about that, huh?"

"Call it a guess."

"Could get me fired."

"He's gonna have bigger things to think about." Travis

went to the door that read *Private*, smiled back at her, asked her name.

"Lexie."

"Lexie. I like it." Turning the knob, he stepped in.

. . . THINNING THE HERD

GRINNING AS he walked in, he ignored the Baby Browning in the chubby hand. Judging by the bore, it was a twenty-five cal. Enough to do the job, but this guy wasn't going to shoot him just for walking in.

Behind the leather-and-chrome desk, Manny Pesco was looking past his best-before date, looking like he sucked lemons. Like most people Travis had history with, Manny wasn't thrilled to see him.

"You're looking like shit, Manny." Two strides and he was sitting opposite, leaning back and making the leather creak, looking around, taking the office in: the big desk, the matching credenza done in leather, single malt in a decanter, a set of crystal glasses, chocolate walls — a man's space — sofa under the window, abstract nude looked like it had been done by a four-year-old, a photo of the mountains in winter on the far wall, one of those putter-practice traps on the floor, a framed shot of the wife and kids on the desk next to a landline and a chrome lamp, MacBook Air open on a desk pad.

"Business been good, huh?"

Manny sat stone-faced, the Browning still pointing at his chest. Looking out through the blinds, Travis let him have a moment, history between them being what it was: crossing paths back when Manny worked behind a different desk on Vancouver's Eastside, a corner office in a warehouse, taking care of Bumpy Rosco's books, working his offshore accounts, keeping his money clean and safe, making Rosco look legit. Manny had a knack for it. Travis headed up the crews loading and unloading the trucks, pulling double duty when Bumpy asked, straightening assholes out and making the odd collection. Did it with a Slugger bat back then. Three strikes you're out kind of thing.

"Take it you're not after a date," Manny finally said, his voice flat. The insurance fraud deal that nearly landed him in Ford Mountain still left a sour taste. Some teamster owing Bumpy twenty grand wasn't making an effort, and Travis was sent in for batting practice. While Travis swung from the hip, the two guys he brought along lit flares and took care of the teamster's truck, not checking the load first. Drums of soybean oil. Highly flammable shit.

The fire ripped through the place and ate a line of trailers, along with the storage units out back, Manny running for his life, leaving the records and ledgers in the office. Diving out a window, he escaped with smoke inhalation, fracturing the tibia in his left leg. Lying on the ground, he watched his thirty-six-foot Sunseeker, which he'd dubbed *Fin Chaser,* smolder under its tarp. Parked it there for winter storage. Just had the twin diesels overhauled.

The depot went by Tasco Trucking, owned by a sketchy offshore consortium, Geovani "Bumpy" Rosco's name not appearing anywhere. Typical of Rosco to buy up real property and slap a third cousin's name on the title. Not that he was the trusting sort, more the sort nobody would screw over and chance becoming a third cousin twice removed . . . by a baseball bat.

The paperwork Manny forwarded on behalf of Tasco to the insurance company showed faulty wiring as the cause, the fire-detection system at fault. No alarms went off. No sprinklers. Nothing the firefighters could do but contain the blaze, according to the initial report filed by the investigation-unit chief, a guy named Levesque.

Some underwriter didn't like it, called in arson investigators who took a different view, who called in fraud investigators who asked about the new Corvette parked in Levesque's driveway.

Tasco withdrew its claim, and Levesque took early retirement, taking the 'Vette on a road trip, Manny seeing it as an opportune time to visit his ailing mother in the old country. Bought a one-way and left for Milan on the next plane out.

The fire set Bumpy back nearly a million. The cost of doing business was one way to look at it; Bumpy's way was to look at the guy responsible for striking the match; the shit had to land somewhere.

Nothing for Travis to do but don his leathers, hop on his Wide Glide and find a no-forwarding address. Catching the ferry to Nanaimo, he hooked up with his old pal Richie Winters at the Sabers MC, partied with the boys and helped set up their first meth trailer. Went on to show them the finer points of smuggling firepower across the border. He did alright for the MC, a means of keeping his head below the reeds, making them a pile of money, the bikers watching his back.

Didn't hear from the old man again until a bunch of Alberta rednecks began hijacking Rosco's trucks. Dope packed inside electronics went missing coming across the wheat fields, the trucks hit at rest stops just outside of Calgary. A couple of Bumpy's drivers had been hospitalized, and the first guy Bumpy sent to straighten it out·had been toe-tagged by the time Travis got the call from Eduardo, a longtime lieutenant. Asking him to do this favor, Eduardo said Bumpy was up for letting bygones go by. A chance to make amends. Offered double the usual fee, Travis said he'd think about it. They settled on triple.

And Travis delivered, got it done inside a week, recovering half the stuffed electronics in back of a barn off a township road ten miles east of Calgary, one of the rednecks eager to give up names if Travis would stop treating him like a piñata. When the rest of the rednecks had been dealt with, Travis showed up at Bumpy's with a suitcase of cash he found at the piñata's, showing Bumpy some good faith. After that, Travis and Bumpy started doing lunch.

"That Blackcomb?" Travis asked Manny now, looking through the tilted blinds.

"You stand up you can see the chairlift." Manny wagged the pistol, throwing in, "On your way out."

"You got coffee in this place?" Travis let an arm dangle over the chrome rest, smiling at Manny like it was good to see him.

Sighing, Manny tilted the barrel at the ceiling.

"That the family, huh?" Travis asked, the portrait on the

desk, wife and kids in front of a canvas backdrop, everybody saying cheese.

Manny said yeah.

"Nice-looking kids. Wife kept it trim, huh? You're a lucky man, Manny. Doing alright."

"How about spelling out what you're after, Travis?" Manny wanting to get this over, tossing the Browning in the drawer.

"Coffee with a splash of cream," Travis said, "but none of that powdered crap."

Pressing a button on his intercom, Manny told Lexie to put on a pot, run to the corner for some cream.

Lifting a pack of Exports and a lighter from his top pocket, Travis lit up, Manny hitting the intercom again, telling Lexie to find something that looked like an ashtray, then said to Travis, "So, you still lighting shit on fire?"

"Here more like an investor." Blowing smoke at the ceiling.

"For you or the old man?"

"This is strictly me."

"Yeah, how's that work?"

"First I got something coming needs a place to land."

"Uh, no." Manny had a pretty good idea what the something was, knowing this guy's history of running dope and guns. "Look around. This look like a warehouse to you?" Jesus.

"But you know a place?" Travis dragged on the cigarette, having fun with him.

"See, you come in here, you want a date, a stag, sensual massage, that kind of thing. White, black, brown, makes no difference to me. Two-fifty a girl, you pick the one of your dreams right off the webpage, stick her in your cart, pay with a major credit card, and the magic happens."

"Easy like takeout."

"You want extras, you work it out, between you and the one you pick. Me, I got nothing to do with the extras, and no way I do fucking storage." The referendum on gambling was about to green-light casinos, the gaming corp standing by with hardhats and shovels. Manny and the other escort services set to make a killing. And now this asshole walks in asking something like that. The years exiled in the heel of the Italian boot, watching an old woman die, all that on Travis, the guy that botched up at Tasco. Goddamn barrels of soybean oil going up like a fireball.

Travis dragged and blew more smoke.

"Think I answered about the storage. Now, if you're asking if I want a partner, I'm going to respectfully say hell no." Manny stood up like he wanted to show him out.

"Ought to hear me out."

"Look, no offense, Travis, I'm pure legit here. That, and this town's already got three escort places, all of us cutting into each other like too many dogs on a bone. Hardly worth keeping the doors open some days. Last thing I need —"

"All that's about to change, Manny. Think you know it."

"Heard city council's got a fourth place putting in an app," Manny said and threw his hands up. "Not much left after the girls get their cut, plus the rent I pay, you wouldn't believe it. Politicians in my pockets, man, you got no idea. You don't want this." Then Manny was grinning, like a bulb went off, saying, "Ah, you read about the proposed gaming laws, huh? That it? Think they're going to allow casinos up here? I got to tell —"

Cigarette between two fingers, Travis curled his hand into a fist and slammed it on the desk, sparks going all over the place.

Manny sat back down.

"Come to you first on account we got history."

"The kind of history nearly got me three to five, had me hiding in Italy on account of it. You cost me . . ."

"Manny, you're a pimp with a storefront, and all that shit you're talking about, that's the past, and yeah, I know about the casinos. What I'm trying to get you to see is the real future."

Lexie came in with a tray, two cups steaming, creamer, sugar, extra saucer, setting it down, not saying a word. Travis tapped ashes at the saucer, most of it landing on the desk, saying thanks, calling her by name, watching her leave, then asking Manny, "You tapping that?"

Manny didn't answer, watching Travis stamp out his smoke.

"What I got goes like this: you come up with a number, bean counter I'm using goes over your books; I come up with another number, you say yeah, and we shake on it. Good for you, good for me."

"Just like that?"

"First order of business, I discourage new competitors, talk merger and buyout with the ones already here. Then we wait and see about the casinos." Travis put his hands on the chair arms, admiring it, asking, "This Italian?"

"And if I say no?" Manny could feel the vice: a wife wanting to renovate, one kid needing an orthodontist, the older one in his first year at UVic. In residence, books that cost two hundred a throw. Family bleeding him.

"Then I go to the next place, see if I get a bite." Travis got up. "Tell you what, Manny, take a couple days, think it over." He extended his hand, waiting for Manny to push his hand across the desk. Handshake like a damp rag. "Know you'll do the right thing."

Shutting Manny's door on his way out, he looked at Lexie at her desk. Smiling, knowing she'd been listening in. Those legs. Those eyes. Not as young as most of the ones he'd been with lately, but there was something about her, Travis asking, "How's lunch with the new boss sound?"

Blue eyes looked up, pink mouth smiling. "Sounds interesting." Then at the clock on the wall. "But kind of early, no?"

He told her he'd be back at noon.

"So we're clear, I book appointments."

"All I said was lunch."

"Then we're clear." She smiled.

"The Ritz's got a bistro, supposed to be pretty good."

"You heard right."

With that, he walked out to the handicapped spot, puffy clouds rolling overhead.

Through the glass, he heard Manny call Lexie into the office, not bothering with the intercom, Manny loud and sounding pissed.

Ducking under the Lambo door, he started the engine and backed out of the spot, on to meet the next asshole, looking at the rearview, catching a glimpse of her walking into Manny's office, thinking ahead to lunch.

. . . EYES ON THE PRIZE

"Sure it's him?" Nav Pudi said into the phone, the reception crackling, the three of them walking through the pines, Veni Gopal and Daljit Rama carrying the bags of pot, their weapons slung over shoulders, the GPS telling Nav Port Mellon was due west. Not far now. The two bodies lay where they fell next to their Wagoneer, half-mile back on the muddy road.

Danny DeWulf was in Whistler, standing in the Village at the top of the lane, eyes behind dark shades, white silk T under an Armani jacket, making like he was waiting for somebody, his own car around the corner. Eyeing Travis as he drove by in the Chrysler, Danny made the plate, saying into the phone, "Just came out of this escort place, sign says *Sugar's*."

"Asked if you're sure," Nav said.

"Yeah, Rosco's guy. Travis Rainey. Fucker with the rocket."

"Okay, stay with him."

"You got it." Danny was moving for his Accord.

"And Danny, no way he spots you."

"No problem." Danny ran when he got around the corner, got to his car and rolled, catching up, seeing the black Chrysler turn right a block ahead.

. . . ZERO TO SIXTY

WASN'T EASY pedaling like that, Grey tearing down Easy Street with the plant under an arm. Cranking it onto Balsam, then Lorimer, he shot the bike across the 99, between a honking UPS truck and a big Chrysler. He didn't chance looking back. Tiny branches snapped, the forming buds dropping off the plant that could fetch him thirty days in an orange jumpsuit. But county lockup wasn't in Grey's plans. He checked behind him, no sign of the cops. Gripping the handlebars, he pedaled, his thighs on fire.

He wasn't fleeing on account of the plant or whatever Mojo and the boys might have stashed downstairs. Pete Melton was trucking down with the second harvest from the Pemberton house, loose-packed in a dozen Heftys in back of his old El Camino. No way he wanted cops at his door when Pete rolled up.

The Pemberton house sat out by One Mile Lake, a place Chip the realtor arranged, nice and remote, did it for an ounce. They had Hydro Henry rig it for a perfect grow climate, the whole main floor lined with six-footers, yielding four to five ounces per plant. At two bills per ounce wholesale, added to the crop near-ready at the McGuire house, they'd more than make up for the Brackendale house falling into RCMP hands back in February. Two more crops from each place and they might even be looking at a bumper year. That's if they lived long enough to see the harvest. This Travis guy calling and making threats had Grey worried.

Cutting across the street, Grey dodged a silver Accord and rode right into the path of a red Benz making a turn out of Northlands. The woman panicked, honking, swerving to avoid the cyclist, ending up on the median with a thump and a grind of sheet metal. The airbag deployed and muted her scream, the C-Class high-centered like a shipwreck on the curb.

If he hadn't been high, his reaction time might have been sharper. He hit his brake, his back wheel sliding, the bike hitting the curb, and man and plant vaulted over the bars, Grey doing the flatland luge over the boulevard lawn. The ass pass across the sidewalk took most of the seat of his jeans, and scraped both palms. A hard stop against a cedar hedge knocked the air out of him. Limping up and over, he picked up the bike and looked to see if the lady was alright, called to her, saying the cops would be along any second, then swung a leg over the bar and cycled down Northlands, leaving the broken plant.

He assessed the damage: ripped jeans, palms scraped, catching his breath. No sign of the cops, Grey wishing he had another joint. At Marketplace, he cruised easy through the Square and onto the Stroll. Fishing out his cell, he punched the speed dial and waited for Pete to pick up, hearing him say, "'S up?"

"How'd things go?" Grey asked, meaning the deal with Rivers and Glinka.

"Made the drop, but . . ."

"What?"

"Benny said that was it, last run they're making for us." Pete didn't mention Benny and Ivan only had half the cash, promising the rest by next weekend. Not the way they did things.

Beck guessing Travis Rainey had been talking to them, too.

Then Pete said, "I'm like ten minutes out, tell you the rest."

"Rest?"

"When I get there. Anyway, you called me."

"Yeah. Had a knock at the door."

It took a second, Pete asking, "Girl Scouts?"

"Yeah, big ugly ones."

"Not selling cookies?"

"Didn't stick around to find out. Right now, I'm leading them astray."

Pete got the picture, saying, "Okay, I'll do a plan B."

"That and give Mojo a heads-up. Think he's zoned out."

"I got it," Pete said. "Gonna do what I did the last time," meaning he'd stash the weed at the storage place out at Alta Lake until it was safe to bring it to the house, same as he did after the Brackendale house was raided.

Grey said, "Yeah," and was gone.

Pete didn't get a chance to ask what Grey was running from them in, knowing his partner didn't believe in cars.

Tucking the cell away, Grey was gliding along the Stroll, his heart pounding like a Keith Moon solo, gut sending up blue-cheese gas. Bumping down a set of stone steps behind

Olympic Plaza, he piloted the Mongoose past the park, weaving through a maze of early-morning tourists taking in Marketplace, most up here for the hiking and biking. He rose up on the crossbar, riding right into the middle slot of the empty bike rack. Timing it, he cleared the handlebars, vaulted, landed and walked it off. Perfect ten. A couple of school-girls applauded, taking him for a rider from Crankworx, the ten-day festival that had ended the previous week.

Throwing them a thumbs-up, he stripped off his jacket and looped it around his waist, covering the torn jeans. Blending with the tourists, Grey was high enough to forget about the fur cap and goggles till the lenses fogged up. Setting the goggles up on the cap, he checked out his skinned palms, picking out bits of gravel.

That's when he spotted the guy in the shiny suit, shirt half open, grabbing at the skinny punk chick by the Greyhound stop, out front of the Pinnacle, jerking her up against a trash can on a post, raising his hand to her, yelling in her face, Grey hearing the slap from across the Stroll.

A Michael Jackson spin, he tugged the goggles down and was back on the bike, ripping it from the rack. Didn't matter he was buzzed, hurting, legs on fire, cops on his tail. Getting his speed, he cranked up behind the guy doing the grabbing and slapping, the black-haired girl trying to fight back, shouting, "Fuck off, Nick!" clawing black fingernails, getting the worst of it, going down on the sidewalk, people stopping to stare, nobody making a move.

Yelling, "Clear!" Grey got air off the curb cut, swishing out the ass end of the Mongoose, doing a perfect whip, the extended pegs on the front forks just missing. The full weight of man on flying bike knocked the jerk into the trash can, putting him down.

Landing it, Grey planted both feet. Definitely a perfect ten. Man, that felt awesome. Getting off the bike, he helped the girl up and said to her, "Who's the speed bump?"

Grunting, Nick tried to rise, his wrist giving out. He rolled on the cobblestones, sucking air into his lungs, a bloody taste in his mouth. Nothing he could do but watch, Dara taking the guy's hand, letting him help her up. She said something he didn't catch, then the asshole that blind-sided him came into focus — fur cap, goggles, jacket around his waist — a couple of tourist girls applauding.

"Need a lift?" Grey asked, pointing at the handlebars, meaning for her to get on, seeing Nick reach inside his jacket.

Too many onlookers, Nick didn't pull the Smith. He rose as Dara hopped up on the handlebars, the freak with the goggles and fur hat pedaling off. Turning on the handlebars, she threw Nick the finger, telling him to consider this her notice, calling him a dickhead.

Lance's Laredo with the portable cherry on top came rolling from the far end of Town Plaza, tourists stepping out of its way. Lance had the four-ways on, tapping the horn. Jimmy held his shield out the passenger window, instructing a cluster of people to step aside.

No way Nick wanted to explain what happened or the Smith with the filed serial numbers. He shoved his way into the crowd, his nuts still aching, skin scraped off his hands and elbows, Hugo jacket ripped, knee bleeding, eyes stinging from the fucking Binaca.

Jimmy Gallo opened the passenger door and stood up on the sill, watching Grey peel away on the bike, had the jacket off and tied around his waist, looked like he traded the pot plant for a chick, the same one from the diner up on his handlebars. Some guy in a ripped jacket was hobbling the other way. Jimmy called to him, but the guy waved and kept going. He got back in, saying, "Looks like our pot grower's knocking over tourists, taking hostages." He burped up sausage. "Still say we let the locals deal with this shit."

•

Fingering the ripped pant leg, Nick limped on, heading to where he left the Camaro, against the curb on Village Gate, disabled without his flip key, note on the dash for the motor league guy. Looking back, he watched the cops in the unmarked Laredo roll away. He pulled out his cell and punched in Travis's number, changed his mind and hung up. No way he wanted to explain why he was late.

Fuck!

He walked back, wondering how long till roadside assist came with a new flip key. One thing for sure, he wouldn't forget the asshole with the goggles, the skinny chick, either. This wasn't done, not by a long shot.

. . . CLEANING HOUSE

"Who the fuck goes around calling us slopes, I mean this day and age?" Mojo was pissed, pants worn low, showing the Pac-Man boxers, black widowmaker covering the sleeve tats.

He was looking at Pete Melton, saying, "Come on, man . . ." Here he was, third-generation Vancouverite, working on his bachelor's at SFU, highest grade-point average, volunteering with the Nordic ski patrol, pitching in at the Food Bank every Christmas. "Slopes. *Jesus!*"

"Redneck underachievers, lighting up to the sound of banjos," Pete said.

"Backward-thinking fucks think we're all about rice, flip-flops and karaoke." Mojo was pissed that his roommate Airdog got attacked, Airdog on the road to his MD, making it happen, peddling dime bags to avoid the rip-off student loans. Airdog had to flag a ride to the local dental clinic, hoping they could replant the teeth.

Frayed jeans, his Nine Inch Nails hoodie, with his hair mussed, Pete looked around Grey's place for anything that looked like evidence, guessing they were going to be raided again, saying, "So the asshole's not into multiculturalism. More important, the fucks are coming for us."

His spiked hair jumping like wires, Mojo helped Pete gather evidence. "I mean where are we, the fucking Ozarks? Slopes, gooks, chinks, slant-eyes, Jesus Christ . . ."

"Forgot zipperheads," Pete threw in, spraying Sparkle from the pump bottle, wiping down the glass table, scooping a few seeds and bits of stem. "Main thing, Airdog's gonna be okay."

"Yeah, with fucking dentures at twenty-two, man."

"The shits for sure, but still . . ." Going around the couch, Pete asked, "Where's the plant?" The heat lamp was shining down on nothing.

"Must've been Grey."

Unplugging the thousand-watter, Pete took it with him, careful not to touch it, damned thing was hot. Switching off the turntable with Mungo Jerry spinning around, he went through the kitchen, tossing the paper towel in the trash, setting the lamp on the mud room floor.

They swept through the rest of the house, filling the hockey bag with anything that might interest the cops. Tucking Uncle Rubin's High Standard Sentinel pistol in his belt, Pete tossed a box of .22-cal hollow-points in the bag, along with Airdog's collection of pipes, about ninety in all (all field-tested), everything from brass to wood to bone to glass. One carved to look like a toilet seat with a working lid, one disguised as a Magic Marker, another shaped like bagpipes. Stuff belonged in a museum. AC/DC roach clips, boxes of Bambu papers in double-wide and assorted flavors, a water pipe that said "Dave's not here" when you pressed it, blunt papers, a postage scale, a couple of stash safes, ashtrays from Amsterdam and Copenhagen that hadn't been cleaned since Uncle Rubin brought them back in '72, hemp wicks, Baggies of bennies, bumblebees, red devils and yellow-jackets. Up or down, they had it covered.

Walking behind Pete, acting as a second set of eyes, Mojo was done with his rant, carrying the Mr. Potato Head bong under his arm. No way it was going in the bag with all the other stuff. Built it himself in a moment of inspiration, finding the toy at a garage sale, added the smoke chamber tube, the Head's body making a natural bowl.

They left the framed photos hanging, the ones Airdog snapped with his Canon: artsy 8 × 10s hanging in the staircase, macro views of bud resin in sunlight, different angles of smoke curling from between painted lips, the lips belonging to Grey's ex, Tammy.

Pete's fawn-and-bloodshot bulldog answered to Goober. He was on his favorite armchair by the front window, flattened out with his eyes half closed, aware the two humans were running through the house. It took Pete several tries, calling and snapping his fingers, before Goob gave a grumble and got down — a major movement for Goob — following the boss to the garage.

Stuffing the hockey bag in the back of the El Camino, same spot Rivers's and Glinka's pot had been, Pete held the tarp up while Mojo set the Head on top of the bags, away from the hot bulb, testing to make sure nothing would slide around. Mojo saying, "No way." Taking the bong back out, saying, "The Head stays."

Securing the tarp, Pete hoisted Goober onto the passenger seat, severing a trail of slobber hanging from the big tongue with his finger. It beat Goob's way of getting rid of it, a quick head shake that would send it ten feet in any direction.

"What now?" Mojo asked, watching Pete flick his finger.

"Stor-All place down by Alta Lake."

Mojo knew the place, the Ah-So-Easy Stor-All, sandwiched between the Express & Freight and some outfit that fabricated granite and marble counter tops. Hardly anybody ever there, nice and secluded.

"Want to take a ride, case 5-o comes back?"

Mojo said he'd board over to the dental place at Creekside, help Airdog get home. "Poor bastard. Got to feel like he Bono'd a tree."

"Yeah." Getting behind the wheel, Pete scooted Goober over to the passenger side, Mojo raising the garage door, checking the street, the perv across the street not in his bay window for a change. Backing the El Camino onto Easy Street, Pete threw Mojo a wave and rolled down the crescent, punching Grey's number into his cell.

Watching the blue funk huffing from the exhaust, Mojo lowered the door, stepping around the oil spot, thinking when he got himself a set of wheels, the thing had to be electric. Back in the suite he shared with Airdog and Tuff Dub — the low ceilings, windows at chest level, clothes piled like anthills — he set the Head on the table, checked around for anything they'd missed. Reaching the open bottle of Jack, Mojo poured three fingers into yesterday's glass and tossed the drink back; he felt it burn its way down and poured one more, drinking it while searching through the pile of clothes. Tossing a Throw the Goat T over the widowmaker, he headed for the door, grabbing the folding knife from the drawer, dropping it in a pocket. *Gooks.* Jesus. He took out his cell and punched the speed dial number for Airdog, thinking, man, what a fucked-up day.

. . . A TOUCH OF GREY

First impression was the guy was out on a day pass, broadsiding Nick Rosco with his flying bike and putting him down. A crazy superboy decked out in goggles and a fur cap, jacket with the sleeves looped around his waist. Now, without the goggles and fur, he wasn't bad-looking, a little frat-boy maybe, nothing the right haircut and an earring couldn't fix. Dara was a sucker for the brown hurt-puppy eyes, windows to the soul and all that.

"Thanks, by the way," she said, turning on the handle-bars, looking at him, flashing the black eyeshadow.

He shrugged like it was nothing, thinking what he wouldn't give for a mint, the ghost of blue cheese still raising hell down below — probably smelled like a camel.

"You kidding? That was the stuff of . . . superheroes," she said, waving the big ring around, "Totally impressed with it."

Grey steered around a man with a suitcase on wheels and a couple with matching backpacks. Leaning forward, he introduced himself. "I go by Grey."

She twisted around again, saying, "Dara." She couldn't offer her hand, needing it to balance on the bars.

Easing the Mongoose to a stop by the gazebo in Town Plaza, he steadied the bars while she got down. Then he walked it over to a busker sitting on the gazebo steps, strumming a three-chord Dylan number on a beat-to-hell acoustic. Grey introduced Dizzie, stringy blond hair looking wet, lanky, as he rose to his six-five. His cargos rode low, showing Bart Simpson boxers out the top, Converse that could fit a circus clown out the bottom. A Blue Jays cap on the ground was weighed down by a fistful of change.

"You do me a solid, Dizz?" Grey asked.

"Whatever you need, dude." Dizzie guessed by the fur cap and goggles, Grey had been messing with a mutant strain of Eight Miles High, the THC levels going to Mars.

Peeling off the jacket, Grey handed it to him, Dizzie slipping it on, the sleeves making it halfway down his forearms. No questions asked, Dizzie donned the goggles and fur cap.

"Just ride around the square," Grey said, showing the route around the gazebo with a finger, "But not too fast; let 5-o chase you a bit."

"5-o?" Dizzie nodded, like, yeah, that sounds normal.

"There's a dime bag in it."

"Let's do it." Dizz picked up his ball cap, pocketing the change, handed the cap to Grey, then held out his six-string Kent. Hopping on the Mongoose, Dizz pedaled around the square, the coins jingling in his pocket. "Better not be a scratch on her," he said, nodding at the six-string.

Slapping on the ball cap, Grey started walking, his ripped jeans showing, asking Dara, "Guy hitting you back there, he, like, your old man?" Holding the door to McGoo's, he followed her inside, checking his skinned elbow, then his palms.

"You serious?"

"I don't know. Blind date, maybe." Brushing past her, going to a sales rack, he propped the guitar up and flipped through some jeans, looking for 32/34s.

"Don't date assholes, as a rule," Dara said, watching him take a pair of Levi's, slipping out of the old and into the new right there in the aisle. Who needs the change room?

The jeans had a nice fit. Dara nodded approval.

Then he moved to a spinning rack of sunglasses, picked out a pair of Ray-Bans. With the tag dangling, he put them on, asking, "How about these?"

"Uh-uhn." She spun the rack, took a pair of Oakleys and watched him switch them. "Go with these."

"You sure?"

"Either one beats the goggles, but yeah, I'm sure." She straightened the frames for him, looking at him, pointing down. "You might want to . . ."

He buttoned the fly, calling to Freddie the clerk over by the cash, telling him to stick the jeans on his tab.

Looking past his bangs, Freddie said, "What tab's that, dude?" pointing to the shades Grey forgot he had on, Grey taking them off, asking, "These on sale?"

"Let you have them for one-fifty."

Grey checked the tag. "Says that, one-fifty."

"Yeah, but you got tax. I'm throwing that in."

To Freddie: "Fine, stick them on there, too. Oh, and appreciate if you stash this in back." Grey held the guitar across the counter, then balled his ripped up jeans, passed them over. "Oh, and toss these, will ya?"

"This like collateral?" Freddie asked, sneaking a look at Dara, thinking Grey must have horseshoes up his ass, chicks always drawn to the guy — had to be the Eight Miles High. Bad-boy pot grower.

"Dizz'll be by for it, soon as he runs an errand," Grey said, asking on the sly if Freddie had any Tic Tacs. Then he headed for the back door, saying, "Oh, and I wasn't here."

"Right," Freddie said, "nice not seeing you. You too . . ." realizing he didn't know the girl's name, catching the Nirvana T-shirt, the girl hot in her skinny jeans, following Grey out. Freddie was wondering how he'd explain Grey's tab to Shawn, the store manager.

... LOOSE LIPS

"THIS IS it, huh?" Travis asked him, the beer bottle in his hand, walking around the Camaro parked in the middle of the overflow lot, gouged down the passenger side, the thing making ticking sounds from being run on the highway. No pavement, no surveillance lights in this lot, nobody around. Travis's Chrysler 300 parked next to it.

Hard to figure Nick for the son of Bumpy Rosco, the hard Nicaraguan with a rep for taking care of business. Acting on a tip from one of his dealers, Bumpy had made the quick call to Travis, told him to take out the Hummerload of Indo Army boys packing Kalashnikovs and C13 grenades, coming up from the city's armpit. The Hummer was spotted crossing the Port Mann bridge into Rosco's turf, Bumpy guessing they were aiming to put his East End meth lab in their crosshairs.

Quitting the all-night poker game, Travis took one of his guys along, stole an Uprise bread truck from out front of a Safeway. Driving an intercept course along East Hastings, his guy in the back helping himself to bagels, Travis stopped by the Scotiabank, across from the gas station at Victoria, getting in the back with the RPG, Travis screwing on the charge, loading the warhead into the launcher, waiting till his guy spotted the Hummer coming.

Up came the rear door and Travis hopped down, stepping away, a bagel in his mouth, putting the launcher to his shoulder, letting the warhead snake and hiss across the intersection, blowing the gas guzzler off the asphalt, leaving three Indos in chunks across East Hastings, a fourth one seriously injured. A mother of two looking to lose a few pounds, pedaling her bike, was pronounced a fourth victim of the crime, struck off her Schwinn by flying Goodrich rubber. Travis felt bad about that part.

Witnesses gave conflicting reports, every set of eyes seeing something different. The *Province* ran the headline *GANGBANG!* The article talking about the mayor's office cranking up the heat in the face of an upcoming election — a personal crusade — the mayor ranting he wanted drug crime off the streets. Councilmen dedicated meetings, and police were put on high alert.

Every storefront within a hundred feet of ground zero had been blown out. Shredded awnings hung like pennants. A tattooed hand was found in a dollar shop's window, gripping a Beretta. It was Bumpy's message to the Indos or anybody else wanting to check out his welcome mat: if you're coming, bring the right firepower.

The rocket attack had Bumpy playing model citizen, leaving it to Travis Rainey to gain a toehold up in Whistler. The man who took the Sabers from two-bit dope deals to running a pipeline for a Mexi-cartel, rigging filling machines and smuggling coke-filled Kinder Surprise by the caseload across the border, dodging DEA, ICE, DOJ, FBI and anybody else with initials on their jackets, Travis finding new ways to add zeros to Bumpy's bottom line.

And then there was Nick . . .

Nick followed Travis around the front of the car, telling him the Camaro just turned over two hundred klicks. Peeling off his driving gloves, he patted a hand along the racing stripe, telling him she purred like a cat.

"Scratches like one too, huh?" Travis pointed at Nick's face, the gouge Dara's ring left, adding, "Nobody tell you Ford's back at making the Shelby?" Travis liked pushing his buttons.

"Fuck Ford. And fuck Shelby." Nick said, having never forgiven Ford for the Granada, worst tin can to ever get shipped out of Detroit. Like the one he drove back in high school, his mom's gold clunker, a Ghia model with a gagging six-banger under the hood. You could hear the knocking and pinging even with the radio on. With all the old man's dough, she should have driven a Caddy. As far as picking up school-aged pussy, the Ghia was a deal-breaker, worse than pimples.

"Only color they had?" Travis stopped, taking it in from the front.

"Inferno orange, you kidding? It's a classic."

"And real easy to spot." Travis caught the torn pant leg, the welt rising on Nick's cheek, the keyed door, asking, "Something you want to tell me?"

"Tell you?"

"Start with what happened to your mule?"

"Didn't work out." He swallowed some of the beer Travis gave him, the brew tasting bitter.

"Like what, she deck you?" Travis was loving this, catching the swollen lip. He took out his smokes, fishing for his lighter. "She key the car, too?" Throwing a thumb to the passenger side.

"Fuck off." The name Rosco let Nick talk to people like that, even this goon his old man sent to set things up, something Nick could have done himself. "Bitch was wrong for this, that's all."

Travis turned and leaned against the paint job, putting together what happened between him and the chick. This pussy son of a gangster he was supposed to babysit, the old man telling him to keep Nick miles from the war waging with the Indos down in the city — actually told him that. Since Travis blew up the Hummer, bodies had been stacking up, and Bumpy didn't want Nick to end up in the pile.

"So this chick refused to show you her generation gap, so you roughed her up." Travis pointed to the welt, saying, "And she did that, huh?"

"Fuck you."

Travis let it go a second time, getting back to serious. "How much you leak?"

"What?"

"What does she know?"

"I leaked dick." Bad enough this asshole was leaning against the new paint, treating him like a kid. "Look, just back off." Nick's day had started out shitty side up, catching it from the old man, arguing about taking a room at the same dive Travis was staying at, the Cadillac Arms, a one-star dump miles outside the Village, didn't even have a pool. Nick checked out some Google images, place didn't have a website; according to the pics the only amenity was a Coke machine in the lobby that looked like it got dragged behind a Peterbilt. The old man wanted him safe, wanted him close to Travis.

But Nick stood his ground, told the old man no, said he knew how to use the .38 under his jacket, all the protection he needed. Had his man Stan book him into the Wilmott, a baby suite on the top floor, heart of the Village. Five stars. Told the old man he wasn't staying with the hired help, told him to stop fucking worrying. Finally the old man gave in.

Whistler was going to be his town. That's what the old man promised. Travis would set it up, and Nick would run it. Time for people to start showing him respect.

"Asked how much dick," Travis said, setting his bottle down, sliding it across the orange hood. Rosco's idiot child wasn't going to land him in Corrections.

Nick drew a long breath, saying, "Even if she knew something, what's she gonna do with it?"

"Chick can ID you, for one."

"For what, putting a hand on her leg?" Nick slapped the driving gloves into his palm, looking at the bottle sweating on his hood.

Travis slid off the hood, snatching the gloves from Nick's hand. Forcing one on, flexing his fingers like O.J., he looked at it, asking, "What's with the holes?"

"For better grip," Nick said. "Look, you done —"

Clutching a fistful of Camaro grill, Travis tore out the bow-tie logo, grunting as he did it. Something he knew Nick wouldn't report to the old man.

"What the fuck?" Nick screeched.

"Yeah, real good grip."

Nick couldn't believe it, the bow-tie logo in the big fist. "That's coming out of your pocket. *Fuck!*"

Travis took hold of Nick's hand and slapped the logo in it, closing Nick's fingers around it, and squeezed, saying, "Send me the bill, okay?"

Nick winced, the jagged plastic digging in his hand.

"And park this thing out of sight." Then, like he was talking to himself, "Guy buys an orange car."

Trying to peel the glove off, Travis saw the kid with dreadlocks pedaling the bike across the lot, coming their way, guessing what he was going to say before he pulled up. Had to be another of Grey Stevens's crew, this one darker, with hair like rope, taller than the one Travis punched out an hour ago, Travis guessing this guy hadn't heard the news yet.

"Yo, you dudes looking for something to mellow you out?" Tuff Dub asked, steering around the front of the Camaro, sizing up the two men, the piece of grill in the thin guy's hand, the bigger one trying to peel a glove off his hand. These guys had to be tweaking, could probably use some mellowing. He hadn't planned on making any sales, just came by to find Airdog, knew he liked working the lots Sunday mornings. Sometimes it started slow, but things got hopping closer to noon, city folk coming up for their outdoor fix, wanting to toke up some Eight Miles High before hiking and biking the trails, ziplining or bungee jumping a hundred and sixty feet over the Cheakamus. High flying. With stoner grins on their faces.

His own all-nighter had him sleeping away most of the morning. Doing hurricane bong hits with the college cutie from Seattle. Black babe named Shawna, all legs and nice high J. Lo buns, her thick lips wrapping around the pipe, the two of them getting wasted then going to town. Peeling himself off Shawna's floor, he made his way over to the Starbucks, pouring a couple of ventis into himself. Became human again. Getting voicemail the only time he tried calling Mojo, he hadn't heard what happened to Airdog right in the next parking lot. Riding his way through the lots on his way home, he thought he could dump a dime bag.

"Talk to your buddy Stevens today?" Travis asked him.

"Who's Stevens?" Tuff thinking these guys could be narcs.

"I got this." Nick sidestepped Travis, tired of the bullshit, getting in front of the kid with rope for hair. Time to show Travis what he could do. "You fucks not getting the message?"

"What —"

Nick shoved the kid hard, knocking him from the bike.

"Hey, chill dude," Tuff said, catching his balance, looking at the guy with the chunk of grill in his hand. "All I said was . . ." He reached inside his pocket for one of the dime bags, show this asshole why he was here.

Thinking gun, Nick dropped the grill and went for the Smith, drawing it out in one smooth motion like he practised, shoving the barrel against Tuff. Trying to twist away, Tuff got his legs tangled in the bike's frame. Jumping in, Travis made a grab for the Smith.

The shot was muffled, the barrel pressed against Tuff as Nick fired. Tuff was jerked back, Travis catching him from falling. The kid looked surprised, wind punched out of him, trying to speak, going limp in Travis's arms.

Nick straightened his arm for a second shot, Travis

snatching the pistol. Couldn't believe it. Letting the kid slump to the ground, the red stain spreading across his chest, eyes searching for answers as he tried to draw breath.

"He . . . he was going for a gun," Nick said.

Travis checked around the lot, Nick's pistol in his hand, the glove still on. Shaking out the rest of the shells, dropping them in his pocket, he tossed the piece back, called Nick a fucking idiot, told him to get rid of it, then told him to pop his trunk. Looking around again, Travis swept the line of trees between the two parking lots. A guy staring at them at the opposite end of the lot looked frozen. Then the guy turned and ran.

"No fucking way you're getting blood all over —"

Coming up, Travis snatched Nick by the throat, could have ripped out his windpipe, telling him again, "Pop it, now, then you lay your fucking jacket down." Travis squeezed his fingers together. "Do it."

Rubbing at his throat, Nick opened the door and got in. He popped the trunk, waited till Travis bent and lifted Tuff Dub, then stuck in the key.

"Your old man gets win—"

Nick cranked the engine, stomped the pedal and peeled away, his door slamming shut, leaving Travis standing holding the limp body, watching the orange Camaro speed off, the trunk flapping up and down like it was waving bye-bye.

. . . GETTING THEIR MAN

THE STITCH stopped detective Jimmy Gallo cold, felt like an ice pick hooking between his ribs. Stooping over, he panted like his old collie, thinking this was it. Should have let Lance do the foot chase, Jimmy packing too many extra pounds for this, the new shoes pinching like a bitch. Why the hell were they chasing after this moron Stevens anyway? Lance had the two of them acting like mutts; something runs, you go after it. Far as Jimmy was concerned, the loot sent them up here to write a fucking report on drug activity, a bullshit assignment to appease the brass upstairs. Lance didn't get that part, trying to turn this into real police work. Warning Grey Stevens the bad guys were circling.

Jimmy watched the guy he thought was Grey Stevens circle the bike around the gazebo, twenty yards ahead of him, the fur cap and goggles on his head, playing cat and mouse. Hands on his knees, Jimmy felt the ice pick go deeper. If it wasn't for the paperwork and the eyewitnesses, he might have winged the bastard, just enough to stop him from pedaling.

"You okay, officer?" Dizzie asked like he hadn't seen Jimmy chasing after him. Taking out the earbuds, he rolled the bike closer, walking it with his feet.

"Be even better after I kick your ass." Jimmy wheezed the words.

Tugging off the goggles, Dizzie said, "These things fog like a bitch. Sorry, man, didn't see you. You need directions or something?"

Lance rolled the Laredo past some strolling tourists, cherry blinking on top. Getting out, he walked over to Jimmy and the kid who wasn't Grey Stevens. The same outfit but the wrong guy. Lance recognized him as one of the too-many buskers the municipality had sold licenses to over the past six months, he'd caught the kid's act outside one of the hotels. Now, making him for one of Stevens's dealers, he said, "Bum with a guitar, right?"

Dizzie stepped off the bike, saying he preferred the term *local entertainer.*

"Anybody with fifty bucks for the license gets to stand on a street corner, shuck and jive," Jimmy said, telling Dizzie to lace his fingers on his head, taking the bike from him.

"Shuck and jive. That like from the sixties, daddio?" Dizzie doing like he was told.

Jimmy dropped the bike, saying to Lance, "Guy's up to his elbows in shit, and he asks me a question like that." One punch, hard enough to fold the kid over, teach him respect for the law, that's all Jimmy wanted.

"Hey, how do I know you guys are the real deal, nobody's showing me any tin?"

"Yeah, we could show you tin," Jimmy said, pulling back

the red jacket, his shield clipped to his belt. "Take you in, show you all the tin you want, do the whole tour, the cell, do the old ink and roll, cuff you to the table, ask our questions. Make a day of it."

"Look, if I did something wrong —"

"Wrong? Come on, kid, I heard you outside the Fairmont, murdering 'Michelle, *ma belle*.'"

"Ouch," Dizzie said.

"Really had to be there, back in the day, you know, to really get the Beatles." Jimmy threw a thumb over his shoulder, telling him to get out of his sight.

Dropping his arms, Dizzie picked up the bike and walked it over to McGoo's, leaning it against the wall, going into the shop.

"You okay, Jimmy?" Lance asked, his partner not looking so hot, face flushed, holding his side.

"Never better." Jimmy climbed into the Laredo, the ice pick downgraded to needle jabs. The radio bleeped, Jimmy taking up the handheld, turning up the volume, holding the whip out the window, the dispatcher coming on.

Taking advantage, Lance walked past McGoo's, ducked into the public can, the door marked *Men's*, damned coffee going through him like rainwater down a sewer drain. Smelled like the place had just been disinfected, new cakes in the urinals.

When he came out the bike was gone, and Jimmy was waving for him to hurry, told him they had a code three, meaning shots fired, Jimmy telling him to drive over to Day Lot 5, pointing to where it was. Lance jumped in, snapped on his seatbelt and cranked the engine.

"Got a wit heard a shot," Jimmy filled him in, "thinks he saw a couple guys stuff another guy in a trunk, drive off."

Lance was rolling, making it to the overflow lot in under two minutes. Three units were already there, light-bars flashing. The witness was a hiker named Jenkins, up here from Mission. Thick glasses magnified his eyes, Jenkins explaining he was myopic, a professor of art history who never carried a cell on account of the electromagnetic radiation. Came up here to get in tune with nature. Took him ten minutes just to find a pay phone and make the 9-1-1 call.

"This day and age, who doesn't carry a fucking cell?" Jimmy asked after they turned Jenkins loose. "Should be a fucking law." Jenkins's statement went like this: reasonably sure he heard a gunshot, two guys, one tall, one not so tall, stuffing what looked like a third guy in the trunk of a late model car that might have been dark. Turned out on top of being myopic, Jenkins was color-blind. Jenkins declared one man took off in a retro-looking car that could have been orange, red or brown. The second man drove off the opposite way, Jenkins not sure which trunk the body was in. He said the dark car's door opened funny, "like a flapping bird wing" narrowed his color choice to black or navy, said it like he was asking a question, repeating how it all happened so fast.

Jimmy tore his notes from the pad, tossed them on the floor of the Laredo. No body. No gun. No casings. And a witness likely to show up at court tapping a white stick.

Lance tuned Jimmy out, felt the adrenaline. This town was set to explode. And this was his shot.

. . . HIGH NOON

FACE LIKE porcelain, not a line or crease. Travis ran his palm across her shoulder, Lexie's skin warm under his touch. Laying his head back on the doubled pillow, he watched her rise on an elbow. Looking at him like she was learning his game, figuring him out, she said, "I mean it. I don't fake, never told anybody that was the best two minutes of my life. I just answer the phones, do the bookings, update the Twitter page."

"Hey, I believe you." He tossed his wallet back on the nightstand. "You just book and twitter."

"Tweet."

"Okay, tweet. Guess I should feel . . ."

"Lucky?"

"Flattered, but in a lucky way."

She was smiling, saying, "I like this by the way," moving her fingers along the silver over his ears, fingers that felt like feathers. She touched the scar a .44 slug had left on his deltoid, not asking how it got there.

After leaving Manny's, he had driven out of town, made the call to Gibbet, waiting for a call back on a side road, expecting to rendezvous to hand off the body packed in his trunk like tinned fish. Thinking of her, he made another call to Sugar's, asked Lexie if she knew who was calling. She said, yeah, the new boss. Told her he was sorry, but he'd have to take a rain check on lunch. Told her it was a life-and-death thing. She sounded disappointed, telling him, too bad, Manny had just gone home with a migraine, leaving her afternoon free.

He had to wait on Gibbet anyway, so he drove back and met her at the bistro, ordered up the linguine vongole in wine sauce, followed it with espresso and cantuccini. The body waiting in his trunk. On his second espresso, Travis put it out there, needing an alibi, asked how she felt about turning back the clock.

Lexie gave him a long look, saying, "How about I make it stand still?" leading him a block from the office to the room Manny kept at the Glacier, called it his VIP room. Handing his car keys to the valet, Travis tipped the kid a twenty, telling him to make sure he parked it in the shade. Then in suite four-oh-two, she gave him all the alibi he could ever want, his cell phone in easy reach.

When they finished they talked a bit, then he reached his jacket lopped over the armchair, fishing for his wallet. Guessing his intention, she told him she wasn't on the menu. "Like I said, I just felt something and acted on it." She could have been pissed off, instead she grinned.

"What's funny?"

"Should've seen Manny after you left."

"Yeah, how was that?"

"Rattled."

"And you liked that?"

"Yeah, I did. Ought to try working for him."

"Been there."

She rose and he watched her step across the room, showing her tan lines, cheeks rising and falling. Her blonde hair curled down her back. She disappeared into the can and closed the door.

He tried Nick's cell for the second time, had to leave a message. Told the dumb fuck he better be in his suite at the Wilmott when he got back, told him to leave the pumpkin in the parking garage, or next time he'd take more than a chunk of grill.

Then he called down to room service and ordered the truffle ice along with a carafe of Italian roast. Lying there, waiting for Gibbet's call, he felt a second wind coming — show her he wasn't that old.

The toilet flushed and she stepped out, smiling at him, comfortable being naked in front of him, coming back to the bed, party-pink mouth smiling. Lifting the blanket, she climbed back in, drawing close, asking, "You believe me, right? I just do the bookings."

"Yeah, I do."

"Wouldn't believe some of the calls. Guy this morning, right after you came in?"

"Yeah?"

"Here for some medical supply symposium. Said he wanted to pay me in syringes."

"The barter system."

"Yeah. Figures escorts are junkies. Had one a week back asking for a Daisy Duke experience. Wanted her bent over the hood of the General Lee, willing to pay extra for the little shorts."

Travis was thinking it sounded like Nick, right down to the orange car.

"Get guys asking for Dolly Parton boobs, J. Lo's butt, somebody else's lips. Hear stuff you couldn't make up, you know?"

He nodded, then threw it out there. "Hey, got something else you could do for me."

She looked at him. "How's that?"

"Looking for some guys sounding and looking like they're from Bollywood."

"Uh huh."

"Guys I'm talking about got scorpions tattooed across their hands." He showed her how the tattoos ran.

"Take it they're not with any convention."

"You do that for me?"

It took her a moment. "Yeah, I can do that." She stopped talking and moved her hand under the blanket, checking on his second wind.

. . . MOJO RELIGION

DARA LEANED back into Grey's sofa, finally calm after he rescued her from Nick Rosco. The music pumping through Uncle Rubin's old-school speakers was hers, *Ready to Die*, the new one by Iggy and the Stooges, her iPod hooked into Grey's Bose dock, hooked into the old-school preamp. Grey's way of making her feel welcome. Grey feeling more at ease since ditching the cops, Mojo and Pete clearing out all the dope-related shit, Pete stashing it with the pot at the Stor-All place by Alta Lake. Grey put all the crap that happened right out of his mind, looking at the girl, Mojo in one of the armchairs by the front window, keeping an eye out.

Dara saying how she carried her tunes with her everywhere she went, sixty-four gigs worth of it, Mojo saying he wouldn't step out the door without his tunes, saying, "Like a religion."

Above the sound system hung a framed photo of Uncle Rubin, the old boy smiling, grey wisps of thinning hair, looking hip in his rose-tinted shades, the shot taken before the cancer.

Dara looked at Grey, talking over the music, saying, "So tell me about this guy on the bike who saved me."

"Like what?" Grey asked, sinking into the cushion, looking at her: the Nirvana T-shirt, legs in skinny jeans, scuffed runners up on his coffee table, pink laces dangling down, her feet going back and forth like a metronome. "Not much to tell, really."

"Mysterious, huh? Okay, how about him, what's his story?" she said, nodding at the Mr. Potato Head bong on the table, its buggy eyes on her, a tube coming out of the back of its head, pipe extending from the top of its black bowler. Pretty cool, she thought.

"The Head," Grey said, telling her Mojo found the toy at a garage sale, still in its original box, how he transformed it in a moment of inspiration, how they'd been toking up with the Head ever since.

"Cool," she said, nodding at Mojo.

Bopping to the music, he slumped low in the armchair by the window, the one Grey painted with black gloss house paint, the fabric crunching every time somebody sat in it, Mojo thinking it was the best chair in the world, the other chair was Goob's, the one with all that fur stuck to it. Mojo's hair was freshly spiked, tattoos of winding serpents in green and red running down both arms. Bondage pants, studs and straps all over the place, a silver skull on a black T-shirt. He glanced out now and then, checking for cars driving by, hoping Pete remembered to bring back Uncle Rubin's pistol, Pete downstairs making chicken broth for Airdog, the poor guy drugged up and sleeping it off.

"Okay, so I know a little about Mojo . . ." she said, looking at Grey, trying again. "Now you. Give me something."

"Like what?"

"Like what do you do when you're not saving us mortals?"

Grey gave a shrug. "I don't know, ski, snowboard the white months, bike and board the rest, take life easy, you know, save up my strength." The last few days had been anything but easy: Travis Rainey calling and making threats, the two cops coming round, then phoning, leaving messages, Airdog getting his teeth knocked out. To top it off, his Mongoose was swiped right after he put new pegs on her. Damn Dizzie for walking into McGoo's and leaving the bike outside, unlocked. Gone, just like that.

Dara nodded and looked back at Mojo, the guy twisting a joint easy as he breathed. One hand, one lick. Done. He tucked it behind an ear.

"Thought you only used him?" Dara nodded at the bong.

"Head's for inside," Mojo said. "Joint's for outside — for later." Taking out a Baggie, he reached for the Head.

Dara watched Mojo load the bowl, fire it up with his Bic. Ladies first, he passed the Head to her.

Taking it, she put her mouth around the end and — holy shit — she understood about Eight Miles High. One toke and she was floating, her insides feeling warm. Best pot she ever smoked — and the girl had been to Jamaica. Twice. Taking another hit, she passed the bong; any more and the Head would be smiling and talking back.

"So, that's what you do, ski and shit?" There was more; she could tell by the way Mojo kept looking out the window, knowing he wasn't waiting for a pizza.

"Yeah, I mean I work," Grey said, taking a turn, talking around the smoke, passing the Head over to Mojo. "It's not all fun and games."

She caught a look passing between Grey and Mojo. "Can I ask what kind of work?"

The electricity passing between these two wasn't lost on Mojo. It did him good to see it. About time Grey forgot about Tammy. High time he got himself laid, and this Dara with the pink laces looked up to the task.

Grey told her how he mixed cocktails at this place called the Cellar, a cool spot, usually with a good crowd. She crossed her shoes on the coffee table, her laces looking neon. If she were at home, she would have kicked her shoes off, freed her painted toes. She liked being barefoot. "You do any of those bartender tricks?"

"Call it flair and, yeah, I do some. Got hooked watching this guy do the egg flip once over at the Star Palace, asked him to show it to me. Practiced it like a week. Then had Niels, one of the buskers, teach me some juggling. Added in a little magic, you know, flaming drinks, multiple pours, that kind of thing. Keeps it fun and the tourists love it. Guess it's my way of showing off."

"I mean, it's nothing to be ashamed of." She took the Head and the Bic from Mojo, winking at him, firing it up, dragging another hit into her lungs. "How about it?"

"About what?"

"Showing me some flair."

"Could happen, maybe later." Grey took the Head and Bic, asking, "How about you?"

She blew the smoke out in a perfect ring, poking her finger through the rising circle of smoke, sending it higher.

"Pretty good, but can you make a living at it?"

"Kind of between gigs right now," she said, her own voice sounding like someone added echo. "That guy you hit?"

"The Nick guy?" He sat the Head on the table.

"Worked for him. Fact, today was my first day." She turned the Head so his eyes weren't directly on her. "Met him over bagels this morning down in the city." She told them how he seemed nice at first, about riding up here in his orange bullshit car, how she ended up blasting Binaca in his eyes and punching his boys once he wasn't so nice anymore.

Grey and Mojo cringed at the thought, both looking at the skull ring.

"Strained the employer-employee relation thing," Mojo said. "Jesus, where'd you find this guy, Craigslist?"

"Through an old boyfriend," she said, looking at Grey, then back at Mojo, recounting how Nick seemed fine at first, giving her some doubt on the ride up, then started with the hands as soon as they turned into the Village, past the welcome sign, telling Mojo how she tried to get away and how Grey came on the scene and biked the guy while he was going off on her.

Mojo pictured it: Grey playing the high hero, on the run from the cops in his goggles and fur cap, a rip in his pants. He grinned and nodded, thinking, yeah, they make a cute couple, this girl with the pink laces, Iggy Pop singing about an unfriendly world.

"So what did this guy want you to do — for a job?" Mojo asked.

"Make a run up here once a week, get paid two-fifty for doing it. I'm guessing dope." She shrugged.

Grey and Mojo looked at each other, getting the picture. Nick had to be with Travis Rainey, the guys forcing them out, the ones who attacked Airdog, the ones Edwards and Gallo warned Grey about. Could be why the two cops came by that morning, tell them about Airdog getting beaten in the parking lot. Mojo took out his cell, said he was putting the word out to the buskers, Grey saying he'd call Rivers and Glinka, give them a heads-up.

"Pretty stupid, huh?" Dara said, sensing the tension.

"You're talking to a guy who rode through town wearing goggles and fur cap this morning," Mojo said, trying to make her feel better, punching a number into his phone, walking to the kitchen.

"You smoking this when you did it, the bike thing?" she asked Grey.

"Come to think of it . . ."

They grinned at each other, and he said, "This is Iggy, huh?" nodding at the stereo.

She told him, yeah, Iggy and the boys still going strong, sipping her drink while he excused himself, went into the hall to make his call. Checking out the odds-and-ends furniture, she guessed the curtains with white flowers that Mojo kept looking out showed a woman's touch. Ten to one, Grey's woman. And by the look of the place, an ex-woman, one that took all the good stuff when she split. A toilet-seat-up kind of place.

Setting her drink on the glass table, she looked at Grey coming back in the room. He looked troubled. "This drink kicks, by the way," she said, licking the sweet from her lips, thinking she should probably go.

"There's more if you want." Grey sat and nodded at the pitcher, frosty from the ice.

Her buzz got her thinking of the Kool-Aid man and his frosty smile, one of the good things from her childhood. "What did you call it?"

"Bimbo punch, but with Meyer instead of regular lemons, brown instead of white sugar." Grey being serious about his concoctions.

"Who's the bimbo?" She couldn't help the grin. Him, too. Their eyes meeting. Chemistry. Eight Miles High helped push it along. "So, who are you into, music-wise?" she asked, thinking she'd stay just a bit longer, then see about catching a bus back to the city.

"Mungo Jerry," Mojo answered for him, coming back in, going to his chair, checking out past the flowered curtains. "Dude can't get enough, plays it all the time."

"That the one *In the Summertime da da da da da*?"

"That's the one."

"Heard it from my mom, stuff she was into like back in . . . I don't know . . . the sixties."

"Shoot me," Grey said, "I'm into the oldies."

"Thought that Elton guy did it, somebody like that."

"He covered it, but his pales," Grey said. "Mungo's the one you want."

"Into anything from, like, this century?" She took in the old-school sound system behind her, saying she hadn't seen a turntable since she was five or six.

Grey made a crack about Iggy being around longer than Mungo, then recited some bands he liked, Dara bopping along to Iggy doing "DD's," her feet looking farther away than they should be. She spread her arms along the top of the couch, felt like she was sinking between the cushions. Running her tongue over her lips, she asked if anybody else's mouth felt like rubber.

Grey and Mojo licked, both said, yeah, like rubber, Dara reaching and turning the Head, sure she'd already turned him away once.

"Not so bad when you get to know him," Mojo said, looking at the Head. "Like one of the family."

"Yeah? How often you change his dirty bong water?"

They were laughing again. This girl alright.

Taking a tissue from her pocket, she tore bits off a corner as she sipped her bimbo punch, letting the bits drop in her lap like snow, thinking about her situation, guessing if it was okay, she'd crash here (no way she'd get a room with the twelve bucks in her pocket), see about catching a ride back to the city in the morning.

When the track ended, Grey went to the stereo shrine, putting on the Mungo, saying they asked for it, thinking he should get over to Nesters for more KD, offer this girl something to eat. Pete and the guys downstairs doing the communal living thing, helping themselves to anything in his cupboards. Nothing new there.

Goober the bulldog trudged and grunted up the stairs, pink tongue hanging out, going right to Dara, sniffing her. Pete followed, clomping in his untied Doc Martens, a messenger bag over his shoulder. Goober licked her hand and went to his chair, Grey making the introductions, Pete saying hi to Dara.

"How's Airdog?" Mojo asked Pete.

"Sleeping off the painkillers," Pete said, sitting cross-legged on the floor. "Couple of weeks they fit him for dentures." Deciding the girl was cool, Pete fished into the messenger bag, pulling out a Baggie of the Pemberton weed, then laid Uncle Rubin's High Standard next to it.

"Belonged to my uncle," Grey said, explaining, not wanting her to freak out, picking up the .22, then taking his vibrating phone from his pocket. Stepping into the front hall, he checked the display and put it to his ear, saying, "Yeah?"

"People coming in, asking for you." It was Teddy B, the sounds of the Cellar in the background, the bar where he worked seeming busy for a Sunday afternoon.

"Cops?"

"Two came by earlier, plain clothes, told them you weren't working today, but not this guy. Dude just came in, with grey streaks in his hair, had a beer. Wanted to offer him a bowl of roofing nails to chew on."

Had to be Travis Rainey, the guy with the threats, Grey asking, "He say what he wanted?"

"Asked when you were in, so I told him I'd have to check the schedule. Pretended to and told him it wasn't posted yet. Guy grunted and walked out. Said he'd be back." Teddy B asking if that was Mungo in the background, Grey saying yeah, then, "Thanks for that, B." Clicking off, he went back into the living room, still holding the pistol in his hand.

"Who was that?" Pete asked.

"Teddy B wanting an extra shift out of me." Grey looked at the pistol, thinking he'd keep it close. He needed to have a word with Pete, figure out what to do. Then he tucked the gun behind his back, smiled at Dara, hoping she'd stick around, then was thinking about sleeping arrangements.

. . . A LITTLE THIS, A LITTLE THAT

IT WAS early afternoon by the time Travis got the call back. Gibbet spoke in that faraway monotone he had, named the spot down by Daisy Lake, told Travis to pull off at the Brew Creek exit and watch for a brown van. Travis hung up, checking the rearview. Gibbet was straight out of some Hitchcock nightmare, the guy the Nanaimo chapter used to call on when a body needed to go Jimmy Hoffa. Nobody knew his real name or much about him or how he did what he did. All anybody knew, Gibbet was the ghost that got it done. Cash up front. No face, no prints, no trace.

The way it worked: Travis left word with Gus, the guy that picked up at Tuck's Secondhand & Pawn out on Loggers Lane, a two-story tear-down with limited hours on the shady side of Squamish. Gus took his number, then hung up. The message got bounced between burner phones and by the time Travis dropped Lexie back off at Sugar's, Gibbet called him back, saying it had been a hell of a day.

Riding to Daisy Lake with the body getting ripe in the trunk, Travis weighed and measured, thinking Nick Rosco was turning out to be more of a fuck-up than expected, shooting the kid in the middle of a parking lot in broad daylight, next to his beacon of a car, then taking off, leaving Travis with the corpse in his arms, looking like a guy about to carry his bride over the threshold.

Taking Nick along to Whistler had been a personal favor to Bumpy, Travis thinking it was Bumpy's way of getting his idiot child out of the line of fire and out of his hair at the same time.

Slipping on the shades, Travis headed the Chrysler southbound along the Sea-to-Sky. Bringing Nick had been a mistake. One that might end with a chalk outline around the fancy jacket, Nick ending up on Gibbet's to-do list.

Taking out his cell, Travis punched in the number of the old road captain for the Sabers MC. After the club was taken down, Richie Winters retired the jacket and said he was done with the life. Riding to his hometown of Salmon Arm, Richie took his savings and put a downstroke on a service station and spent his days getting grease on his hands, doing auto repairs for the local lumbermen in the one-horse town, breaking down a hot car here and there, doing the odd bit of contract work. Travis saying, "Hey, bro. Know who this is?"

"Well, fuck me silly," Richie said and asked what was shaking.

"Nothing but the trees, bro. How about you?"

"Yeah, I been good. Fact, real good. You know, getting by."

"Yeah, and Dell and the kids?" Travis trying to put together how old the boy and girl were now.

"Ah, Dell's back in Nanaimo, you know, but the kids are good, growing like weeds, you know."

"Yeah."

"Yeah, well, truth be told, things went sideways between us, you know. Guess I tore it, final straw was me making a crack about her being an acrobat, all the time holding her cooz over my head."

"You're supposed to *think* shit like that, not say it out loud."

"Yeah." Richie laughed. "So, now I get to see my kids once every couple of weeks."

"That sucks." Sorry he asked, Travis could pretty well write the real story: Richie and Dell sticking together for the sake of the kids, taking it as far as they could, getting bored and drifting apart. She'd always been a decent old lady to Richie, took his shit, carted his drunken ass from bar stool to bed more times than anybody should have to, took care of the bills and the kids, Richie acting like one of them. Far as Travis remembered, the woman never held anything over Richie's head, but everybody's got a story.

With the small talk behind them, Travis got down to it, talking around things the way they did on phones. "You hear much from the boys in Sechelt?" Meaning Benny and Johnny Cash Rivers.

"Last I heard, J.C.'s doing a stretch, and Benny's filling his shoes, you know, doing his thing with the Russian."

"Getting something going for the old man. Already talked to Benny and he's on board, Glinka, too; but word is we can expect some competition. Reason I'm calling, case you want in."

"Yeah?"

"Still got the odd hang-around, ones know their way around?"

"You kidding? Guys are like an open sore," Richie said with that funny laugh of his. "Got a couple working right here, changing tires, doing lube and oil and shit. And yeah, they know a thing or two. Mutt, you don't know, but he's solid, did some prospecting, you know? And pretty sure you met Marty."

"Marty, yeah, rings a bell. Used to go by Bacon, right?"

"That's the one. Hell of a mechanic. Dropped the Bacon handle about fifty pounds ago."

Travis laughed and said, "Helped me out with the clutch on my bike one time. Yeah, guy had the touch alright. Good mechanic." Remembering Bacon from the old Sabers clubhouse, a prospect on his way to full patch, a scar running from one eye straight down his cheek, always with blond stubble on his face, always looked like he was sweating. Liked to carry a wrench.

"Why, you due a lube job, bro?"

"What I got means closing up your shop, but worth your while."

"Yeah?"

"Five in your pocket, two for each of your open sores. That, and I cover expenses."

"How long you thinking?"

"All goes well, maybe a week. More if we go into extra innings."

Meant leaving the kid Jeffy to pump gas, close the garage doors for a week; but the money sounded right, plus Richie was due some excitement. A chance to get out of town, away from the locals moping over their pitchers of beer about the sawmill closing down. He said he was in without another thought, kind of excited about the six-hour road trip, a chance to straddle the Fat Boy and try out the new windshield.

"Oh, and I need you to get some wheels, bro, a van. You know the kind." Meaning plain and stolen.

"That it?" So much for straddling the Fat Boy.

"For now."

"Just need the when and where, bro."

"Just got to drop something off, then get fresh supplies. How about the old arches on Cleveland, you know the place?"

"Just like old times."

He told Richie a time, finished by saying, "Fill you in on the rest." With that, Travis hung up. The flashing lights in the rearview got his full-on attention.

Shit!

He gripped the wheel tight, thinking what to do. The radio car had rolled up on him with those push bars without him even noticing. Travis checked his speedometer, doing twenty-four klicks over. He slowed. Getting as stupid as Nick.

The cop must have hit him with a radar gun. Coasting until he found a place to pull the Chrysler over, one of those tourist lookouts, Travis paused Willie Nelson on the CD singing about there being no place left to fly. Looking at the cop in the rearview, he missed Danny DeWulf, Nav's man who'd been tailing him from the Village, cruising past in his Accord.

Putting on his game face, Travis pressed down the window. Waiting for the officer to call in his plate, watched him get out in the rearview, slap the cap on and do the cop shuffle in those striped pants, hand above his holster, stopping at the window, leaning in.

"Afternoon, officer." Hands in plain sight, Travis smiled.

The uni was Constable Rick Harper. Bending with his black web belt, the big Smith on his hip, radio clipped to the blue vest. He gave his deadpan spiel, asking for license and registration, then asked if Travis knew why he got pulled over.

"Guess I was doing a little over, right?" Not likely this Dudley Do-Right stopped him for having a body in the trunk, the dead kid with rope hair, Gibbet waiting down by Daisy Lake, less than five miles south. Checking his watch as he clicked open the glovebox, Travis fished out the papers.

Looking them over, Harper explained using a cell while driving was an offense, Travis saying it was just a quick business call, apologizing for it.

Asking what line of business he was in, Harper let his eyes search around the interior, impressed with the car, the black leather, Harman/Kardon sound system, the piano-black dash.

"Independent contractor," Travis told him.

"Yeah? Like renovations?" Harper leaned in a little more, glancing at the dual-pane sunroof.

"Yeah, build chalets, add-ons, a little this, a little that," Travis said, thinking he could add arms and drug trafficking, murder, extortion, witness tampering, robbery and hijacking to the list, thinking how it would look squeezed on the back of a business card.

Harper nodded and told him using a cell like the one he had while driving came with a hundred-and-sixty-seven buck ticket and three demerits, Travis saying, "Ouch."

Then Harper was checking out the door, asking, "This got the Lambo doors?"

"Yeah, you bet." Pulling the handle, Travis pushed the door out, then up, showing the cop how it worked, buddying up, offering to let Harper get behind the wheel if he wanted, the P5 under the seat.

Sitting there at the side of the highway, with his striped cap in his lap, Harper gripped the wheel, more like a kid than a cop, putting himself in a ride like this, checking out the instrument panel, playing with the sunroof, asking Travis how he liked the HEMI 8, and the all-wheel drive, asking if the buckets were full leather, how big the trunk was.

Big enough to fit a body in, maybe two if Harper kept playing with the buttons. "Sounds like you're talking yourself into one," Travis said, smiling at him, forcing himself not to look at his watch again.

"You haven't met my wife."

"Yeah, well, I know how that goes," Travis said. "But, I tell you, if you're looking for a set of wheels, you could do worse, leastways, I got no complaints."

Harper slid off the seat and stood next to Travis, putting the cap back on. "A little this, a little that seems to be paying off for you." Smiling, Harper said he was letting Travis off this time, calling him Mr. Romney, the name on the driver's license. Handing it back along with the insurance, he told Travis he ought to go hands-free, then went back to his cruiser. Thanking him and wishing him a good day, Travis got in, closing the Lambo door and turning up Willie, tapping his hands on the wheel, drawing a deep breath, waiting till Harper pulled the radio car into the lane and flicking a salute as Harper pulled a U-ey. Breathing easy now. Thinking Gibbet would be waiting.

Pulling off the shoulder, careful not to pelt gravel at the underside, Travis watched the needle climb, keeping it to the limit, setting the cruise. He passed an Accord with the four-ways going, the driver facing away, taking in the scenery, Alpha Lake showing through the pines to the southwest, the beauty of it lost on Travis.

Maybe he could have saved the five grand Gibbet charged and taken any side road, found a quiet spot among the billion pines and just dug a hole, dumped the body in without ceremony. But he didn't get this far by cutting corners and getting sloppy. Nobody made a body disappear like Gibbet, and that's what he needed. No face. No fingerprints. No problems. Taking care of the details kept you in the game. And as far as payment went, Nick shot the kid; he could pick up the tab.

. . . OUT TO PASTURE

Coming up empty got you benched; in RCMP terms that meant getting reassigned to some shit detail nobody else wanted. It was that simple. Lance Edwards could write a book about it. Sitting at the beat-up desk across from Jimmy Gallo, in a windowless room in back of the Whistler detachment, the kind of space used for storing brooms, he watched his partner draped over another crossword, erasing a word, writing in another. Jimmy told him there were worse places to get assigned, like some First Nations reserve, an outpost with a name like Yahk.

Fifteen years of service. Coming up through the ranks, the CTP at Depot in Regina, Lance put up with a puckered field-coach named Preston. Four years of general duty in Portage la Prairie got him bounced to polygraph in Edmonton, on to major crimes in the minor town of Swift Current, places where winters were whiteouts, like living in a chest freezer, one place worse than the next. He finally caught a break, and was reassigned to the coast, the drug squad at 312 Main, working his first and only case for nine months straight, part of a three-man task force building a wiretap case for the Crown. Gathering enough evidence to get drug boss Artie Poppa to turn on his cartel buddies, ready to name names, trading testimony for immunity. The case was looking solid till Poppa got himself tasered down on Wreck Beach, killed by one of his own, his pacemaker heart no match for high voltage. With Artie Poppa DOA, the Crown had no case, and Lance had no task force, landing him this assignment.

File folders and printouts laid scattered in front of Lance, Jimmy starting a fresh crossword. Far as Lance was concerned, Jimmy was a fifteen-year waste of time, a guy who must have pissed off his own higher-ups. A guy just hanging around for an early pension, happy to sit on his ass and write a report.

"How about you take a break, and we do some police work?" Lance said, patience running low.

Jimmy looked up, checked the time. "Don't know about you, partner, but I'm done at five." Jimmy looked out at the detachment, some of the night-shift guys coming in, saying even Risker had gone home. The only reason he was still there, Lance was driving back to the Beaver Lodge. Jimmy asked how he felt about pizza tonight, saw a sign for two large with an extra topping for the price of one.

"Two guys working with Stevens, one beaten, the other stuffed in a trunk, and you're talking about toppings."

"Alleged."

"Okay, alleged."

"You want to do this today?"

"Yeah, I want to talk to Stevens."

"We tried that. Twice already, plus you been calling him. Guy doesn't want to answer, fuck him."

"Somebody's trying to push him out. Hard. He needs to know that."

Jimmy folded the paper, getting hungry, thinking mushroom, anchovies and double cheese, saying, "Fine. Pizza joint's pretty much on the way."

They were going through the lobby when a bald man came in, stopping, recognizing them, saying, "You're the two from this morning."

They both looked at him, trying to place him.

"The Stevens place. I'm right across the street." He waited till it dawned on the two cops who he was: the perv in the bathrobe, standing in his bay window. Dressed in Levi's and a Roots sweatshirt now, he said, "I'm Roy Scheider. Block Watch." He stuck out a hand.

"Like the guy in *Jaws*," Jimmy said, not wanting to, but shaking the hand.

Roy was nodding, happy Jimmy made the connection, saying they weren't related.

"What can we do for you, Mr. Scheider?" Lance asked, shaking the hand.

"Call me Roy. Well, it might be nothing, but I was looking out around teatime when this van pulls up, two guys eyeing the Stevens place."

"Yeah?" Lance said.

"And they weren't local."

"How can you tell that?" Lance asked.

"The way they walked up to the door, looking around

at everything. Then they went around the back, one going down either side."

"Stevens home at the time?" Lance asked.

"Uh-uhn."

"Happen to jot down their plate?"

"You bet," Roy said, pulling out a folded sheet of memo, Jimmy taking it from him, saying it could be a delivery or the guys reading the meter.

"You tell Stevens?" Lance asked.

"Thought I should report to you."

"You describe the two guys?" Lance asked.

"Suspicious," Roy said, adding they were dark-skinned, both wearing shades, could be from one of those terrorist countries. Definitely not local.

Jimmy took out his pen, wrote Froot Loops on the memo, saying they'd look into it.

"Oh," Roy said like an afterthought, "the one driving had a gun," showing how he held it at his side, looking at Jimmy, saying, "That sound like a meter reader to you?"

. . . IN SYNC

MAYBE HER mother was right about the losers in her life, a long line of them. She wanted out of her mother's basement so bad, it was clouding her judgment. Dara couldn't tell you what she was doing taking a job from somebody like Nick Rosco, promising her two-fifty a week for making a run to Whistler, like duh. Couldn't guess the gig was about muling dope. Couldn't guess how it would turn out. Two hours from home, Nick putting his hand on her, not taking no for an answer. Grabbing and hitting her. Asking for it.

Her last loser was Cam, high most of the time, using his nose like a Dirt Devil. The crowning achievement of twenty years was Cam making the front page of the *Sun*: first person ever slapped with a possession charge at any 420 rally on the planet. Sticking a joint in a rent-a-cop's pocket turned out to be a bad idea, especially since Cam had got the date wrong. Bottom line, Dara sucked at choosing anything with a Y chromosome. So, as much as she liked this Superboy who'd saved her, she was going to take it slow.

Seeing trails coming off just about everything, she followed Grey along the Stir Crazy food bar, all the chopped food fresh in stainless compartments. The place was buzzing with diners, a hundred conversations going at once, Dara able to hear every single word, none of it making any sense. Lots of lights, all of them low except over the grill station. The furniture was black lacquer, the wallpaper a red-and-black stripe, Grey telling her it was all about the ambience.

Picking jasmine over brown rice, she looked under the hanging lights and chose the spot prawns from the stainless trays, smelling the garlic and butter. She scooped some fresh miniature corn, bean sprouts and water chestnuts, added chopped chili and sliced red onions. Handing the bowl to the line cook in his black chef's hat, she pointed to the teriyaki-and-coconut sauce, watching him ladle it on then toss the works on the grill, letting it sizzle, flipping it around, plating it, sprinkling on some sesame seeds and handing it back with a smile.

High enough to be impressed by this, she followed Grey to the cash, taking a sniff at his dish. The black bean sauce smelled awesome, lots of garlic in his, too. They waited while the hitchhiker in front of them unslung his backpack with the cardboard *share a ride* sign and bitched about his tab, saying what happened to this being an all-you-can-eat, being told by the chick working the cash you paid by weight. Who the fuck ever heard of an all-you-can-eat where you paid by weight, share a ride kept up the bitching, demanding a face-to-face with management.

After he was escorted out, Grey paid for their plates, a fifty-buck tab for two plates of stir fry, a club soda and a beer, tossing it on his Amex. Maybe he should have stuck with going to Nesters for KD, but he wanted to get her out of the house in case the cops showed up at his door again. Or worse, Travis Rainey.

The two of them sat at a black table near the kitchen. Chowing down, working the chopsticks, they talked more about music, tasting off each other's plates. Dara dipped a beef strip in her teriyaki-and-coconut sauce and dunked her shrimp in his black bean sauce, listening as he talked about this chick Sarah that used to work in this place, how she was off now touring with her band Walk off the Earth, doing alright, saying they used to party together.

"Yeah, they're awesome," Dara said, remembering the YouTube clip, the whole band playing "Somebody That I Used to Know" on one guitar, Dara saying they smoked the original version. Totally cool.

He tried to keep her from slipping into the shade of what happened that morning, talking about Mountain High, four days of rock and roll on the coming weekend, and the lineup of bands, throwing names around, asking if she knew Moist and Metric, saying one of the Trailer Park Boys was scheduled to MC, the one with the glasses.

"Love that guy." She mimicked Bubbles, jutting her lower lip and circling her fingers in front of her eyes. Then she asked if he was sure about her crashing on his couch.

Checking his wrist for the watch he stopped putting on around the time Tammy left, he told Dara the Greyhounds stopped running more than an hour ago, told her she was more than welcome, Dara saying she didn't want to put him out. With a few bucks in her pocket, the only place she'd be checking in would be the Parkbench Arms. Probably didn't have enough for the bus, either, meaning she'd have to call

Mother in the morning, hand her a line and get her to stick the Greyhound fare on her credit card.

Sipping his Kokanee, Grey watched her eat, getting a flash of the two cops coming back in the middle of the night, banging on his door the way cops did when they wanted in — *thump, thump, thump* — freaking the poor girl out, the couch ten feet from the front door. He forewarned her about Goob's epic snoring, told her he did it in his favorite chair right across the room.

"Can't be worse than Cam," she said, reminding him who Cam was. "And thanks for dinner by the way," she said. In spite of the killer pot, her taste buds were numb; the prawns may as well have been packing-chips. No matter how good they were, she wasn't tasting much, chopsticks shaking as she piloted them to her mouth.

The waitress came round with dessert menus tucked under an arm, Grey swearing by the cheesecake, New York–style with berries and sauce. They agreed to share a slice, then he was telling her about the local buskers getting together at the Plaza later, rehearsing a kind of flashmob gig, planning to do it in the Square to set off Mountain High.

"I love flashmobs," she said. "Rehearsing it, huh?"

"Yuh. Gonna do it to the Hip's 'Little Bones.'"

"Love the Hip and oh, that tune . . ." Using the chopsticks, she tapped the beat on the lacquer.

"What say we check it out?"

"You doing it, dancing?"

"Me, I'm more of a shuffler," Grey said, spearing a marinated square of tofu, popping it in his mouth.

She said it could be fun, then they talked some more about music, the better part of a decade between them, finding bands they both liked, the Clash, the Melvins, Patti, Siouxsie. Dara glad when he admitted Mungo Jerry was just a sentimental thing, his uncle's music. She told him about dropping out of Emily Carr U, having her fill of the eye, mind and hand bullshit — two years of it and the only gig she could land was as a sandwich artist. Tearing tiny bits off her napkin, saying, "Pretty pathetic, really."

"Got the pretty part right." Grey felt his cheeks redden.

Flicking her chopsticks at him, she watched him pick rice off his T-shirt, a couple of grains stuck to the side of his face.

"No idea you were a food flicker," he said, wiping at the rice.

"Yeah, well, some of us shuffle, some of us flick." She grinned at him, eyes going past him to the door, the grin swept from her face. "Jesus Christ."

He turned.

IT WAS the guy he hit with his bike, Nick Rosco, twirling his keys round a finger by the door, bitching at the hostess about having to wait to be seated when there was space at the bar, his hair gelled back, wearing a silver suit this time, looking out of place among the woodsy crowd, most of them college-aged. Finally, Nick's gaze stopped on them near the kitchen, pointing his finger their way, the hostess turning, saying something to him; then he was grinning, flipping the keys, catching them from the air, saying something back, and he was heading over.

"It's alright," Grey told her, Dara scared, wanting to duck out through the kitchen.

"Heard this was a party town," Nick said, stepping up, hands on the back of Grey's chair. "I'm out here looking for action and look who I find."

Picking up a strip of beef and popping it into his mouth, Grey asked Dara, "Sure you don't want coffee with dessert? They do it decent."

"Grey Stevens," Nick said, the name the hostess gave him, the name he heard from Travis Rainey, calling him the local pot grower. Pressing against the back of the chair, he said, "Yeah, maybe you haven't figured it out yet, but you work for me now."

"That right?" Grey chewed, glanced up. "How about we just skip to the end? Want to eat this while it's hot." As Nick leaned in, Grey felt the pistol under Nick's jacket, betting he wouldn't pull it in a crowded restaurant. Doing a half-turn in his chair, easing Nick back, he caught the busker crowd coming through the door like circus cavalry. Eight of them milling around the hostess's stand, everybody talking at once. Catching a bite before going to the flashmob rehearsal.

"For starters, you owe me for the jacket."

"What jacket's that?"

"The Hugo Boss, the one you fucked up when you blindsided me."

"Then you'll go away?" Grey asked, spearing a chunk of tofu, reaching for his wallet as he chewed. Taking a five spot from his wallet, he held it up to Nick, aware of Dizzie heading over. "Ought to be enough left over for a shiny vest."

"Hey, Grey, my man," Dizzie said, coming up from behind, guitar in hand, tossing the fur cap on the table, setting the goggles down. "Real sorry about your bike, man . . ."

Nick straightened, looking up at Dizzie's six-foot-five frame, Zipper and Dimebag right behind him. "You mind, pal? What the fuck we got here, the Bong Show?"

Checking out the fob hanging from Nick's finger, Dizzie asked, "That your orange ride out front?"

"Last guy made a crack about the color . . ." Nick flicked a finger at the earring.

Dizzie jammed the guitar's headstock under Nick's chin,

pressing him into Grey's chair, pointing to the front window, saying with a smile, "Don't fret, pal. Just thought you'd want to know they're towing it."

Pushing the guitar out of his face, Nick crunched the five bucks and tossed it down, saying to Grey, "Catch you later, sport." Looking to Dara: "You too, doll." Then he shoved past Dizzie and the others, walking through the place like he owned it, twirling the key fob, going for the doors, the buskers getting a look at one of the guys making threats.

"Guy's wound a little tight," Dizzie said, tapping the guitar neck. "And didn't get it when I said don't fret."

Nobody else did, either, Dizzie and the buskers going to the front window, looking out at the three-hundred-pound bear hooking up the Camaro, hair on the back of his trunk-like neck. The big man was sweating, had the front wheels off the ground, wheel straps and breakaway chains on. Coming down the steps with the Smith held close to his jacket, Nick rolled a fifty-buck note and tucked it into the barrel, told the bear there were two ways they could do this.

"What's with that dude?" Dizzie asked, coming back to the table, looking toward the window, reaching past Grey, taking the last strip of beef off his plate, biting into it, bending for the crumpled bill on the floor, thinking, finders keepers. Their dessert came, the waitress setting it down with two forks, Dizzie asking, "That the cheesecake?"

"Yeah, want her to get you a fork?"

"Naw, that's okay." Dizzie used his fingers, saying, "Mmm," to Dara, "got to try this."

Then he looked to the front, the buskers and other diners still watching out the window, Nick taking care of business.

. . . YANKING THE CHAIN

"Nothing I could do about it, Geo," Travis said to Geovani "Bumpy" Rosco, keeping his voice level, wanting to tell the old fucker off, but knowing better, standing in the parking lot like he was at attention, the McDonald's sign lighting the lot, boasting *billions served, open 24 hours*. The arches just off the highway, Squamish halfway between Vancouver and Whistler, another hour of driving ahead of him. The old man had been on the phone chewing his ass the past ten minutes, Travis knowing what happened to people that pissed the old man off, the Nicaraguan with a temper, the guy with his fingers in every major dope deal up and down the West Coast.

"This is Nick stepping up, showing my lieutenants what he can do," the old man said.

"Yeah, and I respect that, Geo," Travis said, "but what he did, that's on him."

"Told you to watch him," the old man barked into the phone, "so, this shit's on you."

Moving so people coming and going from the McD's wouldn't overhear the conversation, Travis said, "Look, Geo —"

"Fuck looking. I got to send somebody else? 'Cause if I do . . ."

"I'm getting it done, Geo."

"Yeah, and how's that going, getting the locals on board?" Bumpy's breathing sounded raspy.

"First one comes along, Nick . . . he alienates him."

"With you just standing there?" The old man heaped it back on him, saying, "You want to keep going in circles here, 'cause I sure don't."

Travis stepped farther to the back of the lot, out of earshot of a family climbing out of their suv, going in for soft serve.

"Not trying to piss you off, Geo, just this was a bad idea, Nick coming along. No offense, but I said that more than once." Travis knew he was pushing his luck. Richie and his two guys standing at the back of the white Ford van, waiting for him. "I'm thinking he'd be better back in the city, lie low."

"A chance somebody saw him do this?"

"No, nobody."

"You sure?"

"Yeah." Travis remembered the guy standing by the trees between the two parking lots turning and running.

"Then no need for lying low," Bumpy said. "At least that. And the kid that he . . . alienated?"

"Taken care of."

Silence for a moment.

"And it won't blow back?"

"No way." Not the time to bring up the five grand it cost to cover Nick's fuck-up.

"Just do like I told you, keep him safe." The old man's

raspy breath continued another moment, then Travis got dial tone.

Resisting the urge to hurl his phone at the McSign, he shoved it into his pocket, motioning for the two hang-arounds to hurry up loading the sacks of cement from his open trunk to the van, the two guys working like they were union. Fucking dope out in the open. The one named Mutt shot him a look that said he didn't like people talking to him like that.

"Back in a minute," Travis told Richie and headed for the can, his phone ringing again, the display saying it was Nick.

Picking up as he went through the doors, he told Nick to hold on a minute. Seeing Drew, the night manager, he walked to the counter, brought out a couple hundreds, slid them across the counter along with his keys. "You take care of my ride, get her detailed?"

Drew nodded, said, sure will, knowing the kind of detailing Travis had in mind, the kind that removed prints and traces of whatever. No problem driving the Chrysler home, parking it in his garage till Travis called. Could be a few days, could be longer. Either way, he'd have a nice set of wheels to ride around in till Travis called for it.

Thanking him, Travis went into the can, saying into the phone, "What the fuck now?" He missed the two dark-skinned guys watching him from the corner booth, dipping fries in ketchup.

"Found the chick," Nick said.

"What chick?"

"What chick, the fucking one I drove up here."

"Told you to sit tight."

"Told you fuck that. This chick's got the asshole with her."

Travis unzipped and pissed into the urinal.

"That you pissing?"

Travis slapped the flusher, hard, ignoring the question.

The guy two stalls down glanced over, zipped up and hurried out of there, didn't stop to wash his hands.

"The asshole's our guy," Nick said. "Asked around and caught up to him."

"You do nothing."

"Said I'm taking care of it."

"And I'm still fixing your last fuck-up." Travis stepped to the sink and ran the water. "Tell you what, call your —"

He got dial tone. Clicking off the prepaid, Travis tucked it away, slammed his palm at the soap pump, splashed water on his hands, stuck his hands under the hand dryer. The chick Nick brought up here to mule was with Grey Stevens now, the guy he was trying to recruit, Nick shooting one of Stevens's crew this morning. Grabbing the dryer with both hands, Travis tore it from the wall, wires sparking, drywall breaking and falling. Dropping it in the trash can, wires dangling from the wall, he walked out, went to the counter and told Drew he ought to get maintenance to take a look in there, saying the piece of shit dryer was on the fritz. Slapping a few c-notes on the counter, he walked out, past the dark-skinned guys in the booth, thinking that was coming out of Nick's pocket, too.

Getting out of business with the Roscos was the right move. Get into the escort business right before they start putting up casinos.

"Something wrong, boss?" Mutt Jackson asked when Travis came across the Mickey D lot, the back of the van still open, the three of them standing there in their leather and jeans.

"I tell you to load up?" Travis said, walking by the big man.

Mutt looked at him like, what the fuck did I do?

"So shut the fucking doors; I got to spell everything out," Travis snapped.

Mutt's fingers went in a ball, but he turned and slammed the doors, the doors flying back open. Huffing air, Mutt held it together, kept from ripping the doors off.

"Let's ride; we got shit to do," Travis said to Richie.

Richie got in the passenger side, Marty and Mutt climbing in the back. Richie looked at Travis, "You want, I can drive."

"Fuck it, I'm good."

. . . THAT SHUFFLER THING

THE OLYMPIC Plaza felt alive, its modern, slanted roof, flags flapping overhead, the mountains in shadow looking purple in the backdrop, the night at hand. Visitors out strolling, stopping and sitting on the trim lawn, the old-school boom box near the front of the stage pumping out the music.

Niels, Zipper and Dimebag were decked out for the occasion in a nice mix of purples, greens and orange, their garb as bright as their professions: fire juggler, static-trapeze artist and twanger of the musical saw. They stood out front watching this chick Eva do a righteous Tina Turner shuffle up on the stage. Her shagged hair looked felted under the lights, Eva doing it in spandex and heels. The girl was all curves, sweat and power. Taboo, Super Frank and a few more buskers lined upstage, a couple more watching from the wings, Eva belting out how she can't stand the rain against her window. A pair of shirtless guys were playing Hacky Sack under the lights; Betty Hoop in miniskirt and curled black wig, working a set of hula hoops, Bent Emma contorting while a couple of kids and a dog chased a Frisbee.

"She's hot," Dara said, sitting, pointing to Eva, Dara still high from the pot they'd smoked, still worried about Nick and checking the shadows.

"Got the moves, no doubt . . ." Grey said, working on a beer, Dara on a latte, both looking on as Eva finished to a roar of applause, male voices calling for a "Proud Mary" encore. Eva strutted to the wings, waving her thanks, blowing the boys a kiss, loving it, the lights staying on.

Going to the boom box, Dizzie waved his arms for quiet, said, let's hear it for Eva, waited for her to come back under the spotlight, waited till the applause and catcalls died a second time before saying, "This is it, people," putting on the Hip's "Little Bones," Spike starting it off with a clap, doing a cross-step to center stage, spotlight following him as he snapped his fingers, his hand going back and forth to the beat like he was scattering rice. Dizzie, Zipper and Dimebag formed a second line behind him, taking their marks; more lights came on; Eva, Niels, Stickman and Miss Behave formed the third line, following Spike's moves. Arms shot out in unison, heads bobbing to the beat, stepping to the side in sync, a motion like they were swimming through water, hips rocking side to side, dipping, legs splayed, back to their marks, knees bending, shooting up, clapping to the beat, turning on the spot, three lines became four, then five, the dancers following Spike's moves, working on getting it tight.

"Care to join in?" Grey asked Dara, her pink laces going back and forth.

"Think I got a bit of that shuffler thing." She sipped her latte. "Dance like I just got a new hip," she said, shielding her eyes from the overhead lights, watching.

Grey doubted it. Looked through the crowd, keeping

watch, Uncle Rubin's .22 in his messenger bag, close at his side.

"True. I'm a total spaz. Ever see the *Seinfeld* episode when Elaine danced? That's me." Laughing, she asked again where they were doing this flashmob.

Grey pointed toward the Square. "Be worth sticking around till the weekend; I mean, you're into the music, right?" He wanted it to sound casual, telling her the couch was all hers.

"I don't want to get in the way."

"You won't. Promise."

"That Mungo guy on the card?"

"Mungo's a they, not a he, and I wish."

She sipped some more latte. "So, this be like a date?"

"It'll be like . . . checking out the music, being my guest. I ask you on a date, you'll know it." The two of them smiling at each other.

The flashmob finished a second run-through, the crowd starting to thin, the buskers ready to call it a night. Zipper called over, asking if Grey wanted a lift, Grey looking up, catching them coming past the Olympic rings all lit up, silver with colored stripes.

"Shit." First instinct was to run.

"What?" Dara freaked, snapping around, seeing the two cops from Gretzky's Diner, relieved it wasn't Nick.

Picking up his messenger bag holding the goggles, fur hat and the .22, he helped Dara up, smiling at the two detectives. No way he was ducking them this time.

... SMALL FISH

"So THAT wasn't you?" Lance Edwards asked. His jacket hung open, showing the badge clipped to the belt, the strap of the holster.

Grey slung the messenger bag on his shoulder, cap sticking out. "Me, I'm into the whole PETA thing. Sound like I'd wear fur?"

"PETA, huh? That the one with that Pam broad?" Jimmy Gallo asked, remembering the poster of her in a bikini, marked up like a side of beef, Grey saying, yeah, that one.

"Doesn't bother you what happened this morning?" Jimmy asked, thinking his partner was nuts dragging him down here this time of night, talking to this asshole, like he was going to give them anything. "Your one roomie gets his teeth knocked out."

"Yeah, sure it does."

"How many tenants you got living downstairs?" Lance asked, writing down names, then asked if he'd seen the other two, Grey telling him they left Mojo sitting at home like an hour and a half ago.

"And the other one?" Lance asked, checking his notes, "Tuff Dubb."

Grey just shrugged, saying he was around.

Jimmy saying there was a shooting in the other parking lot. "Witness says a guy took a bullet and got stuffed in a trunk, shooter driving off."

"You're thinking that's Tuff?" Grey took hold of Dara's hand. "Think you got it wrong."

"'Cause you want it to be wrong?" Jimmy said.

"Come on. Tuff's no fighter — guy's a vegetarian."

"Yeah, you seen him around this afternoon?"

"Tuff's got a come-and-go nature." Reaching past the fur cap, Grey fished his cell from the bag, punching in the number of Tuff's prepaid. Let it ring, the call going to voicemail.

Jimmy didn't like the smug on this guy, Lance saying, "Top it off, a neighbor reported two guys casing your house this afternoon."

Grey shrugged, guessing which neighbor.

"And you're all la-di-da." Jimmy looked at the buskers gathering around, listening in. "None of you got nothing to say?"

"Yeah, want to say my bike got swiped," Grey said. "Right out front of McGoo's, in front of your noses."

Jimmy looked at Lance like, do you believe this guy?

Lance gave it another try. "How's your buddy Airdog doing?"

"Sleeping off the Demerol."

Lance looked at his notes. "You hear from Trevor Sam . . . Tuff Dubb . . ." he held out a card, "you call me?"

"Yeah, I can do that." Grey took the card.

"We put out a BOLO," Lance said, then, "I'll let you know if we get a hit, and I'll have a unit drive by your place a couple times tonight."

"Appreciate it."

Jimmy scanned the faces, stopping on Dara, saying, "Girl from Gretzky's, right?"

"Drank the coffee and lived to tell about it."

"You have a name, Miss?"

"Sure, everyone does." She tried to make the smile work, some of the buskers grinning, Jimmy looking pissed. "Dara Addie," she said.

"You staying in town, Miss Addie?" Lance asked.

"Yeah, visiting a friend," she said, hooking Grey's arm.

"Well, if anybody knows anything that might help . . ." Lance said, looking around at the buskers, then turning back the way they came.

"Hey, you guys driving by Nesters?" Grey asked.

"You're kidding, right?" Jimmy asked.

"You want to keep us out of harm's way, right? Plus, they close in like ten minutes, what with us standing here cooperating with you . . ."

Lance started across the grass, saying, "Come on."

Jimmy followed, sure his partner was nuts.

"Think I should mention that Nick creep has a gun?" Dara said to Grey in a low voice, the two of them following.

"Not sure what to tell them." Grey tried Tuff's number again, still getting voicemail, then he tried Benny Rivers again.

. . . UNDERTOW

BACK IN the day, it had been the best place on earth for a solo run, snaking cliffside lanes, the snow-capped peaks hanging above turquoise water on the west side. The Olympics forced the highway upgrade: new bridges, retaining walls, rumble strips, barriers, passing lanes. Cost the taxpayers a steep six hundred million.

Riding back from Whistler on a rain-slick morning in the autumn of '91, Travis left the lid behind and let his Wide Glide unwind on the stretch, gripping the ape hangers, feeling the wind, feeling alive. Got as far as Loggers Creek. A massive slide shut the highway down, gave him a new appreciation for "the killer highway." Turning the bike around, Travis took the scenic route back to the city, up past Pemberton, cutting through Lytton and looping around old Highway 12.

Talking about the chrome on his bike out front of some truck stop near Hope led to a night of hard drinking with Rudi Busch at his private hunting lodge off the Crowsnest Highway, the two becoming fast friends, Travis finding out Rudi ran a few guns on the side, Travis hooking him up with the Sabers, using Rudi's cabins as stash houses for guns and dope. A crack shot who didn't ask questions, Rudi had his sons cut and repack, standing watch over the Sabers' shit, later distributing Bumpy Rosco's coke coming up from the other Colombia.

The cartel boys started out sending their powder in semi-submersibles, three-man crews subbing past patrol boats, transferring their cargo on open seas to Mexican go-fast boats, the coke bouncing across international waves, some of it making its way up the Gulf of California. Sealed bags were taped inside wine barrels and trucked up the dusty roads into Nogales. Ferreted through drug tunnels, handed off to Arizona bikers and taken overland along with truckloads of Mexi yerba packed in fifty-pound burlap sacks marked *Coffee of Molokai*, straight up through Utah, Idaho, Montana and up the back roads of the Kootenai National Forest. Rudi and his boys took the handoff and brought the barrels and burlap sacks across the bramble border into Canada, making a shit-pile more than they ever did operating a hunting lodge. Beat the hell out of listening to fat old men brag about fucking antlers, dropping change in the tip jar.

The war between Rosco and the Indo Army had Travis exercising caution, Rudi hiring on a couple more boys, repacking the coke and yerba in Canada Cement sacks marked *low alkali*. What didn't get routed straight to one of Bumpy's warehouses (owned by some third cousin) was shipped up the Trans-Canada to the Inn Between, a defunct motel outside Pemberton, Rudi's sons tucking the sacks into a false basement wall. A couple keys of coke and a dozen of the yerba had been packed into a metal compartment fitted under an Escalade, the two brothers keeping watch over it, waiting for word from Travis, ready to send it down ahead of Mountain High.

When the rock crowd hit the highway at the end of the week, heading up to the festival, the Mounties would have their hands full. That's when Travis would have the Busch boys drive the Escalade down to Whistler. That's how long Grey Stevens had to become a team player or become history.

Dark now. Driving up through Garibaldi Village in Squamish, Travis had paid the guys half of what he promised, then took a call from one of Bumpy's lieutenants. Eduardo, saying in his queer-ass voice he just received a package holding a CD with a clip starring Benny Rivers and Ivan Glinka being gunned down, the iPhone zooming in nice and close. The clip was titled "Payback," with today's date, the voiceover saying, "this happened three miles outside Port Mellon, just a taste of what's gonna happen in Whistler." Eduardo asked Travis if he needed a few more boys, Travis saying he'd let him know and hanging up, telling Richie and the two in back, "You boys ready to earn your wages?" Relaying the call, letting them know what they were in for.

"How we doing it?" Mutt said.

Looking at him in the rearview, Travis said, "Hard."

Mutt grinned.

Only thing that wasn't clear was what Travis would do about Nick, the fucking heir apparent shooting off more than his mouth, taking out one of the guys Travis had been hoping to recruit. He could take care of the Indos, and with

Stevens and his crew onboard, he could push the dope; but as for babysitting Nick, he might have to put in another call to Gibbet before this was over.

"They got beaver up here?" Marty asked from the back seat, popping a ziptop, belching a beer-blast.

"Yeah, only it goes by 'pussy' these days," Travis said, meeting his eyes in the rearview, feeling wet on the back of his neck. Marty's blond hair cut short, chin scruff failing to hide the vertical scar, Travis guessing he got tagged by a blade. Not too bright, but one tough son of a bitch according to Richie, the kind he'd need for this. Let him belch.

Marty took another slug from his can, wiping foam from his mouth, saying, "Long as it's wet."

Mutt laughing, keeping eye contact with Travis in the rearview, saying, "Fuckin' A."

Travis was thinking the untamed hair and beard made Mutt look like that Sasquatch thing from *Star Wars*, a creased forehead made for butting goats.

"Least they're eager," Richie said to Travis, Richie with the Manson eyes, hair oiled and pulled behind his ears. Man, Richie missed this, thinking back to when Travis first showed up at the Sabers clubhouse, Nanaimo chapter, Richie a full patch, Travis an independent. Richie putting in a good word, getting Travis in tight. Now Richie was working for him. But that didn't matter, five Gs for a week of his time, a chance to cap some hadjis, would do him good, liven things up and get the blood pumping. Life at the garage in Salmon Arm was getting him down.

"Who they got playing at this rock thing?" Mutt asked.

"Heard they got Teenage Head and the Demics. Remember them from, like, the seventies?" Marty said. "And Dread Zeppelin."

"Dread Zeppelin? That for real?" Travis asked, looking over at Richie like, where'd you find these guys.

"Hey, they're a decent act," Marty said.

"Yeah, never know, you might like them," Mutt said, catching Lance's glance in the rearview again.

"How you know what I'd like?" Travis asked, easing on the speedometer, not wanting to attract any more undue attention, catching Mutt looking at Marty with a what's-eating-him look.

"Just saying . . ." Mutt threw up his hands. "Hey, if there's a problem . . ."

"I say I got a problem?" Travis asked, turning his head, looking at him. "Right now, how about passing some of that brew up here?"

Richie looked at Travis, then at the two in back. Jesus.

Reaching across the back seat, Mutt handed a couple of cans forward, getting a couple more for him and Marty, eyes on the rearview.

"These guys do a reggae Zeppelin twist," Marty went on.

"This Dread Zeppelin?" Richie asked.

"Right. See, the dude singing packs like three hundred pounds," Marty said, "glittering like Elvis with the sideburns and grease, the whole bit."

"And you think I'd like that?" Travis said.

"Tell you what I'd like," Richie said, "get some payback for Rivers and Glinka." He was thinking how much longer till they got there, reaching for his pack of smokes, taking one out, looking for the push-in lighter that wasn't there.

"Amen to that," Marty said, then, "Hey, I got to drain the vein, man." He crushed his empty can under his boot and gave up another belch, looked at Travis. "How about pulling over?"

Travis drew a breath, checking his rearview again. The road behind them was black, no one following.

"Third one's the charm." Marty clapped his gut, belching again. Three beers in ten minutes.

"Jesus, like driving with kids," Travis said, looking for a spot to pull over, the construction markers flashing and blinking ahead, a yellow bulldozer off to the side. Richie was glad he didn't ask how much longer.

A road sign announced a detour past the McGuire Crossroad just ahead, nothing but the outline of pine trees, stars overhead, orange pylons reflecting their headlights.

Travis pulled the van to the shoulder past the construction sign, gravel crunching under the wheels. The bend up ahead kept him from seeing the spike strip laid across the northbound lane a couple hundred feet away. "Fuckers got two seasons up here, rain and fucking construction. Been like this since the Olympics."

Marty climbed out, Mutt thinking now was as good a time as any, crushing his foot down on his own empty, popping a fresh can, setting it on the floor, sending a couple more empties tumbling as he followed Marty out.

"Sure these guys can shoot straight?" Travis asked Richie.

"They're solid."

"Guess we'll see."

"Better if you lighten up a bit."

Travis didn't respond, thinking about Rivers and Glinka, thinking he could have used them. Benny was a tough bastard, a good shot, too. It would have taken a squad of Indos to take him out.

"How we doing this, besides hard?" Richie asked, looking out at Marty standing just off the shoulder, legs apart, splashing the gravel. Mutt ducked under a couple of low boughs, disappearing into the trees, twigs snapping under his boots.

"Just talked to Rivers yesterday. Him and Glinka were set to run for us. No idea how anybody got wind of that."

"You got somebody else selling?"

"Trying to swing this pot grower, guy's got himself a network of buskers, playing street corners, moving his shit up here," Travis not saying how Nick Rosco already shot one of them.

"So, who we got besides the four of us?"

"Rudi Busch's boys in Pemberton, sitting on the rest of the stash, waiting on my word," Travis said. "Might have this escort place, use it like a front."

"Escorts, huh?" Richie lit up, thinking of the fringe benefits.

"Guy who owns it used to work for Bumpy, looks like that hockey loudmouth, guy with the fucked-up outfits."

"Cherry?"

"Him, yeah."

"And this Nick guy?"

"Bumpy's idiot son. Need to keep him benched. Old man sent him up, wants him kept safe."

Richie nodded, then said, "Been meaning to ask, that Hummer got blown to shit down in the city . . . that you?"

Travis grinned. "Why they pay me the big bucks, bro."

"Had a feeling." Richie took a slug of beer.

Marty got back in, sliding across the seat, knocking Mutt's open beer with his foot, spilling it, diving after it. "Aw, shit, man."

"Throw all those fucking empties out," Travis snapped at him. "Smells like shit in here."

Tossing out the cans, Marty was thinking Travis was more puckered than his old lady when she was on the rag.

"What, your buddy get lost?" Travis asked, looking out the passenger side, wanting to roll.

"Said he had to take a dump, all of a sudden," Marty said, tossing a few cans out. "Heard him bitching about wiping with leaves."

That got Richie grinning, shaking his head.

Headlights rode up from behind, shining in on them. Travis made out the stripes and light bar on the Crown Vic. The sacks of cement were in back in plain view, a bag of X packed in the spare tire-well under the floor, another one duct-taped under the back seat, the P5 under Travis's seat. "Everybody be cool."

Just four buddies on their way to do a little cottage reno. Travis waited, knew not to step out. Rolling down his window, he let the uniform come alongside, a silhouette in the radio car's headlights. Bringing up his flashlight, the cop shone the beam into the van, asking why they were pulled over.

"No problem, officer. One of our buddies just taking a leak." Travis squinted out. It was the same cop from this afternoon. Travis fished for his name, coming up with it. "Well, Constable Harper . . ."

Recognizing him, Harper gave a smile, but his hand stayed close to the holster. Breaking protocol, not waiting for the 10-28 on the plate, Harper had stepped out of his vehicle, seeing Marty get back in, not wanting to give them time. "Small world." He thought a second. "Mr. Romney, isn't it?"

"Yeah, good memory."

Neither noticed the car pulling along the shoulder, stopping three hundred yards behind the cruiser, its lights off.

"I go by Sam," Travis said, pretty sure that was the name on the ID he showed Harper that afternoon. "Oh, and I had the missus order up that hands-free kit for the Chrysler. Bluetooth, right?"

"Only way to go." Cop eyes searching inside, using the flashlight, Harper looked at the other two. "Driving a van this time?"

"Yeah, the old workhorse," Travis said, tapping the steering wheel, sure Harper didn't miss the interior smelling like a Molson plant.

"Chrysler's not giving you trouble, I hope?" Harper's eyes darting around the interior, then clicking off the light.

"No, nothing like that. Just needed some room, got all our gear stowed in back," Travis said, fingers drumming the top of the steering wheel. If Harper asked to see the registration, they were fucked. Throwing a thumb toward the woods, he said, "One of my guys is off watering the bushes." Realizing he already said that.

Harper nodded, scanning the trees, saying, "Two trips in one day."

"Yeah, no sleep for the wicked. Putting a porch on a place on Cheakamus, one of those log homes. Client caught me this afternoon on my way down, right after we spoke. Panicking on account he's got relatives coming from England or someplace on short notice and needs the summer place looking nice."

"So, you're making hay . . ."

"Right. Guy's willing to pay the overtime."

"Nice spot, that Cheakamus, like a postcard."

"Yeah. Wish we had some time for kicking back, wet a line maybe, but not this trip." Travis kept his hands on the wheel, wondered where the fuck Mutt was.

"Pulling a double myself with this rock festival coming up. Got me signed up for crowd control."

Travis threw in something about sticking the extra dough in the kitty for the 300, Harper saying, "Amen to that."

A transport zipped by, southbound, the rush of wind rocking the van, Harper having to clap a hand to his striped cap. Scanning the trees again, Harper said, "Think your buddy got lost?"

Travis dropped his hand close to his gun under the seat, saying, "Paying for all the burgers and fries he murdered at McDonald's."

Harper gave a nod, then said, "Mind if I have a look in back, Sam?" The hand never moved from his holster. "While we wait."

"Yeah, sure, just doing your job, right?"

"The back open?" Harper asked.

"Think so." Travis and Richie exchanged glances.

"How about you stepping out?"

Waiting till Travis got out, Harper told Richie and Marty to stay put, then followed Travis to the rear with his flashlight on again.

Richie's hand went to the door pocket, touching the big Smith, eyes straight ahead, listening. Travis stopped at the back, Harper sticking the flashlight under his arm, motioning for Travis to open it. Scanning his light over the half dozen Canada Cement bags, yellow hard hats, workers' gear, an Igloo cooler, a Canucks hockey bag, an open case of Granville Island.

"You know I could write you up for the open beer?"

Travis said he'd just had the one, the boys knocking a few back, last chance they'd get till the job was done.

"Better let me see the registra—"

Rushing from behind, Mutt raised his Smith like a hatchet, bringing the butt down in a chop.

Sensing it coming, Harper ducked and hunched his shoulder, taking a glancing blow. He snapped the holster open as he turned, his hand grabbing his pistol. Mutt stuck his arm out and shot him, Harper thrown against the van, a gasp catching in his throat, eyes wide in disbelief, his knees buckling. He tried to stay on his feet, but Mutt fired again, knocking Harper down.

. . . SHE'S TALL, SHE'S HIGH

To A lot of guys, hookers didn't score you points. Got you laid, okay, but the fact you had to pay some chick to fake the play took the thrill from the hunt, like any loser could reach in his wallet, get her to pull up her dress for a back-alley grunt, like it didn't count. Nick didn't think that way. Getting laid was getting laid, so long as the chick was doable, somebody you could look at in daylight. All that *oh baby, oh baby, you're good* shit didn't matter to Nick. Only one that needed to be satisfied was Nick Rosco.

And this place was packed wall to wall with doable. Sitting low in the velvet club chair in his silver suit, he was feeling no pain, the back-to-back glasses of Johnnie Blue on ice the waitress had been bringing were doing the trick. The girl with the tray was well packed into a mini-dress that matched the chair, purple and black and velvet. Nick was thinking it might be her tonight, smiling back, flirting.

A long, polished bar, a dozen beer taps in front of hundreds of bottles lit up on glass shelves. Just name your poison and toss in some ice. Mirrors on every wall, velvet on everything: walls, drapes, chairs, bar front.

He kept the velvet waitress on his radar until the two women came in and started dancing among the couples under the mirror ball. Nick forgot the velvet waitress, these two doing it, writhing, getting his attention along with every other guy's in the place. He sat tall in his seat, hurried his drink.

Big Maxi's Wet Whistle just became the hottest spot in the Village, bar none, fourth place he'd been in tonight. A good crowd, mostly under twenty-five, the chicks ranging from passable to doable. But not one had anything on either of these two. The glitter ball turned like a slow moon over the dance floor, glinting on the dancers moving to the sound of Moby. Pure shit music as far as Nick was concerned, but music wasn't why he was there.

Scoring would erase his encounter with the punk bitch turning all Mary-fucking-Sunshine, suckering him with a ring the size of a golf ball. Gouged his car, rode off with the asshole that decked him with his bike, the guy Travis was trying to recruit. Grey Stevens was a dead man, just didn't know it yet.

Asking around outside Stir Crazy after he paid off the tow truck driver, he found out Stevens tended bar at this place called the Cellar, worked there most nights, but not tonight. First place he went after he had dinner alone in his room. Turned out to be Stevens's night off, the girl serving said try back tomorrow night. Next place Nick went was iKandy's; the place was dead tonight except for a handful of convention guys getting soused. Name tags and bullshit war stories. After that came the Recovery Room, dark and quaint, not a bad spot, but nothing like Maxi's. Must have got half a dozen messages from Travis, trying to keep tabs on him.

Feeling the scotch, Nick put thoughts of shooting the kid and his search for Stevens on the back burner. Time to kick back, treat himself, get laid. He could drop around to the Cellar anytime, see how good Stevens was at mixing drinks with one hand skewered to the bar top by his trench knife.

The two girls were moving to Metro Area now, the pumping beat of "Miura." Flecks of light fell over them, crossed his table. Making like he was into the shit disco beat, tapping his fingers on the table, Nick looked like some game bird the way he was bopping his head, thinking the fucking song was never going to end. The waitress came around, Nick pointing to the empty glass, in need of a fresh Johnnie Blue on ice. No flirting now.

Lexie Poots moved in front of him, full figure, a cougar in a tight dress, legs glistening, blonde hair bouncing around. Tracking Nick down had been easy, Travis asking her to keep him in one spot for the night. Bringing Jaelene along was her idea, the two of them dancing in front of him.

He wasn't going anyplace. His eyes moved like he was watching tennis: the sequined mini covering little of the blonde, the black number riding up the brunette's thighs, legs like an athlete's, hands on each other's hips, fingernails long and painted. The girls close enough for him to touch.

These two had to be pro, dancing like they were doing it for him. Sure beat the usual dance-club type he ran into, the kind that let you order drinks for them all night, then told you to piss off and climbed in a cab. Nick sipped the fresh drink set in front of him, telling the waitress to get the next one ready, feeling it go down, the ice melting in the glass.

Closing in, the brunette asked if he was having a good time, then asked if he was into the music.

Nick saying, "You kidding?" calling her doll, tapping his fingers on the napkin, making like who didn't, asking her name.

Telling him it was Jaelene, she asked his and why he wasn't up dancing, her body swaying to the beat, Nick saying, first you drink, then you dance, having to repeat it on account of the volume, asking her why not join him for a round. Jaelene, with the dark hair and the deep cleavage, slid into the seat next to him, sitting this one out, telling him they were on a club crawl, her red mouth close to his ear on account of the throbbing beat, telling a story about getting tickets from a friend that got them dinner, drinks and a line bypass at five locales of their choice, this the last stop of the night. He didn't notice Lexie fade through the dancers, heading for the door.

"Good choice," he told her, guessing five drinks was just about right. He gulped his down, looked around for the blonde, guessing she went for a powder, then wondered what happened to the waitress. Nick felt an epic night coming, glad he packed the blue pills.

"So what do you do, Nick?" Jaelene asked, her hand on his sleeve, seeing the pistol tucked in his waistband.

"Pretty much anything I want," letting her see the Smith, his way of letting her know who he was.

"And where does a man like that stay?" she said, sounding

like the five drinks were making her tongue trip on words with *s*.

"Got a suite at the Wilmott." His drink landed, and he took half of it down in a swallow, told the waitress to hit him again, asked Jaelene what she was having.

Jaelene said no to a drink, then said, "Nice big rooms at the Wilmott."

"Mine's a suite, big enough for a party." He looked around for the blonde again. "How about you girls be the judge? Come check it out."

"Could happen," she said. "This suite, it got a mini-bar, Nick?" Jaelene asked, leaning close, pumping the cleavage.

"You kidding? Even got a Jacuzzi. I mean, not that I brought trunks or anything, but if you girls aren't shy, maybe we can get wet."

"I look shy to you, Nick?" Jaelene waltzed her fingers up his sleeve, mouth close to his ear so he could hear her over "Bangarang." "Just one thing, Nick," giving him a beak full of the Tommy Girl she spritzed on. "Want you to know I'm worth every penny of the five hundred I'm going to ask you for." Making sure he understood how this worked.

"No problem, doll." Saying it like five hundred was chump change. He wondered what would happen if he tossed a blue pill on top of all the drink he already poured into himself. His guess was he wouldn't need it, not the first couple of times anyway. This chick smelled right, getting close to him. Still looking for the blonde, Nick willing to pay her five bills, too, then pop an extra blue pill for a threesome, let them decide which one got him first. The next drink came, the waitress setting it down and disappearing again.

Thinking with the head that didn't give a shit how much anything cost, Nick reached for his wallet. Flapping it open, he started pulling out bills.

"Not here, up in your room." She pushed the wallet away.

"My suite." Whatever she sprayed on herself was driving Nick nuts. Tossing a hundred on the table to cover his drinks, Nick was up and out of his chair, feeling lightheaded for a second, grabbing the corner of the table. Collecting himself, he took hold of her hand, spinning the orange key fob around a finger, saying, "Follow me, doll," thinking of getting her in the Jacuzzi.

At the exit, Nick looked around once more. No blonde.

"Trust me, Nick. I'm all you need." Jaelene was steering him toward the Wilmott.

"Yeah, uh . . . no problem." Nick told her to keep an eye out for a cash machine. Jaelene told him all the hotels had them.

Finding the Binaca in his pocket, he blasted, got it in his mouth on the second try. The peppermint and Johnnie Blue made him wince.

. . . BEST SERVED COLD

IT WOULD be his night of revenge on the man who killed his friends with the rocket launcher, nearly killed him, too, gave him this face, half of it like a plastic mask, first-degree burns having a way of fucking up your complexion. Fixing on a point, he watched the tops of the pines swaying in the breeze, the countless stars in the night sky. Some kind of night bird gave a screech. Likely looking to get laid. Nav Pudi knew the feeling.

Stretching one foot under the dash, then the other, watching the GPS device in his hand, he pictured doing it with a cleaver, nice and slow, starting with a finger, then an ear when he ran out of fingers, making Travis Rainey scream. The device told him the van was ten miles and closing, coming right to them. Not a street light out here, not a town anywhere around. The middle of nowhere.

The four of them had been sitting in the Lexus since ten. His own cologne did little to ward off that of the others. He rolled the window down, partly to hear the van when it got close.

The coffee he'd drunk to sharpen his edge worked through him. Twice before he'd got out and stood up against the big evergreen. The night air was cool, and he shuddered, held up his wrist, tried to see his watch as he pissed. Getting back in the shotgun seat, he took the device on his lap. Five miles out now. Soon he would hear their tires on the highway, the sound of their engine.

Veni Gopal sat behind the wheel, still as a ghost most of the night, baseball cap pulled low. Could have been asleep for all Nav knew. Daljit Rama was packed behind him. The big man kept banging his knees into the back of Nav's seat. Waiting in the dark was getting to him, said sitting there felt like a thousand ants were crawling up his legs. Got in and out of the car a dozen times so far. Being six-foot-eight didn't help, pushing three hundred pounds, sitting in back of the cramped Jap car with his knees pressed in tight.

"Nearly here," Benji Kumar said from behind Veni, Benji along for some revenge. Bij, the kid killed in the attack on the Hummer, was a cousin of his. Both played for the Surrey Chiefs.

Like on cue, the cell rang in Nav's pocket. He took it out and clicked it on. "Yeah?"

"Three, four minutes tops," is all Danny DeWulf said, calling from the Accord trailing the van, then he hung up.

"Here we go," Nav said, putting the GPS unit in the glovebox, everybody checking their weapons once more in the dark, the clang of metal on metal. This was for the three killed in the attack on their Hummer six months back. What they'd done to Rivers and Glinka that morning was just a start.

The plan was simple; Veni would let the van pass, pull in behind and follow until they hit the spike strip, then rush up on them. Kill everybody except the one who fired the rocket that day — Travis Rainey — take him and the dope to a remote spot.

Danny had failed with the GPS bug, unable to stick it on the van back at the McDonald's in Squamish. Nav had him turn it on and follow in the Accord, staying close enough not to be seen, the bug giving Nav a signal to track. Danny had been calling Nav every ten minutes, staying just out of sight, giving him an update.

. . . BLINDSIDE

"Fuck is wrong with you?" Travis couldn't believe Mutt shot the cop, twice, standing at the shoulder of the highway. Rick Harper lay face down, two wet holes through his back. Still alive. The four of them looking down at him.

"What fuckin' choice I have?"

"You shot a cop." Snatching the Colt from Mutt's hand, Travis growled at him, said sorry to Harper and shot him in back of the head. "Couldn't just knock him out?" Tempted to shoot Mutt, too, he slapped the pistol back into his hand.

"Jesus Christ, I see the spike strip . . ." Mutt tried to explain, looking to Richie, waving the pistol. "And I figure it's a roadblock or something." Mutt looked up and down the highway like there might be more cops coming.

"What spike strip?" Richie and Travis saying it at the same time.

"Fuckin' tire shredder. Right there in the road. Round the bend." Mutt pointed with the Colt. "Saw it when I was shitting."

Travis and Richie looked at each other, trying to put it together, then back at Mutt.

"Yeah, I'm fucking sure," Mutt said, looking at Richie. "Told you, bro, no fucking way I'm going back inside. Not for you, this guy, Rosco — no-fucking-body."

Travis kept from going off on Mutt, forced himself to think. They had to ditch the body and the cruiser. Late Sunday night meant little traffic, so there was a chance. No way the cop laid the strip. Had to be an ambush.

Mutt wiped the big Colt on his shirt and wound his arm, ready to chuck it into the pines.

"Hang on to that," Travis said.

Richie told Marty to hide his car up the back road.

"Got to call Gibbet again," Travis said, going to the back of the van, stepping around Harper. A name Richie knew, having called him once himself, back when he rode with the Sabers. Gibbet, the clean-up man.

Fishing out his cell, Travis tossed Marty a pair of work gloves from the back of the van. Slipping them on, Marty got in the cruiser, the engine still running. Switching the lights off, he pulled around the van and turned up the side road. Mutt dragged Harper's body into the grass, away from the road, the grass tall enough to hide him for now. Richie ran up the highway, pistol in hand, wanting a look at the spike strip.

Travis punched the number into his cell, waiting for Gus to pick up, telling him, "Got another gig for Gibbet."

Silence for a second, then Gus said, "Busy day."

"Telling me. You help me out or not?"

"Doubt he's at church," Gus said, paused, then, "Same as before."

"Can do half now," Travis said. "This one came unexpected." Travis had enough to cover it, but the money was for the motel and expenses over the next week. No way he wanted to go back to Bumpy's bean counter and ask for more, try to explain why.

"You know how this works," Gus said and waited for his answer.

"Yeah, fuck it. I'll have it for you. Just get him here quick."

"All of it?"

"Yeah, all of it." What choice did he have? Sure wasn't a cash machine out here on the lost fucking highway. He'd get the five back from Nick. Let him pay for his own fuck-ups. Take the rest out of what he owed Mutt and Richie, Mutt for shooting the cop, Richie for bringing him along in the first place, vouching for him. Giving Gus the bearings, Travis finished by saying, "Oh, and this one comes with a car."

"A car?"

"Need it taken care of, too."

"Car's extra." Gus telling him another two would take care of it.

He was being milked, but it needed to get done. Travis said, "Do it," then hung up. No point arguing. You want the best, you pay for it. You want extras, you pay more.

Jogging along the highway, Richie had flashes of Gibbet, wood chippers, cleavers, bone grinders. There was a god-damned incinerator he saw on the TV news one time, used for getting rid of animals done in by SARS, bird flu or shit like that. Meat nobody wanted to eat. Richie shook his head, trying not to think of the smells and the fluids — a job worse than shoveling elephant shit. Thing is, Gibbet did it and it stayed done, never left a trace, no bones, no DNA, nothing to worry about, not in over twenty years. And for that he charged five Gs, more if it involved extras or travel. To Richie's mind, the guy wasn't charging enough. In a court of law, physical evidence trumped all else. The Crown could walk in with their witnesses and Exhibit A's and smoking guns, but if they didn't have the body, they had dick, just another Jimmy Hoffa case. Yeah, Richie would charge more, fact, he'd charge the moon. Then he was checking the retractable strip across both lanes.

"Cop sure didn't lay it," Richie said when he got back, Travis nodding, both of them with pistols drawn, wanting to get the hell out of there. He started to punch in Lexie's number, tell her he needed a ride, looked at Mutt, saying, "So we're clear, this is coming out of your end."

Mutt's mouth tightened, and he came toward him, freezing as headlights shone on them, an engine gunning. A sedan bounded across the four lanes from the opposite side road. Brakes screeched, and the car slammed to a stop, four doors flying open.

Travis, Richie and Mutt were caught in the wash of headlights, thinking, more cops. Nav and Benji were pointing machine pistols. The giant stepped from the back, holding a double Glock.

First to drop his piece, Travis put up his hands, eyes on the twin Glocks, the rig looking sci-fi. Sure weren't Mounties. Richie's hands went up, his pistol dropping, then Mutt. The headlights kept them in silhouette, Travis knowing who they were. The one that got out of the passenger side was older, his face marred with burn marks. He grinned and motioned with his machine pistol for Travis to back away from the van.

"It was you, that morning on Hastings, in back of the bread truck?" Nav said.

Travis didn't answer.

"Their names were Bij, Rajeev and Rosh."

"The three got killed. Yeah, well . . ."

"You will die twice for each one." Nav pulled his cell, punched in a number, the scorpion tat showing across his hand. He said something Travis didn't understand, then went right for the sacks of cement in back of the van like he knew what they were. Headlights flicked on to the south, and Danny DeWulf rolled the Accord along the shoulder.

Tucking his weapon under an arm, Veni helped Benji grab up the sacks, piling them in the trunk of the Lexus. Nav fished through the hockey bags, slit the back seat with his Ka-Bar, Danny getting out of the Accord, a MAX-31 in his hand.

Travis stood with his hands raised, watching Nav tear out the side panels, throwing everything out of the back of the van, finding the rest of the stash in the spare's well. They finished loading up the trunk, Daljit holding the double Glock on the three men.

Nav got in the Lexus; Veni and Benji came for Travis, Veni with a fat roll of tape, leaving the giant to show what a double Glock can do. Holding the twin barrels out like he was witching for water, Daljit blasted the side of the van, splitting the night, wanting these guys good and scared. Joining in, Danny raised his MAX-31 and emptied the coffin mag into the van. Glass and tires exploded, the van shuddered, holes punched in one side went out the other. The air reeked of powder. Everybody's ears ringing.

Reaching behind his back, Danny pulled a Model 29

Smith, saying, "Dirty Harry's gun." Raising the barrel, letting the three men have a look, looking from one to the other, stopping at Richie, "You first."

Looking at the gun, Richie said, "Fuck you."

Lights flashed and the howler cut the stillness. Marty whooped and threw the RCMP cruiser in reverse, tearing down the side road.

Danny was switching his aim, Daljit twisting and bringing up the twin Glocks, the magazines empty. Danny got off a shot, struck the trunk of the cop car, kept firing.

Behind the wheel, Marty ducked low as the rear window exploded, then the windshield, his own pistol in his hand, the cruiser jumping backwards, all he could do to keep it on the rough road. Stopping, he fired through the open back, hitting one of the guys getting out of the Lexus, feeling more bullets strike the cruiser.

Cops, Veni yelled from behind the wheel and hit the gas, Nav firing out the passenger window, knocking out the cop light bar. Daljit and Danny grabbed Benji, who'd been hit, and shoved him into the back of the Accord.

The second the howler sounded, Travis, Mutt and Richie dove for dirt, grabbing for their pistols, getting off a few rounds as the Lexus and Accord tore off, Marty trading shots from the cruiser. Gun flashes lit the night, the Lexus disappearing around the bend, screeching and swerving around the spike strip, the Accord right behind it, both heading for Whistler.

Spinning out onto the highway, Marty threw the cop car in gear, tearing after the Indos, making the curve, steering with one hand, firing out the open front with the other. Forgetting about the spike strip, he hit it, all four tires exploding. Fighting for control of the wheel, Marty dropped the handgun, spun out on the shoulder, ended up facing southbound, the howler still going. The two cars disappeared northbound.

Fuck!

Standing with the Walther in his hand, Travis heard the siren over the ringing in his own ears. It stopped, then Marty yelled from around the bend, backing the sorry cruiser along the shoulder. Four flats, no lights, no windows, holes all over it. "Who the fuck was that?" he called, coming to a stop.

"The competition," Travis said.

Marty rolled the cruiser back up the side road, getting it out of sight.

"Getting fucking interesting," Mutt said, tucking his pistol in his belt, lighting a cigarette.

"Wait till you meet Gibbet," Richie said, still looking up the road, thinking five grand wasn't nearly enough for this depth of shit.

"What the fuck we do now?" Mutt said.

"We go get our dope back," Travis said, taking in the holes in the van, fluid dripping from underneath, checking his own clip, thinking they'd need more firepower . . . and a new ride.

"That treetop fuck with George Jetson's gun . . ." Mutt said, dragging on his cigarette.

"Yeah?"

"That fucker's mine," Mutt said, swiping his foot at the busted glass.

Travis looked at him, nodding. "Yeah, that fucker's yours."

Mutt grinned at him, like they had reached an understanding.

Marty came at a trot, shoes scraping on the gravel, his pistol in his hand.

Finding a rock big enough to sit on, Travis felt the cold and damp against his ass. He tried putting together how the Indos had tailed them and set up an ambush. Making a call to the number Lexie Poots gave him, he guessed by her voice that he'd woken her. Apologizing for it, he asked how it went with Nick, saying he could use some good news, hoping the girl wanted some company. Nearly killed, and he was thinking of being with her instead of chasing after the Indos, getting the dope back before Bumpy Rosco got wind of what just went down, something that could be worse than facing a double Glock. Then he looked at Mutt, asking, "Any of that beer make it?"

Forcing back the creaking side door, Mutt climbed into the shot-up van, smelling gas, leaning across the rear seat, the stuffing torn out, dust and fiber floating in the air, moonlight filtering through a hundred holes. Swiping broken glass out of the way, he checked around.

... PAYBACK

THERE WOULD be a next time; Travis Rainey would come for his dope; Nav had no doubt, sitting in the passenger seat. Behind the wheel, Veni was pissed they didn't kill those fuckers when they had the chance, Daljit and Danny showing off, blasting the van full of holes. Veni wanting to know where the fucking cop came from.

"That was no cop," Nav said, trying to figure out what happened before they made their move. Telling Veni to take it easy, he called Danny's cell, Danny in the back seat of the Accord right behind them, Daljit driving, Nav wanting to know how bad Benji was hit, Danny saying he took one in the side, he couldn't tell how bad, just knew they had to stop the bleeding.

"Least we got their dope," Nav heard Benji say over the phone, Danny telling him to keep still. Nav told them to hang on and made a second call, getting Benji some medical attention. Sikander, a doctor back in India, would be on his way from the city, bringing his black bag. Benji would have to hang on.

"We'll get another chance," Nav told Danny, then he hung up, looking out the back, Daljit keeping the Accord right behind them.

"Which one fired the rocket?" Veni asked, checking his speedometer, easing off on the pedal.

"One with the gray in his hair." Nav took out his cell and punched in another number, knowing he needed more guys, sure there would be more than four when Rosco's crew came looking to take their dope back.

. . . GIRL ON THE CEILING

"Sleep okay?" Grey asked, watching Dara come into the kitchen, her hair wet and spiked like she just ran her fingers through it. The ghost of Tammy wasn't hanging around this morning, Grey standing in front of the stack of last night's dishes, scraping at hardened mac and cheese, working at the plate with a J-Cloth.

She said, "Like a baby, and thanks again for letting me crash." Decked in a denim cowboy shirt she'd fished from his closet after her shower, half the domes fastened, the towel around her neck, she said, "Hope you don't mind . . ." she said, meaning the shirt.

"Not a bit." It never looked that good on him. Glancing down at her legs, he felt a touch of guilt for having her here in the place he once shared with Tammy. Bare feet on the tiles. Toes painted black.

Holding the tails of the shirt out, she was playing a little, liking that he checked her out while making like he didn't.

"Wish I had something more . . . *girl*, you know," he said, looking into the sink, scrubbing at the plate, catching the scent of his own shampoo in her hair.

"Freak me out if you did," Dara said, coming up beside him. "You know, frilly and fuzzy pink things in a guy's closet . . ." She looked into the sink of bubbles, the stack of dishes, the remnants of last night's munchie-fest: a double batch of KD and a chopped salad, Pete and Mojo joining in, a bowl of Campbell's for Airdog. Used every plate in the house. Even Goob got into the festivities. "How about I dry?"

"I got it," he said, rinsing the plate, reaching past her, sticking it on the rack, sliding another plate into the suds.

"You hear from your buddy Tuff?" She watched him scrape at the gluey cheese.

He shook his head, saying, "Voicemail's still full, but if you knew Tuff . . ." He shrugged, repeating, "Guy's got a come-and-go nature."

Dara nodded, knowing the nature.

Soapsuds splashed from the sink. Picking up the dishtowel balled next to the toaster, she took a plate off the rack and started drying.

The thing that happened to Airdog shouldn't have. The guy making threats had given him a few days, said he'd call, now Tuff Dub was missing and Rivers and Glinka weren't answering Grey's calls. He'd talked it over with Pete, thinking they should call it quits, Pete not sure, just letting somebody push them out like that. Grey held off making the call to the number Travis Rainey gave him. Now he was looking at Dara, thinking she shouldn't be here, saying, "Hey, told you, guests don't do dishes."

"Tell you what: you stop, I'll stop. We let them soak, the cheese'll come off by itself."

"You take home ec or something?"

"Matter of fact, I did." She laid the dishtowel over the rack, sat at the table, checking out the 2 × 4 making the fourth leg, the screws sticking out. "See you skipped some shop classes, huh?"

"Smartass." Loading up the sink, Grey let everything soak, dried his hands on the dishtowel, saying it was time to get her on a southbound bus.

"Yeah, you're probably right," she said. "One thing I could use first is coffee." She raised her arms, stretching.

"Yeah, no sweat." He looked around for the kettle. To Grey, coffee at home came in an instant jar, like the one he took from the cupboard. Chock full o'Nuts.

"How about we go out? My treat. Least I can do," she said, trying not to offend him. "Bet you got a Starbucks or a Blenz, right?"

"That like a date?" He slid the jar back in the cupboard, looking at her shape under his shirt as she walked into the living room, past Goob snoozing and snoring on his chair. Looking out the drapes, she did a double-take at the guy in the open housecoat across the street, his bay window like a fishbowl, his vacant look that said *institutionalize me*. He waved, she waved back before turning away.

"Think we'll drive," he said, looking around, wondering where Pete left his keys.

"Yeah, I can't do handlebars this early, Superboy," she said, then remembered his bike had been stolen.

Heading for the stairs, Grey went in search of the keys. Halfway down the stairs, he heard Airdog's seesaw snoring, Pete and Mojo adding harmony, the place sounding like a bear's den, starting to smell like one, too.

THE COFFEE was French roast, and the power muffins were hot off the press — raisins, walnuts, dates and carob. The Lift was a Village hot spot on any Monday morning, beat Gretzky's hands down, the outdoor types coming for something hot and fresh-baked before hitting the trails. The couple that owned it, Connie and Gene, made everything from scratch, roasted their own beans, even made their own butter for the scones.

Grey was telling her about the killer bike trails with names like Big Kahuna and Shit Happens and his fave, the Danimal, trails he rode when he needed to clear his head, the old mountain bike Tammy bought him a long time ago, hadn't ridden it since he bought the Mongoose and took up trick riding. "Man, it's so still when you're up there, just you and the trees. Killer trails put you in the moment . . . and the air, man, it's so clean . . ."

Her eyes danced, Dara saying she'd love to try it.

"Anytime you want." Grey feeling a mix of excited, shitty and selfish, wanting more time with her, not wanting to put her on the ten-thirty 'hound but knowing it was the best thing.

"I'll pay you back the ten spot, just need a week or two," she said, tearing a strip off her napkin. She meant the bus fare — borrowing it from him saved making the call to Mother, Dara not wanting any more of her personal shit landing on Grey, first guy that treated her decent in a long time, reminded her of Karl, the guy sharing her mother's bed, a repelling thought in its own right, but still, a stand-up guy like that.

"Not worried about it," he said, waving it off. "So, you go back to your mom's, then what?"

"Then you call me sometime."

"Like a date?"

"Yeah, like that."

He put his hand on hers, stopped her from shredding the napkin.

"So you know, I'm not afraid of that asshole," she said it loud enough for the couple at the next table to look over.

He leaned close. "Thing is, there's bigger ones . . . assholes, I mean."

"You want me on the bus?"

"I don't, but you stay and you're gonna meet more of them."

"I'm a big girl, you know?"

"Yeah." He smiled; she did, too, his hand still on hers.

"And how would me staying work?"

"Couch is yours . . . till you get things worked out."

"Yeah?"

"And I can put in a word at work . . ." Teddy B owed him more than one favor. "Happens we're short a waitress."

Dara's heart was jumping as she rolled the idea around, saying, "Never done that."

"Walk around with a pad, pour coffee, carry a tray. You can do that, right?"

"All that home ec paying off."

"You could do worse than the Cellar."

"But, I wouldn't want to be a —"

"You won't be." He squeezed her hand.

It felt good in a rush, Dara forgetting all the crap that happened yesterday. She leaned across the coffee and muffins and kissed him.

Letting go of her hand, he took out his cell, dialed up Teddy B, got his service, left him a message. "B, got something new for you to try." Then he hung up, knowing Teddy B would call back soon as he could, thinking it was another strain Grey wanted him to guinea pig.

"Superboy's got some sway," she said, smiling at him, the table getting in the way of her doing more, Dara liking the idea, saying, "Yeah, it could work." Happy. She had just dodged going back to her mother's basement, something that scared her more than facing Nick Rosco.

The waitress came around asking if they wanted a top-up.

. . . MAKING A KILLING

CHIP WOODS was thinking it was bad enough dealing with
the East Indians that came in last night, right as he was
closing and catching up with the week's paperwork, getting
the listings and sales forms to the real estate board, time
being of the essence and all that crap. Chalets that sold for
three to ten million going like shit through a tin horn. Chip
Woods was doing alright, raking in his commission, keeping
Val, the wife, in her Prada and Louis whoever, smelling like
Chanel, the two of them riding to the club at Furry Creek in
Range Rovers, his in Baltic blue, hers in Fuji white. Together
alone in the custom rancher in Lions Bay, big as a palace, the
lit pool on the cliff over the ocean. The personal trainer, the
chef, the gardener, the housekeeper. Driving golf balls every
winter at their timeshare in Kaanapali.

Telling them he closed fifteen minutes ago had done
no good. The older one with the scarred face and mustache
walked to his desk and did the talking, sitting across from
him, setting an attaché on the floor, saying with an accent
that they were looking for a chalet to rent, wanted it tonight.
The one in the shades stayed by the door, looking out, like

they were being followed. Not a couple of muggers; they were well dressed, Chip guessed D&G and Gucci, the one across from him doused in Clive Christian, could be a real Cartier on his wrist.

Introducing himself as Sam Nagra, Nav Pudi offered his hand, Chip noting the tattoo wrapped across the top of his hand. The one by the door was Danny deWulf. Giving a grunt, Danny kept his post by the door, arms folded, same tattoo on the right hand.

Chip tipped in at two hundred even last time he got on the scale at the club, but Danny with the shades had him beat by a good thirty pounds, none of it hanging over his belt. Not sure where this was going, Chip kept a hand near the phone on the desk. The odds of punching in 9-1-1 before getting the shit kicked out of him seemed long.

So he showed Nav Pudi some chalets, pics on his MacBook screen, turning it so he could see, showed him the Armstrong place, a Coast Modern three-bedroom with a pool, then the Morton place, four bedrooms and timber-built, saying he'd just listed it, showing Nav on a map the spot by the golf course, saying it was five-fifty a night.

Nav, with the soulless eyes, liked that it backed onto a golf course. A quiet cul-de-sac. He pulled a stack of cash from the attaché, slapping enough hundreds on Chip's desk to cover the first two weeks along with the damage deposit. Nav gave answers as Chip took down some basic information on a form, checked the fake ID, printed out copies, had Nav sign as Sam Nagra and traded the keys for the cash, and they were gone.

The white guy coming in first thing in the morning

looked like he'd slept on a bench — Chip bet he'd have trouble scratching up enough for an Arby's breakfast. Slouching, hair unkempt, denim jacket, jeans with tatters over shabby cowboy boots. Stopping by the Nespresso machine, helping himself to a Styrofoam cup, he sipped it black, reading the framed testimonials grouped on the wall. Doing the zen-breathing thing Val taught him, Chip pasted on a smile and asked how he could be of service.

"Looks like you're doing alright," Richie Winters said, making it friendly, turning from the testimonials, taking in the rest of the place, coming toward Chip's desk. "Am I right?"

"I'm getting by," Chip said, pasting on the realtor's smile. "How about you, Mr. . . . uh . . ."

"Coffee's first-rate by the way," Richie said, taking a sip.

"Thanks. Call me Chip." He extended the hand, force of habit, told him the coffee was Intenso.

Richie finished the sip, shook his hand, and said, "You heard about that kopi coffee?"

"You mean Kona?"

"Think I said kopi. What it is, they got this rodent in Asia someplace, eats the beans and shits them out. People following after it, picking up the kopi shit, roasting it up and selling it, calling it gourmet."

"Never heard of it." Chip guessed he was pulling his leg. "They call it good shit?"

"Think I'm joking, Chip?"

"No. Kopi coffee. I'll keep an eye out."

"Ought to give it a try."

"You bet. K-o-p-i, right?" Chip jotted it on his notepad.

"Not sure how to spell it, Chip."

"No problem. Now, something else I can do for you, Mr. . . . uh . . ."

"You do rentals, am I right?" Richie sipped his coffee.

"Only place in town that does," Chip said, guessing if he tossed around a couple of rental rates, this waste of time would go away.

"Looking for some friends might have rented from you in the last day or two," Richie said, taking the seat Nav Pudi had sat in. Betting the Indos who ripped them off last night hadn't walked into a hotel, where they'd have to secure rooms with a credit card, something that could be traced. Richie bet they'd walked into a place like this and paid cash, the only place that did rentals. "Dark-skinned guys that paid cash. One's got a mustache, face all fucked up, one's this tall."

"Afraid that's privileged."

Richie sipped from his Styro cup, checked out the photo of the wife and kids on the desk, picking up the frame, going, "Hmmm."

"The wife — going for our diamond anniversary this year."

Richie tilted the frame in his hand. "Kids, huh?"

"Yeah, boy and a girl." *The ones in the photo, genius.*

"Friends I'm looking for got tattoos across their hands, a scorpion, tail wrapping around the wrist."

"Like I said, that's privileged."

Richie showed the palms of his hands. "I'm asking you nice here, Chip."

"See, there are ethics, board rules I got —"

Chip was staring at the big Smith Richie took from under the denim behind his back and laid on the desk. Had to be a robbery. "Look, Mister, I don't keep cash on the premises."

Richie slid the gun closer to him. "Just after an address, Chip."

"Afraid I'm going to —"

"Naw, you're not afraid." Richie set the frame on the desk, left the pistol and coffee and headed to the door, adding, "Not yet." He flipped the *open* sign to *closed* and threw the deadbolt. Tipping the blinds, he walked back, saying, "I were you, I'd pick it up and start shooting. Only chance you got."

"Look, come on, I . . ."

Coming around the desk, Richie grabbed the framed photo and struck Chip on the head with it, watched him tumble out of his chair, into the credenza, hand on his bleeding scalp.

"Fuck me, Jesus Christ . . ." Last time he was in a fight, Chip left some fat kid bloody on the floor of the school cafeteria. The sight of his own blood set him off. Charging low, Chip threw his hands wide, going to bulldog Richie to the floor.

Moving to the side, Richie chopped down, cuffing Chip on the ear, smashing his other fist into his pudding gut, watching him fold.

Shaking to clear his head, Chip tried again, ran into an uppercut. Steadying himself against the desk, he sucked wind, throwing himself across the desk for the pistol.

The cowboy boot caught more thigh than nuts, but it stopped him. Chip lay curled under the desk.

"Just breathe through it, nice and steady," Richie said.

Chip stayed down, sputtering blood out of his nose. "You leave right now, I forget you were ever here."

"Never gonna forget I was here, Chip." Tossing down

the photo of the wife and kids, Richie put a boot on it, crunching the glass. He picked up the desk lamp, yanked its cord free, and threw it against the far wall, then swept the phone off the desk, pulling a drawer, dumping it, grabbing the laptop, raising to over his head.

"No, no, okay, not my Mac," Chip cried out, hands up in surrender. His professional life was in there. Nothing on the drive had been backed up in a week.

Setting it down, Richie waited for Chip to get up, wipe the blood from his face.

"So I ask you about these hindudes with the tattoos, paid you in cash, and you say . . . ?" Richie pointed a finger at him.

"Two guys came in . . . last night, one with a mustache, face all fucked up, name of Sam something, other one was big, in dark shades." Chip reached for the laptop, looking at Richie like he was asking permission.

"Go ahead," Richie said, picking up the Styro cup, taking a sip. The coffee had gone lukewarm, so he dashed it on the rug, watching Chip tapping at keys, giving up the fake name Nav Pudi gave him along with the address of the chalet on Nicklaus North, printing out the agreement and handing it over.

Picking the Smith off the desk, Richie tucked it in his belt and went over the rules. "First one: you call this 'Sam Nagra,' I'm going to be back, fuck you up like you've never been. Understand? Good. Rule two: you call the cops . . ." Richie folded the copy of the agreement and reached down for the broken frame.

"Okay, I get the picture," Chip said.

"Long as we understand each other." Sticking the paper

in his pocket, Richie set the broken frame on the desk, headed for the door, looking back at Chip, guessing he left a strong enough impression. "Oh, one more thing, Chip, this Nagra guy pay a pet deposit?" Richie remembering the Indo assholes liked to keep pit bulls around their meth labs.

"A what?"

"Asking if they said anything about having a dog?" Nothing Richie hated worse than having to shoot a dog just doing its job.

"No, we're strictly no pets."

Richie went to the door, thinking the last thing Chip should be worrying about was a pet, saying, "And try that coffee."

Chip nodded. "Kopi, yeah, I'll keep an eye out."

Richie stepped through the door and was gone.

. . . PAPER PLANES

DIDN'T NEED to be a cop to know something was wrong.
Every face in the station showed it. Ben Risker sat behind
his desk, patches on his sleeves, chevrons on his epaulets, a
nylon stab-proof vest hanging off the back of his chair. He
had called the number at the Beaver Lodge a half hour ago,
asked Lance and Jimmy to come in, now telling them to sit,
shutting his door.

The hard drive on the corner of the L-shaped desk had
to be a decade old. A banner about community policing
sagged from its pushpins above a group of photos, mostly
shots of Risker ass-kissing with councilmen, the mayor,
brother officers, a group shot of the entire detachment out
front decked in their Red Serge and black breeches, topped
in their Stetsons. Smiling in most of them, Risker sure wasn't
smiling now, waiting till their chairs stopped scraping, the
strain of being up most of the night registered on his face.
Getting right to it, he said, "One of ours, Rick Harper, went
off the radar last night." He waited, let it sink in.

Lance and Jimmy swallowed that; neither knew the man
other than to say hello. Still, there was this brotherhood

thing. They asked the expected questions, the same ones Risker had been answering all morning.

Jimmy didn't say it, but he was thinking the way some of these boys hit the bottle, it was small wonder one got in his cruiser and went off the radar. A pint of Canadian Club and a wrong turn on a dark road . . . A glance over told him Lance was thinking the same thing.

"Was a couple hours into his shift, the last radio call coming in just before ten, patrolling the 99," Risker said.

"What about his cruiser?" Jimmy asked. "Got GPS, right?"

"Nothing. Shuttle-bus driver called in a spike strip across the northbound lanes in the same stretch. Said he just missed it, dragged it to the side and found a van shot to hell on its side in the ditch."

"Jesus," Lance said. "What about Harper's last call?"

"Called in a plate, one off the shot-up van, but didn't wait for it, must have stepped out of the car . . ." Risker threw in he had a team of bush beaters searching the area, officers with dogs, Search and Rescue, a couple of EMS guys. How many times had he stressed that his officers don't step out until they get the report on the plate, especially when they're riding solo? Rick Harper could end up being a good argument for the license plate scanners the department wanted to install up on the light bars.

"And the van's plate?" Lance asked.

"Reported stolen from in front of a duplex in Squamish earlier in the evening. Family inside having Sunday roast and trimmings. Something they do every week." He turned from the desk and pushed his mouse across the pad, the monitor coming to gray life. Turning the screen so they could see the crime-scene photos: the bullet-riddled van, the casings on the ground, footprints all over. Risker said, "Large caliber and automatic, by the number of shells."

"These people having Sunday dinner, any with priors?" Lance asked.

"Squamish did the interviews . . ." Risker shook his head, read the name off his notepad, saying, "Family named Ta'Kaya. All with the same story. Nobody heard or saw a thing. Father went out for a smoke while the mother dished up dessert, saw it was missing. Called it in an hour before Rick's last transmission." He looked up at them. "Put a SAR copter up over McGuire at first light."

"And the casings?" Lance said.

"Dozens. Nine mil mostly. Forensics is working that along with bloodstains they found. Looks like somebody tried to swipe it away with a boot. Got a mix of tire tracks, footprints, metal, glass, you name it." Risker looked at Lance. "You ask me, I say your drug war's come to town."

Lance drew a breath and nodded.

"Top it off, half-hour ago, the SAR boys stumbled on a cabin near the scene; the place wall to wall with pot plants in the fucking middle of nowhere. Not so much as a fucking footpath leading to the place. Solar heat, more lights than a tanning salon, place sealed up tight, the whole nine yards. Searchers say nobody's been around in days."

"This place got hydro?" Lance asked, thinking Grey Stevens.

Risker shook his head. "Gas-powered generators, three of them. Search team kicked in the door on account of the racket. Probable cause, then radioed it in." Risker rose out of his chair, thinking the same as Lance, saying the higher-ups at 312 were sending up an ERT — emergency response team — meaning Risker would get sidelined right along with Lance and Jimmy as soon as they showed up.

Lance was first out of his chair.

"Means we're done," Jimmy said, following him out, Lance saying he knew what it fucking meant.

Risker got up, too, going in search of a Red Bull or something — the phone on his desk ringing again — thinking, how does something the size of a police cruiser go missing?

. . . NOBODY'S BITCH

THE BEDSHEET was a trailing mess, wrapped around Mutt's foot, pooling to the floor like a bride's train. He was sitting at the end of the bed, one sock on. The tenement sag of the mattress had taken its toll. Fucking thing poking at his back all night left him aching. Travis, the cheap bastard, wouldn't spring for decent rooms, Mutt thinking of the nightlife and the pussy he could be having in the Village. Here he was risking his ass, hadn't even been paid in full. The Cadillac Arms got a three-roach rating in his book, the only amenities being the beat-up Coke machine out in the lobby and a thirty-nine-game Pac-Man table from like the eighties. Plastic ficus with butts in the planter, flanked by a couple of mismatched chairs. The laminate table had initials carved in it and gum stuck under it, and was piled with magazines dating to the Chrétien days.

Travis threw it back in Mutt's face; most of the cash he'd been advanced from Bumpy's bean counter went to getting the mess cleaned up: five Gs for the kid Nick shot, five more for the cop Mutt left at the side of the 99, two more to get rid of the squad car. On top of that he had to call the old man's lieutenant, reminding Eduardo he could use a couple more guys, didn't mention the attack or the stolen dope.

Head resting against the headboard of the second twin, Marty chomped a Snickers without using his hands, the dripping mess hanging from his mouth like a candy turd. Sucking at the chocolate, Marty was getting down to the gooey stuff, his eyes fixed on the TV, some black-and-white classic from the sixties. His hands were busy cleaning his Walther, swabs strewn across the bed. The smell of the cleaning solvent rose over the body odors. He tuned out Travis and Mutt arguing, Travis telling Mutt he'd get the rest of his fucking money, Mutt asking when. Travis went to the can, slamming the door.

Sixties reruns had been playing one after the other, this one with some babe dressed like a genie. Marty said, "Man, I could do with some of that," liking the way the actress was packed into her genie outfit, trying to distract Mutt, get him to chill.

Tearing into a bag of wavy Lay's, Mutt shoved in the chips, his mouth motoring like a shredder. He didn't care about the genie, was looking in the direction Travis went and thinking about that double Glock with the scope on top. Man, a thing like that could take out a roomful of ass-holes. The last tiny vodka from the mini-bar was in his hand, empties scattered on the carpet among crunched bags of mini-pretzels, seaweed Pringles, M&M's, Big Turk and Twix wrappers.

Walking back in from the can, Travis did up his fly, the door between the adjoining rooms open behind him, the scene looking different than back in the days when the Sabers held church, Travis saying to Mutt, "You know they charge like an arm and a leg for that shit, right?" The mini-bar door was hanging open. Pissed at having to go after Nick for more cash, Nick not answering his calls so far this morning, Travis could still picture that fucking orange trunk lid flapping up and down as Nick drove off and left him holding the dead kid in his arms.

"Yeah, well, fuck, if this dump had room service . . ." Mutt said.

Marty tried to break the tension, saying, "Being on TV adds like ten pounds, they say." Popping the recoil spring back, dropping the slide and nudging Mutt with his foot, hoping to distract him. "And man, this chick's got the pointiest tits. Check it out. I give her an eight." Sucking down the last of the chocolate.

Mutt glanced at the screen, flicking the chip packet away, guessing he'd square off with Travis before this thing was through, show him he was nobody's bitch. "Got nothing on that Elly May hillbilly chick."

Marty put his cleaning supplies on the nightstand, saying he read the chick who played Elly May sued Mattel over a doll they made in her likeness, throwing in, "Same outfit that made Barbie."

Richie caught the tail of the conversation as he came in.

"Where the fuck you been?" Travis asked, turning on him.

"Fixing our problem," Richie said, taking in the scene, the room looking like a disaster site.

"Yeah, it fixed?"

Richie couldn't believe the smell in here, like fucking gym socks and Cheezies, threw open the only window as he told them what he found out, the address he got from Chip the realtor. "Couple of assholes with tats on their hands walked in last night, paid cash for a place. Sounds like our boys alright."

"Fuckin' A," Marty said, racking the slide, slapping the magazine in.

Travis clapped Richie on the back, Richie asking what about Nick.

"Far as he knows," Travis said, "the shit's under the bed. Got him convinced everything's cool, told him to hang tight. Gave him a hooker to play with."

"He getting us the rest of our money?" Mutt asked, pissed about Nick getting a hooker.

"Yeah. Don't fucking worry about it," Travis said, looking from one to the other.

They were worried.

"Got Nick jammed up," Travis said. "Could make things bad for him. We take care of the Indos, he'll get our cash, do whatever I tell him. Right now, I need him quiet." Travis said, looking at Richie. "So, what about this place?"

"A chalet out on the golf course. Big fucking place." Their own flea-dive rooms not lost on Richie, the Indos getting that part right. Place even had a hot tub out back.

"Got an address?"

Fishing the slip of paper Chip gave him from his pocket, Richie said it was off the first tee, adding, "Did a little recon on my way back."

"Yeah?"

"Crept up on it nice and quiet. Got a bit of a rise, a line of trees, enough bushes and shit to make our approach. Whole back of the place is glass, stairs leading up. Be like a fishbowl at night with the lights on."

"Any idea how many?"

"Didn't see anybody."

Travis thought a moment, saying, "Then we go tonight."

"Gives you time to get the money," Mutt said.

Ignoring that, Travis turned to Marty. "Meantime, we're gonna need some hardware," telling Marty to make a run to the North Shore shipyards, told him to see this guy Tanner, said he'd set it up.

Marty got off the bed, tucking the pistol away, pulling his boots on.

"Go with him," Travis said to Mutt, Mutt looking sour but getting up, crunching wrappers underfoot.

Reaching into his pocket for the keys to the rental he'd picked up earlier, Travis tossed them to Marty, telling him to switch cars when they got back, told him to see Jeff at the Alamo, the guy the Sabers had a long-standing understanding with. Cash for keys, any car on the lot, right as you came into town. If anyone ever asked, Jeff would claim it was swiped off the lot, just went undetected, happened all the time.

Marty went out the door, Mutt following him, bumping past Travis, the TV left on.

. . . WHAT GOES AROUND

LYING BACK, hands folded behind his neck, Nick was trying to put last night together, guessing Jaelene split sometime before dawn. The blonde one had ducked out after getting his attention on the dance floor, like she had better things to do. This town full of johns. Catching Jaelene's scent on the pillow, he called her name in case she was in the can.

He would want Jaelene again, likely find her at Maxi's or one of the escort places, wouldn't be hard to find in a town this size. Reaching for his wallet on the nightstand, he flipped it open, making sure she hadn't tipped herself on top of the five bills he paid her. The rest of his cash and his credit cards all there.

In that foggy state of half-sleep, he relived the night: watching her go into the can, Nick folding his suit, draping it over the back of the chair, getting into the bed. Jaelene coming out of the can, light streaming from behind, naked except for the vajazzle and heels, climbing across the bed, the great rack, the long legs wrapping around him, Nick waiting for the blue pill to kick in over the booze, the girl riding him cowgirl till it hurt. A wild night. Nick slept like a baby.

Getting up, he reached the phone, his head thumping through the fog. Calling down for room service, Nick asked what day it was, said he was in need of coffee and something to eat; a Danish sounded good. Dragging himself into the shower, he let the water run over him, as hot as he could stand. And when he came out of the steam, he toweled off and wiped the mirror, still feeling like shit.

Looking in the mirror at his eyes, veins like swollen rivers, he smoothed his hair in place. Then he pulled up his silk briefs, buttoned the shirt, found both socks and took the jacket folded over the chair, fishing in his pocket for the Binaca. Looked at the nightstand for his piece. And felt like he'd been slapped.

Fuck!

He checked the drawer, then behind the nightstand, around the floor. The Smith was missing.

Had to be there.

The one he shot the kid with, the one with his prints all over it. Turning around, he scanned the floor, moving faster now, head thumping louder, getting on his knees, checking under the bed, pulling out the drawers, feeling along the top of the shelf in the closet, ripping open the bathroom cupboards, checking back under the bed. The trench knife was under the pillow, but no gun.

Shit!

Had to be the hooker. He remembered taking off the tuckable holster, putting it on the nightstand like he always did when he wore it. Opening his wallet again, all the cash and credit cards undisturbed. If she stole anything, why not that? Had to be fifty grand of credit on the cards.

It had been under his jacket when he ran into Stevens and the girl at Stir Crazy's, showed it to them, let them know what was coming, stuck the bill in the barrel and pointed it at the fuck driving the tow truck. There when he headed to the clubs, ending at Maxi's, talking to Jaelene. Touching it under his jacket, she asked what he did with that, Nick saying whatever he wanted, showing her who he was.

The knock at the door made him jump. Room service. He called, "Just a sec," got into the bathrobe and tucked the terry belt through a loop. Running fingers through his wet hair again, he pulled the door open, halfway through saying, "Put it over there."

The two guys, one fat, one tall, sure weren't room service and didn't wait to be asked in.

"Don't tell me, Jehovahs?" Nick said, recognizing the two mutts who chased Grey Stevens after he decked Nick with the bike, Stevens riding off with his mule.

"Nick Rosco," the fat one in loud plaid said, but he wasn't asking, shoving past him, doing his cop thing, securing the room, glancing into the bathroom, the other one staying in front of Nick.

"So if you're not Jehovahs, let's see some tin," Nick said, looking from one to the other, wagging his fingers, knowing how this worked.

Pulling his jacket back, Lance flapped his shield, saying he was Detective Edwards, his partner was Detective Gallo, Jimmy pulling back the red plaid, letting Nick get a look at the shield on his belt. Both were low on humor since finding out Harper had gone missing.

"A mick and a wop," Nick said. "No *Watchtower*, no saving my sorry ass?"

"You here alone last night, Nick?" Lance asked, walking past him to the window and looking out.

"You kidding? Should've seen the action I had, make you humps drool."

"The kind of action gets you a pain when you pee," Jimmy said, checking the bathroom, the open closet, drawers all pulled open, cop's eyes searching.

"Beats banging the same soggy biscuit," Nick said to Jimmy. "Bet you been doing it since those lapels were in."

The punch came out of nowhere, folding Nick in half.

"Soggy biscuit left me, Nick," Jimmy said, shaking out his wrist. "Now, how about we start with yesterday afternoon, say around four?"

Nick straightened, thought if he puked, he'd do it on the fat cop. He regained his breath, saying, "Listen, Gasso, charge me with something or take your fashion statement for a hike."

The emergency response team was on its way, Lance feeling time running out. "There's another way we can play it, Nick. Detective Gallo here can slip off the wide lapels, keep using you for a heavy bag."

"Know who my father is, right?"

"Guy with you for a son." Jimmy smacked his fist into his palm.

"Funny."

"Bet he doesn't think so." Jimmy slipped off the jacket, handing it to his partner, limbering his shoulders.

"Got a witness saw two guys shoot another guy, stuff the body in a trunk," Lance said, Jimmy shadowboxing around the room. Jimmy thinking he could beat out a confession — that or his next transfer would be to a remote outpost named Yahk. "We're thinking you look right for it."

"Sure you do," Nick said, watching Jimmy punching his way around the room, adding a little bobbing and weaving. Never seen anybody start sweating so fast.

"Right over in parking lot five?" Lance said, draping Jimmy's jacket over Nick's.

"Yeah, where's that?"

"Next to four."

Jimmy feinted in, Nick falling back on the bed, sure he was going to get hit, the trench knife slipping from under the stacked pillows.

"Trimming the toenails, Nick?" Lance asked, picking up the blade, Jimmy stopping for a second, catching his wind.

"Belongs to the chick was here. Into role-playing and shit," Nick said. "Look fellas, I don't know jack about any parking lot, okay?"

"Our eyewitness says different."

"You had a witness, I'd be in cuffs already. Look, why you hassling me?"

"Drug trafficking, money laundering, picked up more than once for running guns, son of Geovani Rosco," Lance said. "I don't know, you tell us?" Playing with the trench knife, he put a finger against its point, checking it out.

"None of that shit ever stuck. Nothing that counts," Nick said. "But good to see you Dudley Do-Rights doing your homewo—"

Grabbing Nick by his ankles, Jimmy yanked him straight off the end of the bed, Nick's head banging the footboard. He reached, helping Nick to his feet, getting nose to nose, saying, "Parking lot five, go."

Holding the back of his head, snugging the sash on the robe, Nick tried to pull back, thought a second, saying, "What time you say?"

"Just before four."

"Was in the Village, doing a little shopping, you know, tourist shit, maybe had a drink someplace."

"This someplace got a name?"

He couldn't come up with one, just that the place was dead.

"Then what?"

"Had dinner at uh . . . La Cantina, got this cute waitress, blonde, left her a fat tip." Nick watched Jimmy going around the room, throwing more punches at the air, sweat circles showing under his arms. How did they let a guy like that keep a badge?

"Alone?" Lance asked, jotting on his pad.

"Yeah, just me, a plate of mussels and a glass of pinot."

"Then?"

"Went trolling, I don't know, three, four places after that, looking for a date, ended up at this place with velvet . . . uh . . . Maxi's, hooked up and came back here."

"This hooker got a name?" Lance asked.

Nick's mouth tightened into a grin. "The way you say hooker. Think you don't pay just —"

Jimmy came in and slammed him in the gut, keeping him from falling, saying, "Say soggy biscuit again, you're going to need medical attention."

Nick gagged, sucking in wind.

"Name?"

"Chick called herself Jaelene."

"Stay the night?"

"Half of it maybe. Woke up alone, got in the shower, next thing you mutts are pounding on the door."

Turning to Lance, Jimmy asked, "Why you suppose these assholes think they can talk to us like that?"

Lance played with the knife, said it was on account of the kind of crap on TV these days, giving guys like Nick the wrong idea how they can treat law enforcement, what they can get away with.

"Gonna be sick," Nick said. "Look, I answered your questions. You got any more, I —"

"Yeah. What's a place like this set you back, couple hundred a night?" Jimmy asked.

"Try five. Want to make a crack how crime doesn't pay?"

"You like getting hit, Nick?" Jimmy asked, grabbing two fistfuls of hotel bathrobe, "'Cause I can hit dickheads all day. You got no idea."

"Explaining my bruises gonna cost you a demerit point."

"Naw, you just got to make it look like justifiable force. With a partner backing you up," Jimmy said, holding a hand up to Lance, "corroborating the story — sure, you got paperwork to fill out — but basically you got no problem."

Nick threw up, the carpet, the robe, the bed, Jimmy's shoes.

Jimmy looked down, kept talking like nothing happened while Lance went to the bathroom for a towel. "Some of the fellows find it a good way to let off steam, and saves on the therapy."

Lance came back, held out a towel, Jimmy taking it, wiping his shoes, saying, "Sometimes for the hell of it, we plant a little shit, then ask our questions down at the station, place where the toilets smell like piss." Flipped the towel to him.

Nick balled the towel and wiped his mouth. "My old man's lawyer's gonna have you for breakfast."

"First he's got to get the phone call," Jimmy said, getting in close.

"Where'd you park, Nick?" Reaching the silver jacket on the back of the chair, Lance went into the pockets, coming up with the Camaro fob and flip key.

"It's downstairs."

"Mind if we have a look in the trunk?" He dropped the key in a pocket.

"Hard to say no to you boys." Telling them the Camaro was in the underground, at the far end.

"See, there you go. Nice and friendly," Jimmy said. "Way to play it, Nick."

A knock at the door. Lance pulled it open. A guy in a white uniform announced he was room service, rolling in a cart, a warming cover over a plate and a carafe on a white tablecloth. The guy looked at Lance with the knife, puke on Nick's hotel robe, waiting for Nick to sign.

Adding a tip, Nick told the guy, "Here you go," waiting till he left.

Lifting the warming cover, Jimmy poked a finger at the Danish like he was expecting it to move, saying, "Not kidding about the surveillance cameras in the parking lots, right up next to the arc lights. Got the boys taking a look, enhancing the pixels for detail." Jimmy lied, knowing all they had was a color-blind witness, but betting he struck a nerve.

Nick didn't say anything, looked at the Danish.

"Didn't know about them, huh? Yeah, city council voted to stick them all over the place." Jimmy said once they reviewed the footage, they'd be back.

"What can I say?" Nick forced the grin. "You got crime happening in a nice place like this, and in broad daylight, I got to say where are the cops, you know what I mean?"

"How long you in town for, Nick?" Lance asked.

"Don't know, thought I'd catch the bike thing."

"Crankworx? That was last week."

Nick shrugged. "Then I guess it's the cheese rolling."

"Yeah, a real crowd pleaser," Lance said. "Do what you want, but don't leave town just yet."

"Not like I got to work a day job."

Lance went for the door, taking the trench knife, saying he'd keep it, but leave the key at the front desk after they checked his ride.

Handing him the warming cover, Jimmy told Nick he ought to try Blackbird, best pastries around.

"Guess you guys would know." Nick put it down, went to the door and took the *do not disturb* sign.

Walking around the maid's cart, Jimmy snapped it from him, gave it to the girl and told her to go right in, following his partner down the hall.

"Yeah, thanks for dropping in, fellows," Nick called, sure he had to throw up again. He shut the door in the maid's face, throwing on the security lock, holding his stomach on the way to the can, thinking he had to find the hooker, get his piece back, Nick having a pretty good idea who put her up to it. Felt like a cracked a rib when he threw up again, this time into the toilet.

. . . MORE THAN A NIGHT

Lexie Poots was a knockout, but she couldn't follow directions worth a shit. He didn't say much about it through lunch, the two of them going back to her place, now Travis was letting it out, pissed because shit like that could end up biting him on the ass.

Lying next to him, bodies touching — the Twin Peaks condo she rented through Chip the realtor, a place she never brought dates from work, not that she did that kind of thing — she read him now, saying, "I'm sorry, but I got you the gun, right?"

"And now I got this Jaelene in the picture. A loose end I don't need."

Trying to clear it up for him, she said, "Followed your man Nick to Maxi's like you asked. Jaelene's a friend who owed me a favor. Asked her to come along, take care of things. No idea who I did it for, and Jaelene's not the type to ask."

"She one of Manny's?"

She nodded. "Look, Travis, I told you I just do the bookings . . ." She could get pissed herself, for him making assumptions. "You think I'd join him, get him drunk, then what, hope he passed out at the table? Not that I would, but if I let a guy like that touch me, we'd be over before we ever got started, right?"

There it was. He pulled back and looked at her. She was right; no way he'd go near anything Nick touched. "You tell her to wear a glove, picking up the gun?"

She smiled. "One thing these girls are all about is the protection."

His own smile told her he was getting okay with it, this guy with the silver wings in his hair, walked in and told Manny Pesco how things were going to be, a guy who got what he wanted.

Reaching his pants on the floor, he fished out his wallet, took out a couple hundreds, held them out. "For Jaelene." He watched her bend and reach her handbag, thinking maybe this was working out. It had been awhile since something like this had worked out.

She looked at the clock on her bedside table, said she had to get ready, due down at Sugar's in an hour, working the afternoon shift today. Then his cell was ringing, Travis guessing it was Marty, giving him an update on the guns. The display told him it was the old man again.

. . . HITTING THE ROOF

Near the end of his shift, Grey got a second call, Zipper spotting the asshole from Stir Crazy. "Heading your way," Zipper said, offering to back him up. Grey told him he had it covered. Pete was picking him up at eleven, none of them taking any chances.

The Cellar was dead, typical Monday night, just a few regulars at the end of the bar, old soldiers trading stories, drinking their days away. The yuppie couple at the booth near the door came in about once week. Tonight, they were having words, her telling him how things were, him getting up, sick of her shit, the two of them taking it outside before it turned into more.

An hour earlier, Zipper had called, told him he had company coming. Staff Sergeant Ben Risker walked in, off duty, and had a scotch, eyes burning through him. Told Grey if the techs turned up so much as a trace of evidence at the grow house in the woods, he'd be back, Risker sure Grey had something to do with Harper's disappearance. Been nearly twenty-four hours now. He got up and left without paying, Grey wishing him luck finding the missing cop.

The door opened now and Nick Rosco walked in. Dressed casual this time, cargos and a polo, he came to the bar.

"Sorry, we're closing in five," Grey said, mopping a rag across the wooden bar top, his uncle's High Standard on the shelf under the bar.

"Johnnie Blue on the rocks," Nick said and sat on the stool opposite, hand slapping the bar.

"Johnnie Blue's neat and room temp. No ice."

"Where I come from, we like to add the chill. Fact we call it a Blue Chill."

Grey shrugged and reached the bottle. Another bullshit drink like Syn — Seagram's and Hennessy — one some rapper made popular. He pulled a glass and set it down, saying, "Would have taken you for more of a Dumbfuck man myself."

Nick looked like he might come across the bar.

Grey smiled and said, "Dumbfuck. That's one hit schnapps, one of cc. No ice."

"How about a Dead Fuck? One hit Smith, one hit Wesson, much ice as you want, won't make a fucking difference."

Plopping in the cubes, three of them, Grey grinned as he poured the Johnnie, turned to the backlit shelves and set the bottle next to the malt scotch: the good stuff. One eye on Nick in the reflection, he let him know, "Take the cops all of two minutes to get here." The landline within easy reach, the pistol even closer.

"For what, a guy wanting ice in his drink?" Nick watched him pour. No Smith. No trench knife. He'd have to do Stevens with his fists, that or a bottle.

An old-school ringtone sounded in Nick's pocket; he

reached for his cell, swiveling away, taking the call, getting into it with Travis. Practically shouting that he wanted a face to face. The old men at the end of the bar looked over at him, Nick asking them if they had a fucking problem outside of the obvious, then getting back to his call.

Putting the lid on the ice, Grey bent and fished around the bottom of the trash can, coming up with a couple of the roofies, the ones he took from the other asshole last night, tossing them in the muddler, crushing them along with the ice, adding it to Nick's Blue Chill, swizzling it around, setting the glass on a cocktail napkin. *Nostrovia*, dickhead.

His back to Grey, Nick said into the phone, "Where the fuck are you now?" then that he'd be there soon as he finished his drink. Clapping his phone shut, he picked up the glass and knocked half of it back in a swallow, looked at it and frowned, asking, "Who the fuck told you crush the ice?"

Grey shrugged. "Call it innovation."

"Idiot." Nick drained it and told him to get it right this time, watched Grey pour another, knocked it back and got up, telling Grey he wouldn't see it coming, asked what he thought of that.

"It's twelve-fifty for the drink, just charge you the one," Grey said, "plus a tip'd be nice," watching Nick walk to the door, trying to slam it on his way out, the hydraulic closure keeping him from doing it.

Checking the clock on the wall, Grey picked up the landline and punched in the number of the burner he'd left with Dara, waiting for her to pick up, saying, "Hey."

"Hey yourself," Her voice was pure honey. "How's my Superboy?"

My Superboy.

"Just about to pour the old boys in a cab and switch off the lights. Going to be up for a bit?" Hoping she remembered he closed up early Monday nights.

"You kidding? Got my veggie bolognese on simmer."

"That's a dish, right?"

"The best you ever had. Made it just for you, Superboy."

"You can cook, huh?"

"Tomatoes, zucchini, onion, basil, garlic over rigatoni. You bet your ass I can, and you better come hungry."

"You didn't need to do that."

"Somebody's got to wean you off the KD." Then she asked if he had candles someplace, the girl going all out.

Telling her to check over the sink, next to the Chock full o'Nuts. When he hung up, he was thinking he'd sign out a bottle of the new pinot Teddy B ordered in, take the back way out, down the fire escape and wait in the shadows for Pete to come pick him up, wondering how long till the roofies kicked in on Nick.

... AIMING TO PLEASE

THEY WERE back across from each other, on either side of the leather desk. Manny working late, checking over his books, Lexie fielding the calls in the outer office, pretty busy for a Monday night.

"Just saying things are good the way they are," Manny said, careful how he let it drop, telling Travis he didn't want a partner, softening it by calling it a tempting offer, Travis wanting to inject a couple hundred K, Manny guessing the cash would be printed on promises with about a million strings attached. The kind of partnership that would end badly — for him. Let Travis in, and there'd be no getting him out, not without taking his pistol from the drawer.

"I go to the next cum-and-go, things'll go bad for you, Manny," Travis said it like he gave a shit, wanting to make this quick, not the reason he came by tonight. "You end up being the competition."

"Yeah, I get that," Manny said, checking his watch; his wife was holding dinner for him, the in-laws over. "Tell you what, give me another day on it."

Looking at him a moment, Travis rose from behind the desk, saying, "Take two. What's a couple of days?"

What he'd really come by for was to collect Nick's pistol from Lexie, ask her if any of her girls had seen the dark-skinned guys with the scorpion tats. But now Manny was watching, and she was on the phone, fixing a john up with a dream date. Walking through reception, Travis winked at her but didn't say a word and went out the front door.

Manny watched him leave, the big man climbing into the back of the waiting cab in the handicapped spot, hearing Lexie on the phone. When she hung up, he told her to make sure she locked up. Switching off his office lights, he locked his office door and went out, hungry for his wife's pot roast, the way she did it with the candied yams and Yorkshire pudding to sop up that gravy. God, it didn't get any better than that.

A minute after Manny's Cadillac drove off, Lexie watched the cab pull back into his spot, Travis getting out.

"Interest you in a drink or something?" she asked, watching him click the exterior lock and switch off the lights, the pink bulbs of Sugar's sign the only light in the room.

"What's the something?" Going around the desk, he drew her to him and kissed her.

Pulling away enough to reach the top drawer, she lifted the tray and took off a key taped to the bottom, reached in the lower drawer for the Ziploc holding the Smith, set it on the desk.

"Thought you meant the other kind of something," he said, grinning.

"I did." Then she unlocked Manny's door and went in. Going to the decanter on the bureau, she poured two shots straight up. Handing Travis one, she nodded to the sofa.

"Two things," she said. "Guy that called before, think it's your guy. Said he was John Smith, but the accent said he was somebody else." She handed him the folded note, the same address Richie got from the realtor.

"He's throwing a party, wants some company." She watched him pocket the note, Travis saying, "Yeah?"

"Told me six girls. Said to make it a nice assortment."

"Like a box of chocolates?"

"Some dark, some light. All of them sweet. Bite into one, see what you get."

"For when?"

"Said the sooner the better. Told him I'd put it together."

He nodded. "You said two things."

She started to unbutton her top. Watching her, he made a quick call to Richie, said yeah a couple of times, then told him to come pick him up . . . said to give him a half-hour. Told him where, told him they were going to crash a party.

When she eased back on the leather, he went to her; her fingers found his buckle and went to work. By the time they finished, the sofa had humped its way against the wall. Polishing off his drink, he kissed her neck, then that pouty Cameron Diaz mouth, asking how about later, Travis feeling good for his years.

"Later could work," she said, fastening his belt, straightening his shirt.

"Oh, one more thing, want you to fix Nick up again."

"Tonight?"

"Doesn't have to be fancy, just something with a pulse — keep him in his room."

"Guess I can do that."

Travis called her an angel, took his cell and punched in Nick's number.

"What the fuck's going on?" Nick sounded pissed.

"You in your room?"

"You're supposed to keep me in the loop?"

"Told you, I'm waiting to hear from my guys in Pemberton, meantime I'm cuing things up with Stevens."

"I'm looking at the fuck right now."

"Told you to back off."

"Yeah, well, fuck that."

Travis let go a sigh. "Not the time for this, Nick."

"You want me taking this to my old man? Tell him how you're going behind my back?"

"We don't do this on the phone," Travis said.

"Then face to face."

"Fine. I'll call you in the morning." Travis hung up, wanting to hit something, Lexie looking at him.

On the other end of the line, Nick was jumping off the bar stool, screaming and hitting *call history*, then *send*, the old guys down the bar staring. When Travis picked up, he yelled, "We're doing this right fucking now."

Drawing a long breath, Travis guessed Nick's next call would be to the old man. Checked his watch: ten minutes before Richie showed up. "Where are you?"

Travis heard Nick cover a hand over his phone, Nick asking Grey where the fuck he was and repeating the location.

Travis covered his own cell and asked Lexie where the

Cellar was, relaying directions, telling Nick he had five minutes, then he hung up again, thinking he should just shoot the prick, do it with his own gun, the one out on the desk, right through the Ziploc. Be done with it. He dialed up Richie, told him to circle the block.

•

NICK KNOCKED at the door, the gun in the bag back in the drawer, Lexie staying in Manny's office. Stepping on the welcome mat, shaking off the rain, he was feeling the roofie fog rolling in, thinking it was just the booze, looking down and reading, *Come on in and get wet.*

Travis repeated what he'd already told him: the dope they brought from the city was stashed under the beds at the Cadillac Arms, his crew on top of the beds watching reruns, the rest of the dope was waiting at the Inn Between up in Pemberton. "Going to see Stevens in the morning, want you in on it," Travis lied.

"Going to kick that fucker's ass."

"He gives us any shit, I'll hold him and you can start kicking."

Nick liked that, glazed eyes looking around, he asked what this place was.

"Old friend of mine runs it. Guy named Manny. Used to work for your old man." Travis was sure Nick was strung out on something, getting stranger by the minute. The main thing was to calm the situation, saying to him, "Right now, I'm waiting on a date." Turning Nick around, he practically shoved him back out into the rain, saying, "Glad we talked,

Nick. Now, go to your room, or you'll miss the surprise coming your way."

"The what?"

Travis held his hands in front of his chest, suggesting tits, Nick thinking the guy was making amends, saying, "So tomorrow . . ."

"Right, I'll call you first thing. Now, 'less you got a problem with me getting laid, too?" Travis grinned and was closing the door.

Feeling the cold rain on his face, Nick stood there, the roofie fog getting thicker. Walking past the stone-and-glass building fronts, he tried to recall driving here, thinking maybe he did, but not sure where he parked the Camaro. Maybe back at Stevens's bar, thinking it was this way. A surprise coming to his room — had to be a girl, maybe the same hooker, one that stole his gun. His hotel was the other way; he turned again. Nothing looking familiar.

Lexie came out of the office, saying, "That fellow's got issues."

"This from the girl who's heard it all." Peeking through the blinds, Travis watched Nick stumbling up the street; he was sure the Wilmott was the other way. Nearly out of view, it looked like Nick took a tumble into some shrubbery. Then Richie and the boys pulled up in a four-door Wrangler, this one dark brown with a hard top.

. . . IN A KILLING FIELD

GRASS WAS wet from the sprinklers, the five of them coming low and fanning out, AKs with suppressors, all of them with ski masks in case of cameras mounted under the eaves, everybody waiting for the signal at the line of trees. The fifth man was Tanner, the guy Travis sent them to see about the guns.

Marty and Mutt had switched the rental, taken the Jeep Wrangler from the Avis lot. Then Marty drove it down to the North Shore shipyards. Tanner met them and led the way to the ocean tug dubbed *Mañana*; the skipper, Ramon Sanchez, cracked open some brew and showed them the store of Russian AKs and ammo hidden behind a false wall. The vessel smelled of rot, but the hardware was first-rate.

Weapons and ammo boxes were strapped under the seats of the Jeep, Marty making the call to the number Travis gave him. Eduardo said he was still working on getting some guys, taking care of paying Sanchez, an online transaction from a bank in Geneva to one in the Caymans. All done with a phone call.

They kept a sharp watch on the ride back, Tanner wanting to come along, telling them he'd been working on and off for a couple of private security contractors stateside since his days of running Kinder Surprise with Travis and Richie. In between gigs right now, Tanner didn't mention the baseballing, his nose a coke highway since laying up in Canada, waiting for the phone to ring. Hearing from Travis got him eager to get back in the game. A chance to play with guns. A chance to smoke a few assholes.

His baby face defied his age, hair as wild as Tanner himself. Plenty of practice with Russian AKs, Tanner did a stint in the ashes of the former Yugoslavia. Left a body count up and down the Congo, hunted Al Qaeda and Islamics, popped off insurgents in Iraq, Darfur, more in the Gaza and Georgia. Now there was talk of North Korea. All the same to Tanner. A resume that had the military contractors stateside drooling.

North of the border things were different, no military contractors up here. Tanner lying low and getting high, starting to feel bored. So when he heard Travis wanted guns, sending his boys to the shipyard, he offered to throw in, not worried what the gig paid.

Making the call from the shipyards, Marty got Travis on the prepaid, Travis saying hell yeah, bring Tanner along. No telling how many Indos would be in the chalet.

Now Richie and Tanner snuck along the line of yews on the west side, the side with fewer windows, making their way to the front.

The lone sentry was having a smoke. Richie unslung the AK and set the big key down, came up behind the man, taking the Smith from the thigh rig holster, chopping him over the head. Then they waited at either side of the front door while Travis, Marty and Mutt crawled across the backyard, all in tactical vests, staying hidden behind boxwoods fronting a drystone wall.

Worming his way to the Big Green Egg grill, Travis belly-crawled up the flagstone steps, waiting at the potted cedars, then the hot tub, smelling chlorine. Nobody at the windows. A stone lion and lawn furniture hid Marty and Mutt.

Hadn't counted on the downpour, a cold August rain slanting down on them. Keeping Richie on the cell, the hiss of the open line, Travis coordinated their moves, Richie and Tanner set to smash through the front door, Marty and Mutt waiting behind Travis. Take the Indos by surprise, lay them out, find the dope and get the hell out of there before the Mounties responded to the 9-1-1 calls.

Lexie would swear he'd spent the evening enjoying her company, the two of them at her Twin Peaks condo, gas fireplace on, bottle of Cristal getting chilled, creating a mood, Travis never out of her sight. Had her order up Peking duck with spicy noodles from the Jade Dragon same time they struck the house. Told her to ask for extra sauce and light a couple of candles, run the shower when the delivery boy came to the door, lay his jacket over a chair, shoes by the door, make sure the delivery guy knew he was there. Toss in a fat tip.

The date Lexie sent to Nick's would put him out of the picture for the night. And with the dumb fuck's pistol in the Baggie, the one Nick smoked the kid with, the one with his prints all over it, Travis had Nick in a good place. The piece could stay missing, or he could throw Nick under the bus if he got jammed up and needed to get a sentence reduced. The Crown would drool over a deal that nabbed them a Rosco. That, or he could just shoot him with it, make it look like suicide.

Hugging the wall, he waved at Marty and Mutt now by the Green Egg. They crept along the flower beds of yellow and red, crawling along the wet pea-stone walk, Travis watching for motion detectors and red-light cameras mounted along the back of the house. He didn't see anything like that, only the outline of the giant Indo through the sliding doors, all the lights on in the place.

Daljit had his back to the glass, decked in leather pants and a widowmaker, a drink on the rocks in his big hand, a thick chain around his neck, a chin like Roger Ramjet, waiting for the rest of the girls Nav said were coming. Glancing out, he guessed the rain was delaying them. Waiting for Sugar's girls that would never show.

Speaking to somebody at the far end of the room, Daljit sipped his drink, keeping his back to the glass. Travis crawled close to the sliding door on the right, these Indos light on expectations, exactly like when he hopped out of the Uprise bread truck, letting the warhead fly across East Hastings, the eyes of the kid behind the Hummer's wheel going wide, the one with the mustache jumping from the back door and rolling. The one that lived.

He signaled for Marty and Mutt to crawl up the steps. Everybody in line. Everybody set. The Indo with the drooping mustache walked to the fireplace, his hair curling at the back of an open Nehru, the bulge of a handgun under the shirt, his face scarred. Travis knew who he was.

Soaked to the skin, they rose, ten pounds of Soviet steel in their hands. Mutt and Marty, AKs with suppressors at the ready, pistols tucked in back of their pants. Tight against the bricks, Travis raised his hand.

A ditzy laugh sounded from inside. A girl's voice saying, "You guys are too much."

Daljit stepped from the window, a tanned chick with disco hair sitting low on the sofa getting his attention. Travis guessed these guys called every escort place in town, not leaving anything to chance. Should have been as diligent securing the place. Far as he could tell, the room opened to a dining room. The foyer was past the massive Empire chandelier hanging above the glass-and-steel dining table, cartons of takeout Chinese, bottles of booze and a stack of plates and napkins.

A second chick, this one black with her hair stacked, came in and sat next to the disco chick. Long legs in a mini-dress, the girl slid her hands up along the back of the sofa. Getting to her feet, Disco got both men checking her out, showing her stuff under the clinging Dior. Moving across the oak floor, she did a kind of slow dance to the center of the room, giving it a lot of hip, doing it for the big man, some pop number playing on the Linn disc changer. Taking his hands, she tried to get him moving his tree-trunk legs, Daljit grinning, looking to Nav like he was asking permission, Nav taking a highball glass, saying something Travis couldn't understand, fixing himself a drink at the wall unit, a drop shelf serving as a bar. Under-mounted LEDs lit the decanters; he scooped ice from a bucket, dropped it in his glass.

No way of knowing how many more were in the house, but one thing for sure, these guys weren't ready for this, underestimating Travis.

"Showtime," Travis whispered into the open phone.

Danny DeWulf came in through the dining room, looking all Bollywood in a sleeveless T stretched over his Charles Atlas build, the word *LEVI'S* across his pecs, cowboy boots over tight leather pants, shades on even though it was night, hair greased in a pomp. Taking a bottle of vodka from the table, he tugged the black girl off the sofa, a Colt tucked in back of the leather. Rocking his hips to the beat, he pulled her close, front to front, doing what looked like humping with clothes on. He put his mouth on her neck, catching sight of Travis at the sliding door. He pushed her off, yelling and grabbing for his pistol, as Travis shot out the wall of glass.

Still firing, Travis was moving; Marty and Mutt rising, weapons on full auto, each blasting out the sliding doors, going through the openings.

The front door crashed in at the same time. Danny was diving under the table, bringing his pistol up and snapping off a shot, Travis catching one in the vest, the shot knocking him back but nothing more. Mutt let loose a burst, dotting the *I* in the *LEVI'S* on Danny's T, putting him down. Swinging the barrel, he took out the chandelier, takeout food flying up off the table, bottles bursting. Both girls screamed over the suppressed auto-fire, leaping into each other's arms, not knowing to drop to the floor. Diving behind an armchair, Nav had his Colt out, Daljit throwing himself into the fireplace opening, his double Glock upstairs.

Firing three-second bursts, Marty and Mutt walked to the center of the room, back to back, securing it, Richie and Tanner in the foyer, firing up the stairs.

Drywall dropped in chunks, the sound system blown apart; the reek of powder filled the space. Daljit raised his hands, crouching by the fireplace opening. Nav dropped his gun, raised his hands, too, and stayed down.

The wind knocked out of him, Travis picked up his AK and stepped over. Crunching glass, he pulled off his mask and looked down at Danny DeWulf, his shirt wet with blood, shades still on. He shot him again, the girls screaming and crying.

Putting a finger to his lips, going "Shhhh," he went over to Nav.

The rattle of suppressed fire continued from the front, Richie and Tanner holding position, exchanging with the Indos pinned upstairs. Handguns popped and voices yelled back and forth, the sound of feet running from above. Mutt did a sweep, ducking through the kitchen and pantry, helping himself to a buffalo wing, stepping over casings littering the marble foyer, Richie and Tanner aiming up the stairs. Spindles hung like broken teeth, wall sconces blasted out, chunks of drywall falling, studs showing like exposed ribs.

Stepping to Nav, Travis grabbed a fistful of silk Nehru and jerked him to his feet, pressing his suppressor into the man's belly, looked at the ruined face. "Tell your fucking buddies playtime's over."

Nav took his time, calling in Hindi.

"In English, fuckhead," Travis said.

Nav called again, "Askay, Veni, stop the shooting."

Silence. Then voices, then more footfalls sounding from above.

"How many up there?" Travis asked.

"Two, three, maybe a girl. Maybe two."

"Tell them to toss their guns, get their asses down here. And I mean fucking now."

Guessing Travis wouldn't shoot till he had his dope back, Nav called up in English, getting an answer in Hindi. Pistols started popping again, bullets striking the front door, the walls, the panes of both sidelights shattering.

"They say no." No fear, Nav looking into Travis's eyes.

Prodding the barrel under Nav's chin, forcing him up on his toes. "How'd you know we were coming up the highway?"

"GPS."

"And my dope?"

"In the trunk." Nav nicked his head to the garage.

"All of it?"

A nod.

"Keys?"

"Daljit."

"In English, asshole."

"That's Daljit," Nav's eyes flicked at the big man by the fireplace, the giant standing with his hands in the air, his captain held at gunpoint. Nothing he could do about it.

Pistol shots followed by the *pop pop* of suppressed auto-fire.

"Fucking neighbors out on their lawns," Mutt said, coming back in the room, first to hear the distant sirens. He swung and fired his AK into the ceiling, drywall chunks and dust falling.

Daljit did it slow, fished the keys out, held them out, Travis snatching them, tossing them to Marty.

Travis called to Richie, the front hall looking like a demo team had been at work, the place shot full of holes. Richie and Tanner popped in their last clips and let the AKs patter like toy guns with the suppressors, more casings spitting across the marble floor.

Travis shoved Nav toward the garage, the sirens getting closer. Marty got Daljit moving, Tanner and Richie coming on the double. Salvaging a couple of breaded shrimp from the dining table, Mutt lifted the ski mask and wedged them in his mouth, chewed, standing over the dead man with the shades. He fired a burst at the staircase, keeping Askay and Veni from coming down, their voices excited, the sirens nearly on them. Brushing frags from an egg roll, Mutt searched the table for one of those plum sauce packets, had to eat it plain, popping open a box of what looked like crab langoon, asking the girls if they wanted a taste, wishing he had something to wash it down with, the bottles all shattered, spilled booze dripping from table to floor. Hearing a creak on the stairs, he fired another burst, the girls whimpering, Mutt asking if they were enjoying themselves so far tonight, asked them to guess what happens if they spoke to the cops. Blew them a greasy kiss, then he headed for the garage.

Nav and Daljit were shoved ahead into the dark of the three-car garage, Travis flicking on the fluorescents. The Lexus and Accord side by side. Tanner covered the door into the house, calling for Mutt to hurry the fuck up. Marty tossed Travis the keys, Travis shoving Nav and Daljit to the back of the Lexus.

The sirens drew ever closer, Travis knowing they were out of time, no time to check the trunk. "Nothing personal," Travis said, the AK coming up, seeing the burns on Nav's face. "That time on East Hastings . . . we had a moment, you bailing out of the back, looking at each other, knowing who each other was."

Nav gave a nod.

"Got lucky that time," Travis said. "Saw it coming, like you see it coming now."

Nav shrugged, knowing how it was, looking at Daljit, Daljit giving away nothing. Marty tilted his barrel and shot the big man, point blank, watching him stutter-step back and collapse, Travis raising his AK.

The power was cut, the garage thrown into pitch. Travis fired where Nav stood, lighting the space, but Nav was gone.

More gunfire from inside the house, Mutt yelling, coming at a run. Marty jumped in the car. Tanner yelped by the door and went down, Richie crouching and firing into the dark of the house, helping Tanner to the Lexus, everybody getting in. Fumbling the key into the ignition, Travis found the headlight switch, mashed his foot on the pedal and threw it into reverse. Tossing the spent AK, Mutt grabbed his pistol and fired at the doorway, diving in back.

Travis sent the Lexus crashing through the garage door, Marty and Mutt firing out the windows, the Indos returning fire from inside the garage, the sirens right on top of them.

. . . DIVOTS

MUZZLE FLASHES from inside the house, the cruiser's siren ahead of them blotting the sound of gunfire. The big chalet sat dark on the edge of Nicklaus North, end of the cul de sac, a Jeep Wrangler parked across the street. Booting the Laredo down Nicklaus Boulevard, the portable red beacon on top, Lance passed the line of privileged neighbors rubbernecking from their front lawns.

A pair of cruisers blocked the top of the driveway, light bars going, their bull bars blocking escape. The one rushing in pulled up and officers jumped out. Four officers already hunched behind their open doors, sidearms drawn across the hoods. The wail of more howlers coming up the 99; sounded like the whole detachment was on the way.

Lance screeched to a stop out front; Jimmy threw open his door, getting his sidearm from the holster. Lance read the situation, hearing a crash from the rear of the house. Guessing what it meant, he was cranking the wheel, no time to think it through, he gunned it, practically knocking Jimmy back in, the door thrown shut. Hopping the curb, Lance gunned the Laredo across the lawn, through the sprinklers going in the rain, sending their Styrofoam cups flipping from the holders, coffee sloshing everyplace, a packet of french fries flying like rice at a wedding.

"What the fuck!" Jimmy yelled, clutched for a hand-hold, his head knocking the roof liner, the door sill, then the window. Felt like he was being punched.

Cleaving through flowers, gripping the wheel, Lance charged down the setback, rocking and ripping through shrubs, taking out a wheelbarrow planter. Stones slammed the underside, smashed a headlight. Cranking 4L on the fly, he got some of that torque-on-demand, digging wheel ruts through a raised bed, the Laredo feeling more Brahma than SUV. Timber ties thumped the undercarriage. Vincas, shastas and clumps of earth went flying left and right, the two of them bucked and tossed, Lance not caring this was his personal ride.

Jimmy clutched for the bottom of the seat and grab bar, tried to keep from being thrown around, pistol somewhere on the floor with the fries. Fucking partner was going postal. One headlight beam jumping up and down, Lance piloted around to the rear of the house, all four wheels pitching dirt clods.

The Lexus tore through the garage, leaving the metal door jagged and hanging. Nav ran from the garage, cutting across the backyard, Askay and Veni firing at the fleeing Lexus, then at the Laredo charging around the side, then at the officers yelling at them to throw down their weapons. They jumped in the Accord and tore across the golf course, exchanging fire, slowing for Nav to jump in the back. A couple more men running out into the night.

Veering off the driveway that hooked around the house, Lance accelerated onto the golf course, springs bottoming out. Best guess, he made out four or five heads inside the car ahead. He didn't see the Accord take off away from them across the course. Leaving the unis to secure the house, he gave chase, Jimmy yelling for him to fucking stop.

Muzzle flashes showed from the back of the Lexus, the bullets punching through Lance's grill and rad. Jimmy fumbled for the single-stack Smith on the floor, the Lexus racing across the Nicklaus course. Snapping open the glovebox, he grabbed Lance's handheld, tried calling in a code five, tossed around the cockpit like he was in a gale, his head banging the roof.

Lance fought the wheel, the Laredo bouncing off the ground, biting in, the speedometer needle climbing, fading siren sounds coming from behind them as more roll-outs rushed to the house. He didn't give a shit how the pros played the hole. Dodging the large bunker, he ripped up the green, his foot to the floor, keeping his wheels straight, mud and green slamming the undercarriage. Shooting for the path, the brake lights of the Lexus ahead of them lit the way, somebody in back still shooting at them. Going for the second green, they dodged the pond, swaying onto the path. Lance kept his foot mashed down on the pedal, the engine screaming, tires leaving a muddy swath through golf green.

Another muzzle flash and the windshield exploded, Jimmy throwing up his arms, Lance ducking low. Steam poured from under the hood, Jimmy breaking protocol, firing from a pursuit vehicle, pointing the service piece he'd never had to fire in fifteen years on the force. He was firing it now.

Lance clutched the wheel; he was gaining on the bastards, his single headlight on them, wasn't letting them get a lead. Jimmy kept up the return fire. The trunk of the Lexus flew open, tore off and tumbled, Lance's Laredo smashing over it. A figure in back shoved an automatic through the window. Bullets whumped into the grill, the second headlight was gone, a front tire blown out.

Lance fought for control, misjudging the trap, his front wheels hitting sand doing seventy-five, the rough sucking the front end, vaulting the Laredo up and over onto its roof, crushing the cherry. Airbags deployed.

Upside down with the roof caved in. There was that moment when they both thought they were dead. Trees were on top, the night sky on the bottom. Jabbing his thumb, Lance got his seatbelt to release, drawing air into his lungs. Taking a mental inventory before moving, he watched the taillights of the Lexus disappear, no other vehicles in pursuit. He could hear its engine gunning down the right side of the hole, making the ideal lay-up.

His partner was throwing up, or down. Lance wasn't sure. Pushing the spent airbag away, he felt the collapsed steering wheel digging into his ribs, couldn't tell if anything inside was broken.

Vomiting, Jimmy tried to get himself upright, wiping at the puke on his face. Tasting the sour, he thumbed at his belt, feeling a sharp jab in his shoulder, another in his hip.

"You okay, buddy?"

"I look okay?" Jimmy's seatbelt was stuck, the sagging webbing of the shoulder belt holding him suspended, his head pressed against the crushed roof-lining. Puke slid up his nostrils, and he tried blowing like a dolphin to get it out, sour and stinging. If he still had the Smith in his hand, he would have accidentally discharged it in Lance's direction, the crazy fuck.

The dispatcher's voice chirped across the handheld — fucking thing still worked, sounded like it ended up in the back of the vehicle. Dispatch asking them for a 10-73.

Pushing broken glass aside, Lance shoved at the deflated airbag, crawling out through the crushed opening where the windshield had been. It was quiet out on the course. The Lexus was gone. He could still hear sirens far behind him. Above him, rain clouds were parting, stars shining.

Pushing his arm over his head to keep his neck straight, Jimmy fumbled behind him for the handheld, wondering what the ten-code was for the worst case of vehicle pursuit he'd ever seen, his numbskull partner writing off his personal vehicle, nearly getting them both killed — Jimmy just up here to write a fucking report.

. . . A BLANK SLATE

"HEY," NICK yelled out, looking around for something to bang against the bars. Couldn't believe he'd got picked up by the county Mounties. Couldn't remember it: hauled in for intoxicated and disorderly conduct. Here he was in the drunk tank. Bastards took his belt and shoelaces.

Calling out again, Nick heard jingling, then a door opening, didn't know it was the same cop who did the processing, standing looking at him with that pissy cop look. "You rang?"

"About my phone call?"

The duty cop's name was Efram. Going gray and round, he had to grin, saying, "There I was, dunking my donut, just waiting for one of you shitbirds to start singing; and here you are, the shitbird too drunk an hour ago to remember his own name, demanding his phone call. To this I say —"

"*Fuck you, pig!*" Springing from the opposite steel bunk, Nick's teenaged cellmate clutched the bars, ugly look on his face, bandage on his forehead, another wrapping his arm. A big kid for his years, freckled, broad shoulders and thick through the chest, red hair sticking out in all directions. Spit flying as he spoke. "We got fucking rights, you know that?"

Efram didn't flinch, saying, "Like the right to remain silent."

"Listen, my man here gets his fucking phone call; you understand that, you fucking swine?"

More spit flew from the kid's mouth, Efram taking a step back, staring at the kid they hauled in after a vehicle chase on the 99, apprehended in his daddy's Olds Intrigue. What was left of the pile of scrap metal got hauled to impound after the kid lost a game of chicken with a concrete highway divider. Needless to say, alcohol was involved.

"Unlike you, my young offender," Efram said, "your shitbird buddy's not being held, just sleeping it off." Efram looked at Nick, pretty sure he had no recollection of last night: picked up by a patrol, found wandering the Village. "And that, my friend, doesn't come with a phone call."

The kid smacked his palms against the bars, calling Efram a swine again.

"Hey, kid, thanks," Nick said to him. "I got this." Stepping up, smiling at Efram like he was trying to reason, saying, "So how about it, officer? I'm sober now. Really sorry for any trouble I caused."

"Up to me when you're sober," Efram said, thinking what this guy needed was a psych test, the way he'd been behaving, the garbage coming out of his mouth. Johnson, the arresting officer, had found him pissing on the Fairmont sign in the Upper Village, pants around his knees, not sure where he was going or where he was staying, had trouble spelling his name. Palmer, in a second unit, came upon the

Camaro a half-hour later sitting in a puddle of antifreeze and engine fluids over by the Badlands. The driver's side looked like somebody had taken a belt sander to it, half the inferno-orange paint scraped off, the door crumpled, side mirror hanging limp, the chassis high-centered on a curb. Judging by the skid marks, Palmer figured the shitbird tried to hump his ride free of its concrete anchor, gunning the ss engine, ripping at its undercarriage. Punctured the rad, tore off the tailpipe and exhaust. God knows how bad he mangled the suspension and the axle. All that with little more than two hundred klicks on the odometer, still had that new car smell.

A crying shame guys like Nick Rosco had more money than brains. Efram hated every single last one of them. Closing the outer door, Efram thought back on Rick Harper disappearing while on duty Sunday night, the shootout on the golf course. Shitbirds like Nick Rosco and the red-haired kid had no place on his radar, not today.

"How about we play by the rules?" Nick yelled after him, the kid standing by the bars, yelling, "Fucking right."

Nick's throat felt raw after that; he went back to his bunk, his head pounding.

Throwing himself back on his own metal bunk, the kid was saying he wished he had a drink or something, then, "What'd they get you for anyway, my man?"

Nick wasn't entirely sure. Last thing he remembered, he was leaving the escort place, Sugar's, pissed off at Travis for keeping him out of the loop, treating him like a kid, just like his old man always did. He'd been at the Cellar, wanting to square things with Grey Stevens, getting the call from

Travis, going for the face to face, Travis trying to square things by sending him a hooker, Nick heading to his hotel when things got fuzzy, made a wrong turn somewhere. After that, it was pretty much a blank slate.

Man, what his old man would say if he found out he got himself tossed in a drunk tank. Again. And wrecked his car. Again. Better yet, if the old man found out he lost his piece, the one he used on the kid. Jesus Christ. Nick tried to recount the Johnnie Blues: one in the Wilmott's lounge, two more that Stevens poured, a couple at the clubs he wandered into, a few more at Maxie's. Not enough alcohol for this level of blackout. It didn't make sense.

The red-haired kid, whose name was Luke, kept on loose talking, getting up and pissing every five minutes in the toilet with no lid, once in a while actually getting the stream into the porcelain. Filling Nick in on what a rush it was to get chased at high speed along the 99 north of town, pedal to the metal till he lost it and smacked up his ride, cops swarming all over him, pointing guns in his face. Dragged him out and took him away in an ambulance, cuffed to the safety arm of the stretcher. A uni stood watch while the vet stitched up his arm and forehead. The kid bitching, this fucking one-horse town didn't even rate a real hospital, the nearest one down in Squamish, asking Nick what was so world-class about this place. Sixteen years old and he knew everything, bullshitting about how crashing his old man's wheels beat any ride at the PNE, said the airbag felt like getting punched by a girl, nothing compared to what his old man would do. Nick thinking how his own old man would have handled it back at sixteen. Done it with a belt. Or a shoe.

Getting up, the kid unzipped and aimed again, three feet from the toilet, his elbows cocked and his hands behind his head, saying, "Look Ma, no hands," laughing like the whole thing was funny. Nick smelling the kid's piss.

. . . BELOW THE SALT

It was Pete's voice, a whisper over the cell phone.

"Where the fuck are you?" Grey sat up at the end of the couch, never made it to his bed last night. He stretched, the dawn showing through the drapes, birds chirping outside.

The way Grey spoke into the phone had Dara and Mojo waking and looking over, Dara in mid-yawn, curled on the other end of the couch, her shoes off. Mojo slumped in the chair by the window, spent all night keeping watch, pissed there wasn't so much as a bong load in the place. The only coffee was that shit Grey had in the jar.

Pete was at the locker, the Ah-So-Easy, picking up the Pemberton stash, had Airdog and Goob with him. Doing it at daybreak to draw less attention from watching eyes, leaving themselves plenty of time to get to the Olympic Plaza for the early flashmob rehearsal, the buskers looking good, pulling it together four days ahead of Mountain High.

"Just got here," Pete was saying in a low voice. His headlights washed over the two guys standing at their car at the far end of the line of units. "I'm eyeballing these guys . . . Shit . . ."

"What?" Grey said, Dara sitting up, looking at him, reaching a tissue, starting to shred it.

"They're looking over," Pete said, wishing the barrier had stayed up after he used the swipe card and pulled in.

"Who?"

"Unit down on the end. Two guys loading sacks or something in their trunk."

"The guy that decked Airdog?"

"He says no," Pete said.

Grey heard Airdog's voice from the passenger seat. "This the safety?"

"Just roll the fuck out of there," Grey told him. "Now."

"Right," Pete said, not whispering now, wedging the phone between his shoulder and ear, shutting his car door. The keys of Pemberton pot were under the army surplus tarp in the middle of the unit, the sack of pipes and paraphernalia next to it. They'd have to come back.

Pete put his hand on the gear shift, looked over his shoulder, catching a third guy coming down the driveway. On foot, he was heading right for them, passing under a light. Pete caught the grin, the straggly hair, jeans over cowboy boots. Must have hopped the gate.

A blue Chev Express was stopped in front of the gate, blocking the exit, its lights off, exhaust puffing from its pipe. Pete couldn't see anyone else inside.

Richie had been watching the house on Easy Street since they got back from shooting up the chalet, Richie drawing the short straw, shivering with the dew while Travis was with some chick, Mutt sawing logs in his motel bed. When Pete Melton rolled out of the drive, he followed the

El Camino, keeping far enough back with his headlights off until Pete turned southbound on the 99. Travis wanted the place watched, pissed off the dope wasn't in the Lexus's trunk, pretty sure it didn't fall out when the cops shot the trunk lid off, suspecting the Indos had worked their own deal with Grey Stevens.

Eyes red-rimmed on account of the bennies, Richie was running on next to no sleep. He put it together as he walked toward them: the two guys had a stash in the locker. From what he'd been told, the pot Stevens was growing rivaled any kush they could channel up through Seattle, the reason Travis hoped to get these guys on board.

Coming around the angled stretch of building, Richie saw the two guys at the far end looking up, knew who they were, both Indos stopping, looking like deer in the headlights, holding the cement sacks they stole from the van. So Stevens *was* playing footsie with the Indos. No choice now, Richie had to do this solo. Walking down the driveway, he sized it up: the two guys in the shitbox Chev were no threat. The two Indos said something to each other, set down their sacks and reached for pistols, then fanned apart. Richie thinking, here we go.

●

"GETTING THE fuck out of here," Pete said into the phone, reaching for the car door, Goober in the middle, Airdog with the pistol.

Richie tapped a cigarette on his Export pack, coming to

the driver's side, asking Pete for a light, letting him see the Smith under the denim.

"Don't smoke, man," Pete said, fumbling to get the key in the ignition, Airdog not sure where to point the .22, the guy at the window or the two coming their way, both holding pistols.

Richie watched, the Indos exchanging quick words between them, figuring their move. Sticking the smoke in his mouth, Richie reached a hand in and took the keys from Pete, pitching them against the locker door. Then plucking the cell from Pete's hand, he tossed it, too, the phone's shell breaking into pieces.

"What the fuck . . ." Pete got that much out, the Indos both raising their pistols, this turning into some crazy *High Noon* scene.

Askay had been upstairs getting a hummer when the shooting started last night, wasn't getting caught with his pants down a second time. Bullets had ripped through the floor, he'd seen his friend Danny killed, dead under the dining table, Chinese food all around him.

Dev Singh had come up from the city last night just ahead of the takeout. When the shooting started, he got pinned down by automatic weapon fire, so much for the hookers. Now, he held his pistol straight out. This was payback.

Askay went along the passenger side of the car, Dev intent on the guy that looked like a biker. He stood easy, hadn't drawn a weapon, just standing there with an unlit cigarette. Coming around the El Camino, Dev snapped off the first shot, firing too fast, Richie bringing the big Smith up in a smooth motion, same time Pete shoved open his door, catching Richie as he fired. Pete rolled out, scrambling for his keys.

Dev fired again, Richie crouching and shooting back, Askay firing into the car, Airdog ducking down, arms over his head. Pete grabbed the keys and flung himself back into the car, rapid fire all around them, louder than any Foo Fighters concert. Bullets flying, Pete jabbed to get the key in, Airdog trying to pull Goober down.

Blown off his feet, Dev was flung back and down, a dark, wet spot spreading across his chest, Richie reaching for his spare clip.

Askay yelled, getting low against the passenger side and stuck his arm into the car, trying to shoot at Richie. Goob jumping and clamping his bulldog jaws on the wrist, Askay's gun going off, the bullet striking Richie in the gut. Dropping the gun, Askay jerked to free his arm.

Jamming the stick in gear, Pete slammed his foot down, and the El Camino jerked forward, leaving Richie and the Indo exposed, Askay clutching his bloodied arm. Richie stumbled back, still sticking in the clip as he fell back against the locker door.

With Dev down and no gun in his hand, Askay kept his eyes on Richie, scrambled for the plum Ford and was struck by Pete trying to do a three-point turn. Goob was barking like mad. Askay rolled as Pete slung his arm over the seat and mashed the pedal, backing up the driveway, crashing through the barrier, into the side of Richie's van, clearing it out of his way, throwing the El Camino into drive, fishtailing away on the gravel.

Pressing himself against the locker, Richie breathed through the pain, feeling the wet spread. He took aim at Askay in the Ford as it peeled off after the El Camino, but the gun was too heavy. Dropping his arm, he touched a finger to his wound, pushed off the wall, making it over to Dev lying on the ground, a big hole in his chest. Sounded like a lung shot, from that wet sound. Dev stretched his fingers for the pistol on the ground, eyes on Richie.

"Didn't get it all, huh?" Looking into the open locker, half the cement sacks and the bags of pot they stole from Rivers and Glinka still there. Richie swept Dev's pistol away with his foot, grimacing at the pain. "Guess we're both fucked." He was in no shape to carry the sacks to the van. No time to call Travis either, guessing he'd hear the whining sirens any time now.

Richie shrugged and raised the Smith in both hands and shot Dev in the face, the recoil knocking him back. He tried to make it to the wall.

•

GREY WAS shouting Pete's name into the cell.

Dara and Mojo were up, wondering what was going on.

The connection was gone, Grey still yelling into the phone. He had Lance's card out, punching in the number, nearly dropping the phone when the knock came at the door. The three of them looking at each other. Moving to the peephole, Grey opened the door, pulling himself together.

Lance stood on the porch, side of his face looking like bruised fruit, looking at Grey and the other two. Taking out his own ringing phone, Lance looked at the name on the display, then at the phone in Grey's hand.

"Who says we're never there when you need us?" Lance said, grimacing as he tried to smile.

"Got a call," Jimmy said, one eye black, nose swollen, waiting at the bottom of the steps. He threw a thumb over at Roy Scheider's house. "Your neighbor spotted another suspicious vehicle, said it was parked up the block." Expecting a smartass response.

"It's Pete . . ." Grey started, looking at Lance, not sure he was doing the right thing. "Called from this storage place . . ."

"One down by Alta Lake?"

Grey nodded. "Guys there with guns. I heard a shot, then lost the connection."

Jimmy started limping for the Tahoe — the staff sergeant had given them his own vehicle, warning Lance not to go golfing in this one, didn't want to see so much as a scratch on it. Jimmy had taken the keys from Risker, no way he was getting in with Lance driving. He knew the storage place, could partially see it from the highway, looked like a strip mall that never got finished, corrugated metal siding, garage doors painted green, a boom gate out front. Getting in and grabbing the handset, Lance called in the code three, asked for additional units.

Racing down Easy Street, neither cop looked over at Roy Scheider standing in his window. Lance knew they were running out of time, the ERT was on its way. He suspected Stevens had left out half of the story, but still, nobody could act like that, not without landing an Oscar. Jimmy hit the howler and lights, planting his foot on the pedal as they got on the 99.

•

"THIS BLOWS sideways, you know we're all fucked?" Mojo said, guessing he didn't need to remind Grey he just sent the 5-o to where Pete and Airdog were picking up the Pemberton pot, pointing them right to the stash.

Nothing he could say, Grey stood there, Dara slipping an arm through his. The three of them on the stoop above the uncut grass, Goober's turds all over the place. It was getting light now. Roy the perv watched them from his fishbowl window. Dara waved over. Roy raised his hand.

"Now what?" Mojo asked.

"Fuck if I know," Grey said.

"We wait for Pete and Airdog," Dara said, "then we go check out the flashmob." Leading them back inside, she put on a pot of water, getting out the shitty instant Grey kept in the cupboard.

. . . SHOOTOUT AT THE AH-SO-EASY

MARKED CROWN Vics flanked the entrance, the gate in pieces on the ground. The Express van sat on the opposite shoulder with its side caved in. Officers decked in Kevlar vests and ballistic helmets secured the scene, feeling they'd been under siege since Sunday. Another Crown Vic pulled in and parked next to the Coroners Service SUV. Two ambulances and a fire truck were parked along the row of units, their emergency lights flashing.

Staff Sergeant Risker stepped out of the Crown Vic, a Remington twelve-gauge under his arm, donning his cap, ready to take charge. A Starbucks in his free hand, he walked past the Tahoe, the one he'd assigned to Lance and Jimmy. Stepping around markers where shell casings had been removed, he went to the city detectives standing by the open storage unit at the end, the two of them looking beat to hell. His men were working the scene, marking evidence bags, taking measurements, snapping photos, getting it on video. Risker said he'd bet a paycheck some of the casings matched the ones found at the McGuire side road, still nothing on his missing officer.

He went past Lance and Jimmy to where ME Swann crouched by the one body on the pavement, looked like a tackle box open next to him, the vic's arms and legs splayed out like he he'd been making snow angels when he took one in his chest, a second round taking off most of his face. Blood pooled under the body, the Armani jacket sopping it up. The .380 next to the dead hand was double-action, a polymer frame, real light and real fast — just not fast enough, Risker thought. The scorpion tat was black and ran across the hand, tail and stinger wrapping around the wrist. The second dead guy propped by the wall was dressed in jeans, looked like a bum, took one low and just off center. From the blood smears, Risker guessed the bum killed this snow angel, then made it as far as the locker, and died propped up with the fifty-caliber cannon in his hand.

Risker put it together pretty much the same way Lance saw it: a shootout over whatever had been stashed in the open locker, which was completely empty now, at least one of the perps driving away. Connected to Harper going missing and the shootout at the chalet. Risker called to Lance and Jimmy, telling them a rockslide on the 99 south of Daisy Lake had buried all the lanes, happened just a half-hour ago, bad enough to stop traffic in both directions, the ERT that was coming up would be on the wrong side of the rocks. "Transportation minister's going in front of the news cameras, telling folks it's the worst slide in a dozen years. Take scalers and engineers best part of the day to clear the mess and free up the lanes," Risker said. "Gives us a window, maybe make some headway before they get here and take over."

An officer was photographing Richie propped against

the corrugated tin. Jimmy saying Risker may as well take the twelve-gauge under his arm and go for mallards.

"Come on," Lance said, heading toward Pete.

"Jesus," Jimmy muttered, limping after him, sent here to write a fucking report, in the middle of a drug war.

Lance let the fire engine pull past him, looking at Pete Melton standing by his El Camino parked on the berm, knowing the fucker had more to tell.

Pete watched the two dicks coming, the crime scene boys working like ants, taking their photos and samples and shit. Pete stood where he'd been told, phone with a cracked screen in his hand, the line open, whispering without his mouth moving, saying, "They're coming." A quick glance at the back of the El Camino.

Airdog whispering back, "Go to them for fuck's sake." Lying corpse still, sandwiched between bags of Pemberton weed and the sack of pipes and paraphernalia all packed around him. Peeking out, seeing the two dicks coming.

After the gunplay, the Ford had screamed out of the lot and taken off in the opposite direction. Before the first wail of the sirens, Pete and Airdog drove back onto the lot and hurried loading the cement sacks and bags from the Indos' locker into Pete's locker, running back and forth, then piling the bags of the Pemberton pot into the back of the El Camino, getting out of there, parking up by the road, moving like mad just before the first patrol car rolled in. Airdog getting under cover, Pete waiting next to his ride to deal with the cops.

Afraid to move, Airdog wondered what the pot Pete sold to Rivers and Glinka was doing in the Indo locker with the cement bags, getting a sinking feeling about it. Guessing Glinka and Rivers never made it back down to Squamish. Maybe he got away lucky, his tongue probing the sockets where his front teeth had been.

Goober, on the passenger seat, had his head out the window. Pete clicked off his cell and moved down the berm, away from the El Camino, meeting the tall cop halfway, the fat one limping behind him. They started firing their questions, some of them the same ones he'd already answered. Still rattled, his ears ringing from the gunfire, Pete told it the way he'd been rehearsing in his head while he waited.

Out of his league, Pete, the introverted pot grower, the guy with the green thumb, tried to tell the two dicks enough without telling them anything, his story going like this: the dead guy against the wall must have dogged him here in the van. Just out for some pre-dawn air, Pete cruised down the 99, saying Goober liked to go along and hang his head out the window, the dog not built for walking. Said he pulled off the Blueberry exit when he noticed the van in the rearview, sure he was being followed, worried on account of what happened to Airdog and maybe Tuff Dub, too. He drove in here to shake him, hoping for a turnaround. The Indian guys were at their locker, loading bags into their trunk. Next thing, the guy following him was there, pulling a pistol and everybody was jumping and shooting. One of the Indian guys went down, and Pete panicked, backing the El Camino through the gate, broadsiding the van. He stopped down the road on account of it being a hit-and-run, too freaked to drive farther, made the call for help, lucky his phone still worked. Then the plum Ford came racing out, going the opposite way. Pete just standing there waiting for the cops to show.

"Said the gate was up?" Jimmy asked, the notebook in his hand.

"Yeah, when I drove in." What he wouldn't have given for his Oakleys from the glovebox, slipping them over his lying eyes, the fat cop looking at him in that funny way cops have. "Guess it was down when I left. Not sure. Maybe the dead guy pulled it down, before he got dead. I don't know. Happened so fast."

"Drove right through it, then hit the van?" Jimmy asked.

"The whole place was going fourth of July. Bullets, hello? Man, look at my car, all banged to shit."

"Same guys we warned you about," Lance said.

"Guess you were right."

"Yeah."

"Think you'll catch them?"

"With civilians like you cooperating . . ." Jimmy said.

"So, the two guys were over there, loading something in their trunk?" Lance said, pointing to the end of the lockers.

"Yeah. Guess I surprised them when I pulled in. You know, with my headlights on. Other guy pulls up behind me, next thing the bullets started flying, and I pulled Goob down and backed the hell out."

"Who's Goob?"

Pete pointed up at the El Camino, Goober looking out the window, his tongue lolling out. Saying again how it happened so fast. Pete wished it was Grey instead of him, Grey better with this kind of impromptu.

With Pete Melton's account, they may as well be asking

the mutt what he saw. Jimmy looked at the ugly dog, knowing whose shit he stepped in back at the Stevens' place, not liking the beast any more than his lying owner. Took him twenty minutes to scrub the bits of shit from between the treads of his shoes.

"How come you called Stevens, not 9-1-1?" Jimmy asked.

"Got him on speed dial; man, it happened —"

"Yeah, I know, real fast." Flipping his notebook closed, Jimmy started to limp away, thinking he could do with more of that Tramadol the nurse at the clinic gave him last night, label on the bottle saying one every three hours or as needed. Jimmy fucking needing it.

The med-techs were setting Richie's body in a bag, loading it on the gurney, zipping it closed with their blue gloves, the two techs working like it was routine, passive about handling a body that was still warm with the life gone from it. Shutting the back of the ambulance, they snapped off the blue gloves, got in and drove off, a half-wave, half-salute to the fat detective as they left — just another day at the office.

Man, Pete felt he could use a hit from Mr. Potato Head, these guys with the prying questions, Airdog lying there with all that pot, the rest of the dope down in the locker.

Lance was looking at him, wasn't buying the dumb act. Intel had Peter James Melton down as a person of interest, discovered his green thumb around the time Stevens's uncle was diagnosed with cancer, suspected of being involved in setting up a number of grow-ops up and down the Squamish-Lillooet corridor. Melton was sharp enough to stay under the radar, but not sharp enough to see this game was likely to get him killed. "You or Stevens ever rent a locker here, Pete?" Lance was looking at the El Camino, dog with its tongue hanging out the passenger window, tarp pulled tight over the back.

"Me, hell no. Grey, you'd have to ask him, but I doubt it." Then he forced a smile. "Still trying to tie us to the grow-op you found, huh? Where was the last one?"

"McGuire," Lance said, putting the brakes on the fist he wanted to send Pete's way. "Place where one of ours went missing Sunday night."

"Yeah, right." Pete said he was sorry about that, meaning it, Lance calling over the last uniform Risker had left at the scene, putting up the police tape. He asked him to call in the K-9 squad, then get hold of the owner of the building. The uniform's name was Stenzel, and he said he'd have to clear it with Risker, Lance saying, "Then do it." Looking at Pete, Lance said he was going to have every last locker opened. Then he took his cell, calling Rinckey, the Crown prosecutor, getting on the business of a warrant. Looking at Pete, then at the El Camino, Lance told him to stick around.

Pete shrugged like he had all day, saying, "Yeah sure," thinking, fuck me.

. . . IF IT QUACKS LIKE A DUCK

Benton, the handler with the shepherd, showed up a half-hour later. The dog was near-black, named Kilo and eager to get to work, tugging at its thick leash. Hickcock Carlson, the owner of the facility, arrived on the handler's heels. From the look of him, Carlson had been dragged from his bed, his hair unkempt, a windbreaker over track pants, flip-flops on his bare feet. Despite appearances, Carlson didn't seem to mind. No need to wait for a search warrant. He handed Lance a master key from a ring of keys, told him it would open every lock at the place, told him he'd have no shady business here.

At Lance's say-so, Benton let Kilo move at will along the line of lockers being opened by the uniform. Starting at the near end, Kilo sniffed and moved along the lockers, some near-empty, some filled to the rafters. Standing next to Pete, Lance was saying how some of these dogs could even sniff out guilt, not just dope.

"You're kidding," Pete said.

Lance said it had something to do with T cells.

Nearly at the opposite end, Kilo stopped and barked at unit fifteen. It had a different padlock from the one Carlson provided to his customers. The master key didn't fit. Kilo was told good boy, then told to sit.

Getting busy with the bolt cutters, Jimmy snipped the lock, and the uniform hoisted up the door.

Putting on the poker face, Pete stared at the cement sacks and compressed keys of Mexican grass the Indos couldn't load into their Ford, piled on top of the tarp in the locker, the one Pete paid cash for Sunday morning, laying an extra hundred down, promising Kenny, the guy that ran the place for Carlson, a dime bag on top. Pete making like he was seeing it for the first time.

"Ew wee," Jimmy said, eyeing the score, setting the bolt cutters against the wall, taking out a pen knife, cutting across the top corner of one of the sacks, sticking his finger in, tasting it and grinning at Pete like, I got your ass now.

Lance felt the rush of a transfer back to 312 Main coming on, maybe even a rung up the ladder. They were looking at a major score, tying this to the shit going on between Rosco and the Indo Army. For Jimmy, it might spare his sorry ass from being assigned to Yahk.

Watching the dicks grinning at each other, Pete put together his own mental tally, estimating the street worth at somewhere between a hundred-and-fifty and two hundred grand, the sacks he and Airdog moved after they stuffed the El Camino with the Pemberton pot, both rushing back and forth between lockers to get it done, stepping around the dead biker as the sirens got louder. Pete now thinking about their prints all over the sacks, no time for latex gloves. It was a stupid move, Pete the shits at quick thinking. He felt himself sweating at his pits, his El Camino right up the slope, a hundred feet between Kilo and all that Pemberton pot. What the fuck was he thinking? Keeping himself from looking toward his car, he stared into the locker. Slipping on the latex was a cardinal rule. First thing the cops would do was dust for prints, match them to the ones they had on file.

The dog handler led Kilo back toward his K-9 unit, Kilo barking and straining on the leash, nose aimed at the El Camino. Goober in the passenger seat had his tongue hanging out, barking back, the handler misreading his sixty-grand's worth of police dog, thinking it was just dog barking at dog, snapping a command at Kilo in German, the dog settling down, whimpering a complaint, then getting in back of the unit.

Lance waited for the K-9 unit to pull out, then looked at Pete. "You okay? Look a little pale."

"With what I been through?"

Lance looked at him a moment, then told Pete he could go.

"There a reward on something like this?" Pete couldn't resist.

Lance was smiling, walking with him.

"Calling it in, you know? A bust this size."

"You understand we're going to run prints?" Lance said.

"Standard procedure, right?"

"Something like that." Lance walked to the El Camino, favoring his right leg, wincing. "You know what, Pete?" he said, patting Goober at the window. "Bet you a week's pay you got more than a spare tire under that tarp."

Pete felt the sweat roll down under his shirt. Whatever color he had left in his face disappeared.

"Thought I'd miss that, or just let it slide?" Lance knowing the slide he needed to worry about was the one on the highway blocking the fucking ERT from getting up here and taking over, knowing his time was running out.

Pete stood while Lance lifted the back off the tarp, velcro holding it down, the cop looking at the spare, standing spitting distance from Airdog lying among the ferns with the Pemberton pot just past the ditch.

"Should've taken the bet," Pete said, getting in the car, guessing it was time for him and Airdog to lawyer up or split town, maybe leave Goob with Grey for a while, jump the border and play hide-and-seek with Homeland Security on his way down the Coast. Slip through the cracks. He got her started on the third try, reached over and ran his hand over the back of Goob's neck. Lance Edwards told him not to make any travel plans, then was hobbling back down the berm, Pete driving away from Airdog, fumbling for his broken cell phone.

. . . TURNING THE SCREWS

By the time they came for him, Nick's back was sore as hell from lying on the bunk. Must have nodded off after feigning a nap to get the red-haired kid to shut up. Nick opened his eyes to the sound of a key scraping, the outer door opening. From the light streaming in, it had to be after nine; the kid was gone, but the piss smell lingered.

"You two mutts." First words out of his mouth, Lance and Jimmy coming into the cell wing, next stop after the Stor-All place, standing outside the bars. "Somebody give you a taste of your own medicine?"

The two cops looked like they'd had the shit beat out of them, the taller one with a splotchy bruise over one side of his face, each favoring a leg. And the guy coming behind them looked like they pulled him from a hallway at law school, a frat boy in a poly suit tailored by Stevie Wonder. The fat cop made a remark about Nick's accommodations going downhill, then introduced the frat boy as Stone Rinckey, the Crown counsel.

"Big whoopidy-dee-fucking-doo," Nick said, then, "What kind of name is that, Stone Rinckey?" Getting up, he stretched the kinks in his back, Rinckey with a three-day growth of stubble, Nick guessing the frat boy was going for a hip, older look, get the local babes to take him serious.

Rinckey didn't answer.

"So what the fuck is this?" Maybe not the best way Nick could have started. Pointing to the Band-Aid over the tall cop's brow, face bruised, yellow on its way to purple, he asked, "Somebody do that, or you boys have a lovers' spat?"

Stepping up, five years of dealing with shit-heels like this, Rinckey said, "Got this place smelling like a baboon's cage, Nick."

Lance and Jimmy grinned, liking this suit already.

"You want, we can get Efram to hose him down," Jimmy offered.

"Guy has a couple of drinks, you fucks turn it into a federal case." Drawing against the bars, Nick looked at Rinckey, that horrible taste in his mouth suggesting his breath could peel paint, saying, "Don't look like the guy comes in to take my lunch order."

"Little early, but you want, we can fetch you a sandwich. Me, I'll stand back and watch while the detectives help you eat it," Rinckey said with a smile. "Who I am is the guy who serves you up to the judge. And how I work the docket makes all the difference."

"All this for drinking a little over the limit, smacking up my car. Judge going to what, go *tsk tsk* at me?"

"We're not here about last night."

Nick not listening, "I give up my license for what, three months? Ride around in back of a limo. Think that's tough?"

Nick shrugged. The family had lawyers for this kind of thing, to deal with guys like this.

Sparring was one of the things Rinckey loved about the job, but he knew the emergency response team was on its way, meaning this could get plucked off his docket, too; somebody with more juice down in Vancouver getting to work a deal with Rosco. Taking out his pocket square, he held it against his nose, asked the detectives to escort Mr. Rosco to an interview room — get away from the baboon smell.

Jimmy got Efram to open the door, cuffing Nick's hands in back, nice and tight. Nick bitching he wasn't even under arrest, Jimmy shrugging, leading the way.

Walking behind the three of them down the hall, Rinckey threw down a little Law 101 for Nick, saying, "You were charged with dangerous driving a year back. You have recollection of that, Nick?"

"I beat that, got off clean," Nick said, walking between the detectives, hands cuffed.

"What you got was a suspended sentence."

"Yeah, drew some probation, reported to some schmuck with a worse suit than yours. So what?"

"Suspended means it comes back and bites you on the ass, meaning like now."

"Yeah, see, this kind of shit bores me," Nick said. "So talk to my lawyer. Better yet, talk to the fucking bartender slipped some shit in my drink."

Down a short hall, walls of framed photos of officers and awards for community service, Nick was shown into a room of cinder-block walls painted in some sixties shade of green. The lunchroom doubling as an interview room while renovations took place. A metal table and a couple of chairs, a Frigidaire left over from the last gold rush, looked like somebody beat it with chains. A Mr. Coffee machine, its carafe with a good inch of goo at the bottom, next to a microwave by an electrical outlet, a yellow Post-it taped over it warning to only plug in one appliance at a time. The microwave's window looked like it had been used for detonating Pizza Pops.

"The maid quit?" Nick asked, thinking they may as well have stayed in the detention cell, smelled nearly as bad in here. Told to sit, he looked up at a faded print on the wall showing a Mountie in Red Serge on horseback, pines and a mountain range in the background. "Not like the interview rooms they got downtown, metal bars on the table, cameras mounted in the corners, two-way mirrors. Real nice. Room painted pink — color that makes us perps relax and start singing."

Lance leaned back against the counter while Rinckey set his ass on the chair opposite, scraping the legs across the lino floor. Jimmy uncuffed one hand and re-closed the cuff on the table leg, forcing Nick to lean to the side.

"What, I'm a flight risk?"

"Naw," Jimmy said, "just like fucking with you."

Rinckey looked at Jimmy, then got down to cases, asked what Nick knew about the chalet getting shot up, told him they had an officer missing, the shootout at the Stor-All, all of it happening since Nick came to town.

"Told you boys yesterday, just here for the cheese rolling."

"The shooting at the parking lot, got a witness, puts you and Travis Rainey at the scene." Rinckey watched Nick, taking a stab the second guy at the scene was Rainey after he'd been spotted around town, a known associate of Geovani "Bumpy" Rosco. Sure to be hip-deep in all this.

"Bullshit."

"Only thing he wasn't a hundred percent on," Rinckey said, "is which one pulled the trigger on Trevor Sam."

"Who?"

"Kid you shot in the parking lot."

"You fucks got dick," Nick said. "And I don't know anybody named Rainey."

"Witness and surveillance tape say different." Rinckey saw the jaw tighten. He continued, sounding confident, "Puts you both there." What he really had was Todd Jenkins from Mission, eyesight of a bat and color-blind to boot, not sure what he saw. The surveillance equipment sure wasn't fucking IMAX, the tech that explained it to him blamed poor compression and low frame rate, wondering why the city even bothered installing it.

Ballistics was looking at a single casing found at the scene, and the techs were getting a crack at the impounded Camaro, a day after Lance and Jimmy had a look, feeling under the seats, popping the trunk. But without a body or the weapon, Rinckey had basically nothing. The only thing to do was get these assholes to turn on each other.

From the time of arrest, Nick couldn't have been involved in the shootout on the golf course last night. Two toe-tagged stiffs in the morgue, another banger in critical condition rushed down to Squamish General, not expected to pull through. A three-million-dollar chalet shot to hell. A smorgasbord of shell casings all over the house, several handguns and an AK with its serial numbers filed down. A couple of hookers scared witless, too afraid to talk. A single arrest and the guy with the tattoo hadn't said a word.

The mayor's office was screaming for Rinckey to do something about it. Rival gangs butting heads had a way of messing up the gaming review, and the proposed casinos meant multi-millions of dollars, hundreds of jobs. Rinckey needed to make this, and this was his best shot, getting Nick Rosco to trip.

"You gonna charge me, do it, otherwise . . ." Rattling his cuffed hand, Nick demanded his call again. The last thing he wanted to do was call Dobbs, the family suit. His old man would find out the second he hung up, Dobbs having an appreciation for who kept him in pinstripes. And answering the old man's questions would be a whole lot worse.

"That fresh?" Nick asked, looking at the Mr. Coffee. Caffeine might ease the fierce Cirque du Soleil going on in his gut.

Lifting the pot, Lance checked the sludge moving in the bottom, more gray than brown. Risker's rule about the last guy fixing a fresh pot wasn't working.

A look passed between Rinckey and Jimmy, Jimmy nodding to the door.

"How about I get you a soft drink?" Rinckey offered, Jimmy waiting for him to get up and leave, then uncuffing the wrist.

"More like it," Nick said, rubbing the wrist, calling after him to make it a Coke, calling Rinckey frat boy, then, to Jimmy, "What you got me for is what, humping a curb?"

"That what you were doing, humping the curb? Thought you were having second thoughts about the color orange?"

"You got dick," Nick said, rising to get up, Jimmy shoving him back in his seat. "Hey, like I told you, I came up to see somebody racing cheese wheels —"

Jimmy kicked the chair legs out from under him, turning and picking a phone book off the counter by the coffee pot, saying, "Want to lawyer up?" Jimmy reached and grabbed enough shirt to stand Nick up, saying, "Help you look up the number." Slapping the phone book into Nick's chest, Jimmy whumped his other fist against it, knocking Nick down, head slamming the lino. Tossing the phone book aside, planting a shoe over his throat, Jimmy cut off Nick's wind, asking his partner to pass the coffee pot. Handing it to him, Lance checked his nails, thinking about the ERT, knowing he and Jimmy were about to be benched and told to turn over their case files. At least Jimmy was finally doing something, working their case.

Watching Nick turn colors, Jimmy took his foot away, pulled up the knees of his pants and bent down, holding the back of Nick's neck and pouring in the sludge, Nick gasping and flapping his arms, trying to jerk his head away. When the gagging and sputtering stopped, Jimmy drew close and said, "When the boy scout comes back, you give him what he wants, or I take you back to the cell, solo, and you make a play for my gun. Then it's gonna end bad."

"Fuck —"

Jimmy's knee cut off the words. Getting up, he asked, "Think I won't do it, Nick?" Then he helped him up, slid the chair under his ass and shoved Nick into it, telling him not to tip back so far, not bothering with the cuffs this time.

Coming back in, Rinckey looked at the faces, guessing

what he'd missed. Zipping the tab on a can of Orange Fanta, he set it in front of Nick, saying they didn't have Coke, watching Nick drink like a man who just spent a week in the Mojave.

Getting that sludge taste from his mouth, Nick felt the bubbles tickle his throat, let a belch roll up from the depths, took another sip, eyeing the three of them.

"Okay, let him finish, then put him back in his cell." Rinckey reached for his case, got ready to leave.

"Hold on," Nick said, waiting for Rinckey to turn and sit. It wasn't the fat cop that scared him. The hooker that ran off with his Smith, had to be Travis put her up to it. And if Travis took the deal . . . The hell with what his old man thought, no way Nick was doing time. "Let's say I give you Rainey, then what?"

"Excellent changes to our federal witness protection," Rinckey said, seeing Nick's wheels spinning. "A new identity, a new town."

"Cut off from my old man's estate?"

"We'll fix you up, Nick. Besides, you know how proceeds-of-crime works, right?" Spelling it out, Rinckey told him how anything tied to criminal enterprise meant forfeiture of assets relating to the crime. "Meaning you go down on a murder rap connected to trafficking, you're going to get dick more ways than one."

Nick let the last of the Fanta slide down his throat, making his eyes water. "So I give you something on Rainey, and I walk."

"Depends on the something."

"Look, I give him up and he turns on my old man, what's that make me?"

Jimmy leaned in. "Makes you the one won't get ass-raped for the next twenty years."

Rinckey sat back, knowing he had to cut him loose, but letting Nick take it around the block. Nick went to take a sip, the can empty.

. . . LITTLE BONES

GETTING THE steps down, the buskers were looking good, Niels, Zipper, Dimebag, Dizzie, Taboo, all of them making it happen. High-fives all around. A couple more run-throughs and they'd be set to kick off Mountain High, only four days away. The mid-morning vibe in front of the auditorium was humming, the buskers carrying on with rehearsals. Eva had gone back to the city, too afraid to stick it out; Bent Emma the contortionist was thinking about it, but the rest of them refused to be scared off, going out only in groups, looking over their shoulders, almost glad when they saw a cop drive by.

Waving to the auxiliary cop on the bicycle who didn't wave back, Grey guessed the local law figured he had something to do with the officer going missing down by McGuire on account of the grow house they found in the woods, betting it belonged to him, same as the Brackendale house. Cops forgetting they needed proof. When the cop pedaled out of sight, Grey dug in the messenger bag, finding one of the blunts he rolled under Uncle Rubin's .22.

A huge thermos of steaming coffee sat on a folding table

by the stage, a stack of paper cups with sleeves next to it, making the morning damp tolerable. Zipper stood pouring a cup, going on how this flashmob gig would get sick ratings on YouTube. Dimebag and Dizzie were giving Airdog their consensus on this latest batch from Pemberton. Mojo splayed out on the grass, feeling like he was hovering over it, enjoying his morning buzz, saying it was amazing what you could see in clouds, then babbling something about the wonders of non-polar molecules.

Sitting cross-legged close to Grey, Dara drew off the blunt he passed her, trying to keep up, sure she was hearing power lines overhead that weren't there. Grey was trying to understand how the weed Pete sold to Rivers and Glinkas ended up in the Indos' locker, not having a good feeling. Neither of them answering their phones since Pete made the handoff at the motel. Holding the paper cup at an angle, he let Goob lap at the coffee that had gone cold. Goob wasn't fussy, he loved anything with sugar.

Dimebag took the blunt from Dara, toked and passed it to Dizzie, the two of them going on about the Pemberton strain, sounding like they were talking about a twenty-year-old Ardbeg, calling it mellow with hints of this and notes of that, the THC levels hitting new highs. Dizzie asked Pete what he thought, wanting to get the word from the guru of green.

Lost in space, Pete just grunted, reliving the shooting at the storage, the Mounties carting away the sacks of dope from the locker with his prints all over them, Airdog's, too. Man, what he wouldn't give to get into the evidence locker. He reached and stroked Goober's flank, the bulldog lying on his side with his tongue lolling out, no idea he'd be eating inch-thick porterhouse the rest of his days; sinking his teeth into the hand with the gun had just seemed the right thing to do.

"These guys are kicking ass," Dara said, watching the buskers rehearse, leaning an arm on Grey's shoulder, saying again she loved the tune, Airdog saying the Hip were tops in his book, sounding funny with his front teeth gone. Then she was thinking ahead to her first shift coming up at the Cellar, snapping on her name tag, sitting people down, passing out menus, reciting the specials. Coming home to Grey and showing her appreciation, maybe moving from the couch to his bed, the two of them putting out a heat like Witherspoon and Phoenix did in *Walk the Line*. Miles from her mother telling her what to do.

Home. God, she was thinking of his place as home.

Grey nudged her. "Another hit?" He opened the messenger bag, feeling around for another blunt.

She saw the .22 inside the bag, asking, "You ever shoot that thing?" Sure her words were out of sync with her lips moving.

"Hit a paper target once."

"Paper, huh?"

He held out the blunt.

"I'm way past Technicolor, Superboy," she said, her mind racing, a collage of thoughts, thinking about calling Chip the realtor, the number Grey gave her. Chip was the guy that came around door knocking, handing out calendars and fridge magnets and free-appraisal bullshit, his name and photo all over everything, like he was marking his territory.

West of the highway was his. She'd been thinking about renting a place — her first place, in spite of rents up here being steeper than the slopes: seven bills just for a studio you could hardly turn around in, a toaster oven and a fridge the size of a backpack, a toilet, sink and shower. But it didn't matter, she was going for it.

Could sell her boyfriend's killer pot on the side. She looked at him. God, her boyfriend. After the split with Cam, she'd promised not to use that word anymore, the one move her mother would approve. That was before Grey flew into her life . . . on his trick bike.

"Earth to Dara." Grey tapped her wrist, startling her, asking if she felt like grazing on breakfast, a bunch of them talking about heading over to Gretzky's. "Buttermilk flap-jacks — get a stack like this for like five bucks."

She said why not the Lift, remembering the shit coffee at Gretzky's, Grey promising her the pancakes were the best, Dara saying, "Guess anything beats more KD."

"Yeah, you should get that looked at," Mojo threw in, looking at Grey.

"Got this recipe for a KD pizza . . . got a macaroni crust."

"I look like I'm gonna eat something with a crust?" Airdog asked.

"Make you a KD smoothie. Can't go wrong, it's like nature's perfect food."

"Goob eats better than you, man," Mojo said.

She remembered the fat cop in the red jacket recommending the key lime pie at Gretzky's, Dara thinking she'd go for that.

The flashmob took position for one last run-through,

the mid-morning sun edging above the boughs of the giant cypress to the east, Dara feeling the warmth against her cheek. Sipping cold coffee, she made a face and tipped her paper cup for Goob, scratching behind his ear. Goob rolled close like an overstuffed sausage, lapping at the coffee. It was good being Goob.

"Heads up," Dizzie called into the mike at the front of the stage, squelch ripping through the speakers.

Grey turned.

Nick Rosco was cutting across the grass, coming his way, his clothes rumpled.

"I got this," Grey said, snatching up the messenger bag, guessing this was about the roofies in his Johnnie Blue, Nick coming to do something about it.

. . . DRIVING THE PLAY

Closing the gap, Nick was saying to him, "About that drink you served up . . ."

"Like it with the ice, huh?" Grey felt more like floating than fighting, but he wasn't backing down. His hand went in the bag, fumbling for the pistol.

Nick came straight in and caught him reaching. Following a right with a left, he kept on swinging, connecting, knocking Grey on his ass. The .22 dropped to the grass, Nick kicking at him, Pete and Mojo charging in, grabbing and shoving him back, Dara trying to kick him.

Snatching the .22 off the lawn, Nick covered them, the flashmob stopping, everyone looking.

"Shit!"

Pete had them all turning back the other way. The Indian guy from the Ah-So-Easy was walking between the auditorium and the Olympic rings, two guys flanking him. Askay spotted Pete and headed for him, crossing the field.

Nick made the three Indos with windbreakers over handguns, one of them with his sleeve pushed up, a tensor bandage on his arm. Figuring they were coming for him, he hustled back toward the police station, punching the number of Travis's burner into the cell he'd got back with his personal effects, hadn't charged it since he got here, the phone dead, Nick cursing Bluetooth. Three Indos against him with a fucking gun you used for shooting tin cans.

Taking Dara's hand, Grey steered her toward the stage, Mojo and Airdog right behind them, Pete tugging Goober by his collar. Grey had his own cell out, his eyes on the Indos as they fanned out. Making the call, he waited for Lance to pick up, asking how he was fixed for time, giving him enough to pique his interest. He led everyone past the front of the stage, Dizzie watching them coming, reading the play. Taking his mark on the grass, Dizzie gave the nod for Lamar to hit it, letting Grey and the others slip past the line. Dizzie stepped out to the "Little Bones" guitar riff; Askay stopped up short, the second and third lines closing around him, arms and legs in motion as the drums kicked in. Swallowed by the moving web, Veni and Ram shoved buskers out of their way.

Past the stage, Grey steered Dara for the Stroll, Mojo and Airdog splitting off down an alley, hurrying past the Slopeside Cafe, ducking into Can-Ski, going out the back and into McGoo's.

Goober strained against the hold Pete had on his collar; it wasn't in his bulldog nature to turn from a fight, intent on Askay with the tensor on his arm, wanting another taste. Askay stopped, a half-dozen buskers circling him. He lifted the windbreaker enough to show the grip of his pistol, then caught sight of the auxiliary cop on the bicycle circling on the far side of the park, one of the buskers yelling to him, this guy's got a gun.

Pete picked the moment and broke off, tugging Goob along. Askay shoved Zipper and Dimebag out of his way and went after them, Pete making his way through the tourists on the Stroll. Veni and Ram chased after Mojo and Airdog, following them into Can-Ski, looking around, going out the back door. Ram went onto the Stroll, eyes searching.

Veni opened the door to McGoo's in time to see Mojo and Airdog running out the back with longboards, Mojo yelling for Freddie to stick them on Grey's tab. Veni chased through the store, pushing a lady into a rack of clothes and crashing out the door, taking out his gun.

Lance stood blocking his path, the badge on his belt and the holster showing, his right hand above the grip. "Alright pal, let's see it."

"See what? I am a tourist. I am legal here." Veni's eyes darted left and right, looking for escape, gun still in his hand.

"Got a carry permit for that?"

Jimmy came leading Ram, had his hands cuffed behind his back, his service piece out and aimed at Veni, saying, "Looks like he wants to go for it."

"He's still deciding," Lance said. His hand didn't move. The auxiliary cop rode up on the bike like he was backup. Jimmy guessing this wanna-be cop could squirt the perp with his water bottle.

Veni slowly put his hands up, Lance taking his piece.

●

First thought was to get to the Village cop shop, but the way Grey's luck had been running, they'd shoot him just for walking in. Pete caught up, pulling Goober, saying their best chance was to get over to Lorimer, cross the 99 and make their way through backyards to his place and bolt the doors, pull Tammy's flowered curtains and wait for the cops.

Nick had his .22, and Pete's El Camino was sitting in front of the house, being a bitch to restart after Pete got back from the Ah-So-Easy, long past needing its plug wires sprayed with the silicone 3-in-One Pete forgot to pick up at Canadian Tire last time he passed through Squamish.

Weaving through the mid-morning tourists, they practically ran to the Village Gate, Grey wondering what was taking Edwards and his fat partner so long.

Crossing the Marketplace lot, they got as far as Lorimer, Dara with her arm hooked through his, Pete and Goober right behind them, Goober's tongue trailing. That's when they saw the guy with the bandaged arm coming through the line of cars to their left. Turning to his right, Grey saw Nick coming up Lorimer from Blackcomb Way, the .22 in his hand. Must have circled around the block and cut them off.

From across the Marketplace lot, Askay saw Nick, too, saw he was armed. No idea who the hell he was.

Grey led Dara, Pete and Goob into the street and onto to the wide median. Nick and Askay stopped a dozen feet apart on the sidewalk, sizing each other up.

"That fucker's mine," Nick said, pointing at Grey, thinking he could shoot this guy with the wrapped arm, the tattooed hand saying he was Indo Army. Nick's chance to show the old man he'd been wrong about him. Show anybody else this was his town.

Askay hadn't pulled his piece, just stood and grinned as the silver Accord pulled alongside the curb, coming from behind Nick, slowing as it passed the three with the dog on the median. He held the grin, cocky now, telling Nick to get more bend in his knees, plant his feet wider apart. "Adds power and speed," he said. "You want, I can show you."

"Any idea who I am, you dumb fuck?" Nick caught the Accord rolling up, the tinted passenger window rolling down, Nav Pudi leaning over from behind the wheel as he pressed the button, lowering the passenger window, smiling behind the mustache, looking like he'd just spotted a trophy buck.

"Rosco's kid," Nav said.

In spite of being the only one pointing a piece, Nick was getting how deep the shit was. Looking over, he saw Grey on the boulevard, hitting redial on his phone.

"Where the fuck are you?" Grey yelled into the cell.

"Cleaning up after you," Lance said, sounding pissed, watching the auxiliary cop escort the two cuffed Indos to the station, saying to Grey, "How about you stay in one spot?"

"I'm over at Gateway. You know this guy Nick Rosco, right?"

"He bothering you?"

"Running his mouth at the wrong guys, the ones with the tattoos."

"Shit."

"Yeah, by the look of it, I'd say you better get here quick."

"Alright, don't —"

Disconnecting, Grey said to Dara, "Come on," changing his course, leading her south along the median toward the police station. Pete picked up fifty pounds of Goober and followed.

Nick turned from Nav to Askay, the Mountain High pennants flapping from the light standards. Stevens and the two with him were hurrying away down the median. Nick said, "Want my advice, you assholes back the fuck off."

Nav's teeth showed white from behind the mustache again. Here was the son of the one who gave the order: Travis Rainey firing the rocket from the back of a bread truck. Three of his friends dead on East Hastings, one just a boy. He said something that wasn't in English to Askay; then, to Nick, "You have a phone?"

"You see what I got in my hand," Nick said.

Nice and slow, Askay reached in a jacket pocket, tossing Nick his burner, Nick catching it in his free hand.

"Call the one with the silver hair," Nav said.

"Tell him what?" Nick said.

"Tell him I have his dope."

Finger on the trigger, Nick punched in the number, waiting for Travis to pick up. "It's me."

"Fuck you want?"

"Guy here says he's got your dope?"

Silence.

"Tell him if he wants it, to come and get it," Nav said, waiting till Nick repeated it, then told him to hang up.

Holding the phone out, Nick wanted this over, looking for a way out, seeing Stevens and his friends running off.

Askay didn't take the phone back.

"Now, you call your daddy," Nav said.

Nick hesitated, then pressed in the number, waiting seven or eight rings, hearing his father's voice come on the line.

"What the hell's going on, Nick?"

Looking to Nav, Nick felt his throat going dry. "Dad?"

The older Rosco kept on talking, "Why is it, I ask you to do this one thing —"

"Shut up," Nick said. "There's a man here —"

"What man?"

"Tell him adios," Nav said, reaching, guessing Nick's next move. Nick swinging the pistol, Nav picking the double Glock off the passenger seat. The burst split the morning. Nick thrown back across the sidewalk, shiny jacket turned to pulp.

The cell fell from his fingers. Didn't know what happened, Nick was looking up at the pennant wagging above him on the standard, clouds rolling, coiling into shapes, his father calling his name.

Askay bent for his cell, wiped away some blood, put it to his ear and said, "You hear it, old man?"

"What the fuck's going on . . . put Nick back on."

Askay clicked off, stepped over Nick and got in the Accord, screeching from the curb.

Somewhere, a siren wailed. Drizzle touched Nick's face. He heard the sound of running feet as the car sped off, the darkness spreading along the edges of his daylight.

. . . BY THE TAIL

LANCE AND Jimmy left the cuffed Indo Army boys with
the auxiliary cop, Jimmy feeling new pains since the crash,
bitching his jaw felt like he should be sucking breakfast
through a straw. Jogging ahead of him, Lance was weaving
through the people on the Stroll. It was a mistake letting
Pete Melton go at the storage place, wrong releasing Nick
Rosco from the holding cell, too, Rinckey with nothing to
hold him on. Travis Rainey was waging a turf war with the
Indo Army. Lance was sure it was him and his crew that
shot up the chalet last night. Same guy they chased across
the golf course, Lance wrecking his fucking Laredo.

They had the locker full of dope, but nothing back from
forensics on the casings found at the McGuire side road, no
word on Risker's missing officer or the parking lot shootout.
The rockslide on the highway was holding the ERT back.

His footfalls rang on the pavement, then he heard the
pop of auto-fire. Running faster now, dodging pedestrians,
leaving Jimmy in his wake. He shoved his way through the
crowd gathering in the Marketplace parking lot, telling
people to get back, the body of Nick Rosco on the ground,

a .22 next to him, a couple pointing in the direction the Accord went. Lance crouched next to Nick, his own phone ringing, reading the display: Grey Stevens again.

. . . FAST FOOD

THE ACCORD circled the block, cut them off from the cop shop. Grey practically tugged Dara off her feet. First time in his life he wanted to hear sirens, see some flashing red and blue. They cut through the lobby of the Northern Lodge, in one Starbucks door, out the other, into a side entrance of the Viscount. Down a marble hall and through its lobby, a maze of luggage and patrons, bellboys in red with gold stripes on their pants. Pete couldn't run holding Goober anymore. They left him there. Back outside, they made the traffic light, weaving through the parked cars in Lot 1, security cameras aimed from the overhead cluster of lights.

The Accord rolled west along Blackcomb, wipers swishing back and forth. Grey yanked Dara onto the Trail, hiding them in the row of cedars, making their way through Peace Park. Parents folded newspapers, getting up from park benches, urging their kids out of the drizzle, abandoning the swings and slide.

A group of teens rollerbladed past in helmets and elbow pads, said hi to Grey. Dara stopped on the footbridge, needed to catch her breath, tying a lace. Giving her a minute, Grey kept watch for the Accord through the cedars. Then they moved toward the slope, the drizzle picking up, feeling cold on their skin.

Stopping at the Base, he pulled it together. She held on to him, hair matted, sirens wailing somewhere in the Village. He led her up the slope, exposing them to the road, looking over his shoulder when he got a better vantage, trying to raise Lance on the cell again, not getting a signal now, hitting redial.

Moving upslope to a line of hay bales, the ski lift idle to their right, they kept to pickets of red frost-fence that lined the slope marking the cheese rolling course set for tomorrow. An event tent had been pitched on level ground above them, rain pattering on its canvas top. An event organizer moved boxes under its canopy, middle-aged and plump, the woman had her hair pulled back, orange safety vest over khaki shorts. Nikes. White socks. A pissed expression.

He tried again but couldn't get a cell signal, cursing, catching Dara from slipping, taking her hand and moving to the tent. The tag pinned on her vest said the woman's name was Janice.

First words out of her mouth: "This area's restricted. You can see that, can't you?" Deep brows striped her forehead, eyes belonged on an owl. Janice had been pissed most of the morning, the student volunteers bringing up the cases of cheese just left them out in the open, leaving her to sort it out, going off someplace, saying they'd be back once it stopped raining.

"You can't see the fence?" She pointed like maybe they'd missed it. Janice stood blocking their path, pointing toward the Adventure Zone, saying, "That's where you should be. You're out of bounds."

Grey looked back down, seeing the Indo with the tensor on his arm at the base of the slope looking up at them, coming along the fence line.

"No?" Janice said, seeing they weren't moving, "Then you'll help me with these cases. We need to get them back downhill."

"These here?" Dara asked, going to the stack.

"Yes, take them down past those bales, please and thank you," Janice said. "I'm just here to hang pennants, not move cheese. God, if my physio saw me up here . . ."

Dara lifted a cheese wheel from the top case, eleven pounds of cheddar, a festival sticker on top, saying, "Sure, lady, be glad to help."

"You're a dear."

Grey got a signal, punched in the number, telling Lance they were being chased, where they were, hanging up and telling Dara to come on. They could make it to the line of pines, use it as cover and descend to the road by the time the cops showed.

Dara took a wide stance, pulled back and rolled the wheel down the course.

"What in God's name . . ." Janice practically yelled and moved to stop her, grabbing at her arm. "Are you crazy, you carry them —"

Dara's slap cut the air. Janice was knocked to the wet grass, sliding, her fingers clawing at the mud and grass, guttural sound coming from her.

"Want your cheese down the hill or not, lady?" Dara lined a second orange wheel between her knees and let go, the wheel rolling downslope, hopping, rolling, hopping, rolling, gaining speed. Janice crawled and pulled herself up against the folding table. Her hand went to her stinging cheek, Dara's skull ring leaving its mark.

Askay stopped in his tracks, gun in hand. Whatever it was, it was orange and running at him like a deer. No, it was rolling. He sprang out of its path, slid down a few feet, got up, taking aim at the second one. Fuck, it was cheese. It struck him, swept his legs from under him.

"You can't do this," Janice yelled, pulling herself up, the iron taste of blood in her mouth. Sid and Nancy were destroying the cheese, assaulting the man below. Some sick game. Probably high on drugs. Let them have it, God! She had young children at home to consider. This was never part of the deal.

Dara was bowling a third wheel down the slope, getting some technique into it this time. Askay, down on the ground, rolled out of the way, dropping the pistol.

Grey grabbed Dara by the hand, and they made their break, hurrying for the trees, Grey angling down, careful of his footing.

Sid and Nancy were fleeing, Janice watched the one down the slope get to his knees, then turn and run back the way he came. Her handbag with her phone in it was on top of the box of pennants. Hearing the wail of more sirens down in the Village, she grabbed it, punching in 9-1-1. She was just a volunteer. Mother of two, for Christ's sake.

. . . ON THE JONES

LANCE IGNORED the call from Risker. Stevens and the girl were rolling cheese over on Base II, the bastards pursuing them. Officers were on the scene now, keeping the crowd of people back. Forgetting the pain, Lance was running for the suv parked in front of the station, Jimmy shouting at him, wanting to know what the fuck he was doing.

Not sure why, Jimmy followed his partner. He couldn't believe the hoofing he'd put in on account of Stevens, more than when he was a patrol cop on the Eastside, a beat of junkies and hookers. Making detective meant wearing a cheap suit, conducting interviews, sifting evidence and making notes. Once in a while putting on a vest and taking part in a raid. Didn't have to run down suspects, climbing up fucking mountains. Winded, Jimmy popped another pain-killer as they crossed Blackcomb Way and ran over to Base II.

Gather intel and write a report in a quiet mountain town — like fuck. It had been one thing after another. Middle of a turf war. Now this.

His partner's ass in Jimmy's face, he duckwalked up the slope to the open event tent, its pennants flapping. A uni was taking a statement from a sobbing woman in an orange vest, one Janice Beltram. Jimmy got to the table behind Lance, a new pain starting in his hip, told the uni to turn his squelching radio down, setting his ass against the table, sliding it a foot, catching the woman from falling, saying he was sorry about that, checking out the freckles on Janice's pudding-on-a-plate tits, trying to catch his breath.

"Your shoes . . ." she looked down at them.

"What?"

"They're caked with mud."

"Yeah." He felt his sweat soaking through the shirt, likely leave salty crescents on his blazer again. With any luck, the slanting rain would save him a ten-buck cleaning bill.

Lance and the uni were heading for the tree line; wiping his forehead with the back of his hand, Jimmy said to her, "Here, let me have a look," giving medical attention, taking Janice's chin with his index finger and thumb and looking at the mark Dara's ring left. She smelled nice.

"She hit me. Sid and Nancy, I call them. They ran that way." She pointed to the tree line.

Jimmy noted no ring on her finger, saying, "Might want to put some ice on it." Janice saying he might be right, noticing he was in pain, too, asking if he was alright, Jimmy saying he couldn't think about it right then, being on duty and all.

Lance and the uni were at the trees, Lance calling back to him, Jimmy getting up. He handed her his card, saying he'd love to get her statement, check in on her, hoping Janice was a badge bunny. Then he was moving, putting a little extra in the limp, guessing she was watching. Making the trees, following Lance and the cop back down the slope.

Back in the Tahoe, Lance was taking a call when Jimmy got in, clapping his shoes together, knocking the mud off. Settling on the seat, he dialed the fan to high, keeping the windows from fogging. Lance was rolling, passing the uni getting into his own unit, putting Risker on speaker phone, the staff sergeant filling them in, Nick Rosco shot to pieces right over on Lorimer, every available officer looking for the Accord. Went on to tell him the DOAs from the Stor-All had been toe-tagged: one Dev Singh, no fixed address, priors for possession for the purpose of trafficking, importation of over fifty kilos of coke, an Indo Army tat on his hand. The one with the fifty-cal was Richie Winters, formerly with the Sabers MC, owned a service station over in Salmon Arm. The dope at the locker was being tagged into evidence. X and coke in the cement sacks. Still no word on Constable Rick Harper, Risker telling Lance he was downgrading the search.

"Top it off," Risker said, "the cavalry just arrived."

"Shit."

"You should see these guys, the way they're dressed."

"Worse than Jimmy?"

"Got MP5s, all decked out in black. Look ready for war. Team leader's Hudson, wants a word. As in now. Said I'd relay it to you."

"Sorry you couldn't find me." Lance clicked off and hit the lights.

"What the fuck now?" Jimmy said.

Pulling onto Blackcomb, Lance headed for Stevens's place, guessing that's where Grey and the girl were headed, the crazies close behind.

. . . KILLING THE DEAL

Lexie came off the sofa, slapping the shape back into the leather cushions, aligning the seam of her romper, tiger stripes with a big zipper down the middle, showing cleavage. Slipping a foot into the peep-toe platform. Goddamned things killing her feet, but giving her calves some shape, Lexie wanting to walk so you'd never guess she was a Prairie girl, grew up scattering feed to chickens. Reaching the other shoe, she was thinking of one of those long shoehorns, let her get her shoes on without bending, her club dress too tight for it.

Travis had come to her place late last night, the two of them jumping into bed, fell right to sleep after, sharing her sink in the morning, him shaving with her lady Bic, her putting on her face, letting him use her toothbrush. Switching on the *Morning Lift*, she heard the DJ talk about the shootout at the golf course. She didn't ask about it as they drove to Sugar's, Travis eager to get Nick's pistol from her drawer.

Now he was doing up his cuffs, tucking in the tails of his shirt, tucking the Walther into the back of his pants. Travis watched her fluffing, Lexie wanting to leave no trace of them getting biblical on Manny's leather sofa.

"He scare you?" Grinning at the thought of a guy like Manny scaring anybody, watching her fuss, liking the way she packed the dress.

"Not when I'm with you." She straightened his collar for him and wiped the lipstick from the corner of his mouth, asking, "You hungry?"

"I could eat." A war going on, cop sirens bleating around town, a million things to take care of, and he was thinking about stopping for breakfast with her.

"You like crepes?"

"That like pancakes?"

"Pretty much. There's a place called Libretto Sociale over in Function Junction. They do them righteous, with a fruit reduction to die for."

Hope not, he thought. Taking the shot-up Lexus, Marty had driven Tanner to get stitched up last night, bullet clean through the shoulder. Richie helped himself to a blue Express van off the Avis lot, dropping Mutt off at the Cadillac Arms, then let Travis off a block from Lexie's. Richie parked the van up on Easy Street, halfway down the block from Stevens's, and kept an eye on the place.

The dope hadn't been in the trunk of the Lexus, the Indo with the mustache lying to him with a gun held to his head. Travis guessing Stevens could be working a deal with the Indos, thinking the Indos might turn up at his house. Richie waiting out front.

First thing in the morning, Travis and Lexie took a cab to Sugar's to get Nick's pistol. Eduardo, Bumpy's lieutenant, called and started bitching about how Travis handled last night, not waiting for more backup, every news program

272

reporting the shootout, Eduardo blaming him for the task force on its way, told him Bumpy wanted to talk. Travis hung up and switched off the phone.

Soon as they stepped through the door, Travis and Lexie got into it, his mouth on hers, Travis stopping long enough to go out and tell the cabbie not to wait, handing him a twenty, telling him to keep the change. Coming back in, bolting the door, putting out the *closed* sign, he pressed into her, working his way across the room, bumping the reception desk, Lexie reaching in a drawer for the key, opening Manny's office door. Couldn't keep their hands off each other, this girl far from the ones that used to hang around the clubhouse back in the day. Had him at hello the day he stepped onto the mat that said *Come on in and get wet*.

Now, helping her pull the sofa away from the wall, he was hearing more sirens, asking her, "You got vacation time coming?"

"Why, you taking me someplace?"

"How about someplace hot?"

"Thought you were buying into this place?"

"Think I'm done working with assholes. Thought you might be, too."

She took a look around, making sure everything was like they found it, going through the door. "Yeah, could do with one less asshole."

Freezing at the threshold, she put her hands to her mouth, her breath catching.

Manny was sitting with his legs crossed over the reception desk, grinning at her, playing the man like Travis did the first time he walked in here. The Baggie with Nick's gun lay on the blotter, in easy reach. His grin widened when Travis came to the door and looked past her. Manny asked him, "Can't you read?" He pointed at the brass plate on the door: *Private*.

"No time for your bullshit, Manny." Travis eased her aside, got in front of her, ten feet from the desk.

"Getting ahead of yourself, no?" Manny asked, picking up the bagged gun, swinging his feet down. "Coming in here like the place is already yours, screwing the help." Manny's finger curled around the trigger through the plastic. "Should be asking me like this: 'How long you been sitting there, Manny?' Throw in a look of surprise. I don't know, maybe go for sheepish." He aimed at Travis's middle. "Humping away with the photo on my desk, front of the eyes of my children."

"You know it's just a photo, right?" Travis smiling.

"Like crapping where you eat."

Travis took a single step.

"Far as your offer, don't see it's gonna work."

"So, how you want to play this, Manny? Going to shoot me?"

"This was meant for me, right after the ink dries, am I right? Maybe shoot me, make it look like a robbery. In front of the eyes of my children." He looked at Lexie. "Traitorous bitch."

Lexie got behind Travis, like she wanted him to protect her, her hand moving. She drew the Walther from his belt, stepping away, pointing it with both hands, holding it level. Same time Manny pulled the trigger.

Click.

Travis turned, not bothering with Manny, saying to her, "Thanks for the thought, Lex." Smiling at her. "But you point one of these bad boys, you be sure you can do it." He adjusted the way she was standing. "Get the stance right. Lean forward a bit. Keep this arm straight, bit more bend to the knees. That's it. You're a natural, you know it?"

She aimed the Walther at Manny, wide stance in her peep-toe platforms.

Manny was ripping the plastic off, standing now, trying again.

Click.

"Come here." Travis took her by the shoulders and kissed her, taking the Walther from her hand, slipping it back into his belt.

Manny's jaw clenched. "I really got to watch this?"

"How about Maui, you ever been?" Travis asked her, going to the desk, picking up the ripped plastic, taking the Smith from Manny, wrapping it and laying it on the blotter, shoving Manny back in the chair.

"Yeah, Maui's good, but, you know one place I've always pictured?"

"Yeah?"

"Bora Bora."

"So nice, they named it twice." Travis smiled, hearing another siren race by.

"You know I'm right here, right?" Manny said, staying in the chair.

"And all the time you're sitting there, thinking how this would play, and you didn't check the load." Travis shook his head. "It's that kind of thing, Manny, makes me have second thoughts." He went to the door, checked the lock, looked out, then tipped the blinds. Loving the look on Manny's face when he turned back, like he knew he was about to die. Travis stepped over to her. "This asshole owe you back-pay, anything like that?"

"Nothing worth talking about."

"Take out your wallet," he told Manny.

Manny hesitated, then raised an ass cheek, removing his wallet, slapping it on the desk, thinking of his Baby Browning in his own desk drawer. No way he could get past Travis and get to it.

Taking out the cash, about five hundred bucks, Travis handed it to Lexie, called it severance, then took out the credit cards, tossing the wallet in the trash bin. "Which one's got wiggle room?" Travis asked him.

Manny sighed. "The Visa. It's platinum."

Knowing he was lying, Travis tossed the Visa and a couple of gas cards in the bin, kept the Amex, saying, "Don't leave home without it." Then, to her: "How about it?"

"Could just report it lost," Manny said, "get it canceled."

"Yeah, you could. But then I'd be back."

Manny shrugged.

Travis snapped his fingers. "Let's see your car keys."

"My Caddy?"

"How we're getting to the airport. Don't worry about it, Manny. You can pick it up at the Park 'N Fly."

"Thanks." Manny took out the keys and laid them on the desk, knowing he'd never see the Caddy again, saying, "Don't forget to write."

Taking Lexie's hand and the wrapped Smith off the desk, Travis led her the back way out, leaving Manny sitting at the desk. Anytime now, Manny would notice that he pissed himself, feel the warm wet turning cold around his ass, the chair wicking it up.

Going out the steel door, Travis checked the alley, his hand on the Walther. Taking his cell with the other, he turned it back on, saw Bumpy and Eduardo had left a half-dozen messages while he and Lexie were on Manny's sofa — checking up on Nick, wanting to give Travis shit for not babysitting last night. Now the old man's line was busy, so he dialed Eduardo again, the queer-ass filling him in on what went down two blocks away. Now he understood the sirens. Nick shot dead on the pavement, the old man beside himself, going all Tony Montana, screaming and grieving, hadn't got to throwing blame around. Yet.

Lexie walked with him to the top of the alley, her overnight boyfriend with the silver in his hair costing her a job, wanting to take her someplace hot with an even hotter credit card, driving off in her boss's car. Now he was giving some gangster shit on the phone, telling him to come and do it, then he tossed the phone into the Dumpster, threw Nick's pistol in there, too.

Then they went back around the front of Sugar's, Travis looking around, clicking the fob, opening the Caddy's doors. "How about we take a raincheck on that breakfast?"

"Long as you're taking me someplace hot."

"Wouldn't joke about it."

Through the second thoughts and calling herself crazy, she was thinking what to pack: the La Perla one-piece, the barefoot sandals, picturing fruit drinks with umbrellas, getting highlights in her hair. Probably go topless. Thinking he'd like that. Man, she really was nuts.

Driving nice and slow out of the Village, making it back to her rented condo, he watched her pack, keeping an eye out the window, used her phone to call Richie, wanted to warn him to get out of town, but getting no answer. Taking her suitcase, he set it in the trunk, and they drove to the Cadillac Arms. What was left of Bumpy's advance amounted to just over two grand. Along with Manny's Amex and what he had in his Vancity account, they'd be alright for a while, till he figured things out.

Manny got to go home to the family in the photo, got to keep his escort business a while longer. Wait for gambling to come to town.

Driving north on the 99, Travis cruised past the Cadillac Arms a couple of times, then circled around back before parking out front of room four. He told her to wait in the car, left the keys hanging from the ignition in case she wanted to play the radio.

. . . KNUCKLE DOWN

No IDEA what happened to Richie, Travis was done with Bumpy Rosco, the idiot son catching a bullet and Travis catching the blame. After he grabbed the cash, he'd head up to Pemberton, split the rest of Rosco's dope with Max and Axel Busch. Call it a parting gift. See what their old man Rudi would give him for the rest, likely have to take ten cents on the dollar. Rudi would get them across the border, fix them up with new passports. For that, Travis would leave him the Caddy. No way he'd get it across the border with Manny's name on the registration. Call Drew at the McDonald's back in Squamish, tell him to hang on to the Chrysler awhile. He'd miss those Lambo doors, but what can you do? Once stateside, he'd wait on the new ID, then catch a flight from SeaTac to Bora Bora.

A dozen cigarette butts had been crushed outside the motel room door. Mutt lay on one of the beds, watching reruns, this one just ending, about a car that talked, an open pizza box on the bed, a bunch of half-eaten crusts. Smelled like hell in there. Mutt looked up as Travis came in. "'Bout fuckin' time?"

"You hear from Marty?" Travis wondering if Tanner made it.

"Not a word." Mutt sat up. "Heard on the news there's a rockslide on the highway."

"Yeah?"

"So maybe they didn't get through, and with Tanner bleeding like a bitch . . ."

"What about Richie?"

"Nothing from him either."

"Shit."

"Yeah, shit. So let's talk about my money."

"Starting to bore me with that."

"That so?" Mutt was looking serious.

"Want your money, take it up with Rosco." Travis going to the adjoining room, gathering his clothes, shoving them in his bag.

Knocking the crusts from the box, Mutt swung his legs off the bed and followed Travis. "I'm taking it up with you."

"Forgetting you shot the cop? And the money I had to pay Gibbet." Travis looked past the curtains, Lexie waiting in the car. Tipping the mattress, he pulled the double-sided tape from the seam, reached inside and pulled the banded hundreds from under the fabric. Shoving them in the bag, he turned, Mutt standing with his arms on the door frame.

"Done with pushing my buttons?" Mutt said.

Travis dropped the bag. Nobody to get between them now. "Not your buttons I'm gonna push."

"Figure half that's mine."

"Then come get it."

Mutt charged in, Travis reaching behind for the P5,

Mutt catching his wrist, throwing a blow from the hip, knocking Travis back; the Walther dropping to the floor. Mutt grabbed a handful of shirt, popping buttons, taking one on the side of the head, shoving Travis back into the wall, going for a choke, trying to corkscrew his thumb into the windpipe.

Dropping his chin, Travis snapped in a head butt, thumbs going for Mutt's eyes, the two of them twisting, rabbit-punching, crashing down between the beds. Mutt was like iron, younger, stronger, wrapping his legs, freeing a fist, punching, pulping Travis's nose. Twisting, Travis got free and got to his feet.

Mutt threw himself, shoving Travis into the other room, the TV playing the *Munsters* theme as it crashed to the floor. Clubbing down with his fist, Mutt kept trying for the throat, Travis grabbing the wrist, worming his left hand down, grabbing Mutt's belt, twisting and bringing his knee up into his groin. Mutt let go and rolled off. Travis tried to get up, Mutt grabbing hold, both punching at each other. They stumbled into the bathroom, bouncing off the vanity, both throwing short punches, Travis tripping over his bag.

Mutt stood over him, looking at Lexie standing at the entrance, holding Travis's P5 in both hands, a wide stance, drawing down on him.

"You order a hooker?" Mutt said, wiping blood from his mouth, watching her drop her aim from center and squeeze off a round, hitting him in the thigh. He dropped, crying and cursing, clutching the leg, and she picked up the bag, saying she just did the bookings.

She carried the bag out to the Caddy, Travis following

her out, bleeding from the nose, saying, "That was better, by the way. Nice and smooth."

"Yeah, I'm a quick study," she said, opening the trunk, setting the bag inside, then tossing in the P5. She was in this thing now.

"Get in," she said, fishing the keys from her pocket, going to the driver's side, getting in, kicking off her shoes to drive, telling him there were Kleenex in her bag. She started the Caddy and rolled out of the lot, heading north.

... THE LAST PUPPET SHOW

THEY WENT around securing the doors and windows. Watching out the front, Grey let some light through the slit in the drapes. The sun was high over the pines where the street made a crescent and hooked around to Balsam. Roy Scheider was in his housecoat, standing in his bay window. Block Watch on the job.

Mojo and Pete sat on either side of Dara on the couch, her tearing bits from a tissue, them with expressions like Grant Wood's *American Gothic* — add a little freaked out. Airdog sat cross-legged on the floor, Goob with his head in his lap. Twisting joints kept his hands busy, lining them on the coffee table, Mr. Potato Head watching.

Pete was still taking a stab, tallying how much marching powder had been in the cement sacks. Bags of it in the empty locker, likely uncut, and compressed kilos of yerba; God, he hated that fucking cop dog, Kilo. Six figures slipping through his fingers. Like winning the lotto, then losing the fucking ticket. But more than that; his fingerprints were on the sacks, Airdog's, too. When the cops did their crime-scene thing, the two of them would be royally fucked. Latex gloves were Pete's own rule. Nobody worked the grow houses without donning a pair. Getting greedy while feeling rushed was just plain stupid. Now he was left wondering how to play this. Should have left Airdog out of it, bad enough the guy was waiting on new teeth.

"Here we go," Grey said, tensing, looking out the window.

All heads turned.

The Tahoe rolled off Balsam, onto Easy, pulling into the driveway, stopping next to the El Camino with the Pemberton pot hidden under the tarp, Lance and Jimmy getting out, walking around it.

"Put that away," Grey told Airdog, meaning the joints and Mr. Potato Head on the table, going to the door. Airdog tucked the joints and the Head on the shelf by the old-school stereo, under Uncle Jerry's photo, leaned the Mungo Jerry album in front.

Lance and Jimmy came to the stoop, Grey and Dara stepping out. Jimmy was still thinking of Janice Beltram, the woman with the pudding tits, saying, "You know they got this thing called a lawnmower?"

"Thinking of putting in a zen garden," Grey said.

"You ID the guys chasing you?" Lance said, coming up a couple of steps.

"Didn't get a great look," Grey said, looking at Dara, Dara nodding. "They were in an Accord, something like that. For sure it was silver. The windows were tinted, couldn't see inside."

Dara said, "Yeah."

"Soon as they pulled up, we were out of there," Grey said.

"It was Nick Rosco they wanted. Guns came out and we were running, calling you."

Jimmy said they should drag them all in, stick them in the cell, let the ERT sort this shit out.

"And you didn't see who shot Rosco?" Lance said.

Both shaking their heads.

"We ran and they came after us, one of them chasing us up the hill."

"Guy you rolled cheese at?" Jimmy was asking.

"Slowed him down," Dara saying how she nailed him.

Grey was looking past Lance as the silver Accord swung onto Easy from Balsam. He pointed and the two cops turned, the car rolling like somebody was checking for an address, the passenger window rolling down.

Lance moved first, hand going for his piece, seeing the twin barrels pointing out the window. Jimmy saw it late, hand going under the plaid.

•

Spotting the Tahoe's cop stripes past the old shitbox, Nav called it too late, both cops moving, raising service pieces, the guy from the boulevard on the stoop pulling the girl inside. It was a stupid move, driving by on their way out of town, hoping for a parting shot at Travis Rainey, thinking he might be here, knowing Rainey had been trying to recruit the local pot growers.

Askay had the twin barrels out the window, letting off a steady burst, dotting the El Camino, the one that had pulled into the Stor-All. Knocking the fat cop off his feet, he punched holes in the siding, taking out a coach light, the picture window. The tall cop dived off the steps, sending a bullet thumping into the trunk, Nav roaring away.

Lance scrambled to Jimmy, crouching next to him, a bullet caught him just above the hip, lots of blood. Grey and Dara came out, running down the steps, Dara yelling, "Oh, my God."

"Go . . ." was all Jimmy said, pushing at Lance.

Lance hesitated a second, Dara saying she had this. Then he jumped into the Tahoe, backing out and tearing after the Accord, fumbling for the handset.

... MAN DOWN

GREY STRIPPED off his shirt, balled it and handed it to her, taking his cell and making the 9-1-1 call, guessing Lance was doing the same, the Tahoe tearing out of sight, siren wailing, lights flashing. Airdog stood at the door, Pete holding Goober back, Pete saying they had to split, move the pot again before more heat showed up. He went running for the keys to the El Camino.

"You going to be okay?" Airdog asked, looking at Dara, pressing Grey's balled-up shirt at Jimmy's side, Jimmy grimacing, blinking the rain from his eyes.

"We're good," she said. "Go."

Airdog followed Pete, grabbing the joints and Mr. Potato Head, hurrying back out and down the stairs.

Dara pressed, staunching the blood, hair matted to her head, telling Jimmy to hang in there, the cop grimacing, saying through gritted teeth to take it easy, reaching the pain killers in his pocket.

"Sorry. Not trying to hurt you." Blood on her hands. Rain coming down. Sticking his head out his door, Roy Scheider in the bathrobe was yelling the ambulance was on the way, other neighbours coming out of their doors, looking.

"Pull me out of this shit," Jimmy said, his hip on fire, pill bottle in his hand, trying to flip off its lid.

"Help's on the way," Grey said, kneeling, taking the pill bottle from him and popping the lid.

"Mean that." Jimmy nodded at a turd a half foot away, rain softening it.

Grinning, Grey handed him a pill. Jimmy took the bottle from him, popping Tramadol like they were Tic Tacs, looking back at the turd, saying, "Going to have to write you up for that." Grinning back through the pain.

Dara pressed the shirt, telling him to lie still. Pete and Airdog getting into the El Camino, Pete coaxing it to start, backing down the driveway and taking off.

. . . SCREAMING HORSES

"You fucks are mine." Lance hit the wipers, hands grabbing the wheel, his foot mashing the pedal, the Tahoe going flat out, screaming southbound on the 99. He shot past a couple of cars, crossing the double lines, another suv pulling to the shoulder, giving him room. Lance forgetting about the crash last night, setting aside his pain, telling himself Jimmy was going to make it.

Calling it in as he tore away from town, he threw the mike down, hoping to hear the howlers coming from behind, joining in the chase. No units would be coming from the south, the road crew still clearing the debris, the highway down to a single lane, flaggers dealing with a mile of backed-up vehicles in either direction. No way the assholes in the Accord would get through. He pressed his foot down, wanting more out of her, the Tahoe flying.

Passing a delivery truck on the right, the Tahoe swayed, close to clipping the guardrail. Three-hundred and fifty-five screaming horses. Felt like he was leaving the ground, the pines blurring by.

An overpass, the highway just two lanes here, Alta Lake to the right. Weaving around and passing cars, some pulling to the shoulder, Lance rode the double lines through the Highlands intersection. A gravel truck with a pup forcing him to crowd the northbound lane, cars honking, swerving out of his way, high beams flashing. Passing the Lake Placid exit, a pair of cyclists in the rain. Any number of exits the Accord could take, the assholes lying low till nightfall, Lance betting they'd stayed on the 99, wanting to put some miles between them and Whistler. Brandywine Falls coming up. The rockslide somewhere south of Daisy Lake, its waters showing past the trees to his left.

The highway was double northbound and single south-bound lanes here, Lance riding the solid lines like he was on a track, a river running to his right, past the concrete dividers. Then he caught sight of the car up ahead. Light-colored and going flat out. It had be the Accord, flashing its brake lights as it disappeared over a rise.

The slide was just several miles ahead now, his radio squawking, the mike out of reach on the floor. It didn't matter. Lance was gaining, bearing down, foot to the floor. Going rhino. Coming over a rise, passing more cars, he saw the Accord ahead, sure it was them, and nowhere for them to go. Traffic was starting to back up southbound, the Accord having to slow.

Closing the gap, Lance watched the passenger turning and bringing up the twin-barrels, getting a bead on the Tahoe. No backup in the rearview. Lance was riding them down solo, engine screaming. Doing this for Jimmy. They raced like that, passing the line of cars, the Accord riding the empty northbound lanes, giving the southbound traffic jam a show.

Sweeping back and forth across the northbound lanes, not giving the guy with the double Glock a shot, Lance gained. The driver of the Accord swerved, too, the gunman trying to get a bead.

The PIT maneuver, just like he'd been trained. Lance drew up, the driver of the Accord doing what he could to keep him from pulling alongside. The guy with the Glock was halfway across the seat, firing a burst, windows exploding, glass flying everywhere.

Same time, Lance made his move, his bumper lined with the back wheels. Cranking her to the right, he jolted from the contact, bullets ripping into Risker's Tahoe. The smack of metal on metal at highway speeds. Ahead, a flagger stood in front of debris and construction equipment, holding back the southbound cars, the guy not sure what to do. Two cars speeding in the wrong lanes, the patter of gunfire, the flagger dropping his sign and jumping out of the way.

Passing the line of waiting cars, Lance kept turning, doing the nudge, the Accord losing, the guy with the Glock thrown around, bullets tearing through their roof, the car going into its spin. Lance cranked his wheel, both vehicles doing a crazy asphalt dance, tires screaming, metal grinding. The PIT-compatible airbags holding, not smacking into his chest.

Riding the brakes now, he kept the Tahoe from swerving and shuddered to a stop. Heart pounding like crazy, Lance watched the Accord spin away onto the shoulder, flipping over, then rolling a couple more times down into the ditch.

More flaggers and road crew were jumping, people

getting out of their cars, pointing and taking pictures. A long patch of rubber behind the Tahoe. Drawing his weapon, Lance got out and hobbled for the shoulder, begging these fuckers to make a play.

No takers.

Both men were trapped upside down in the crushed car, both airbags deployed, the windshield in fragments, fluids leaking. Askay was out cold, his head bleeding. Nav was looking at him, the double Glock on the ground near the vehicle. Kicking it away, Lance knelt down and asked, "How you fuckers like that?"

The ERT and county Mounties arrived on the scene just ahead of the fire truck and ambulance, guys in black flack vests with high-powered rifles jumping all over the place, somebody asking if Lance was okay, Lance saying he could use a drink. Hands clapping him on the back.

Lance sat on the road, his body shaking. He was pretty sure he was grinning, too. When he could, he would ask one of the guys in black to find out how Jimmy was doing.

. . . BRIGHT LIGHTS, BIG CITY

"Yeah, so last night kind of change the way this is going?"
Grey said it casual, offering her the Rice Chex, Patti Smith
doing "Fuji-san" in the background. The morning sky promising a decent day.

Taking the box, she shook some into her bowl, pouring
milk over top. She looked at him, her foot finding his under
the table, sliding it up his leg. "Going in the right direction,
but what is this thing?" Making him work for it, loving how
he got all awkward, couldn't find the words. She bopped to
the tune, saying, "I scare you a bit, huh, Superboy?"

He felt his face flush. How could she look so good, the
Nirvana T-shirt she'd had on since she got here, hadn't even
touched her hair. Took Tammy an hour just to put her face
on. He poured the milk, offering it to her. "Felt right, I guess."

"That's what you got, this thing just felt right? You
guess?"

"Okay. Felt really alright. What about you?"

Liking the color in his cheeks, she walked her toes up
his leg, saying, "Your bed sure beats the couch. Can tell you
that much."

He looked under, the foot now in his lap, the toes painted black. Shoveling in a spoon of cereal, he crunched down, pretending to ignore what the foot was doing.

Pete walked into the kitchen, caught the foot in Grey's lap, making like he didn't. Setting the overstuffed backpack down in the hall, he was ready to take Rivers' back road down to Port Mellon, disappear for a while, doing it solo, sure the cops would be coming for him, Airdog opting to stay and take his chances.

Grey straightened. "You sure you want to do this, man?"

"With these task force assholes all over the place, my fingerprints on those sacks . . ." Pete said, letting it hang. He looked at Goober following him in. They had already said their goodbyes, the group of them passing Mr. Potato Head around last night. "Sure, he won't be a pain?"

"Kidding? Goob's family, you know that."

Pete nodded.

Dara got up and hugged Pete, wishing him luck.

"Just till it cools down," Pete said, adding, "Just make sure he doesn't KD my dog."

"No way. I'm weaning him off that shit." She put her hand up like she was swearing an oath.

"Thanks." He kissed her cheek, guy-hugging Grey, the two of them clapping each other on the backs. Hoisting the backpack on his shoulder, Pete went out the door, Goober wanting to follow him.

Out on the porch, Dara held Goob's collar, Grey next to her. Same spot they stood when Jimmy was shot.

Pete got in the El Camino, bullet holes across the back, a couple more down the side, and coaxed it to start, thinking he really needed to spray those plug wires. Farting blue exhaust, the old Chev rolled out. That was it. Blue exhaust all the way around the bend.

"How far you think he'll get?" Dara asked.

"Before he changes his mind?"

"Before that thing croaks."

When Pete was out of sight, they stepped back in, finished their cereal in silence, then went back to bed. Snuggling under the blanket, Goob made it a threesome, Grey and Dara drifting, then waking when they heard another car pull into the driveway, Grey thinking it was Pete coming back. He went to the front window, saying, "Shit," then hurrying to throw on some clothes.

A sand-colored Rover parked over the oil stain Pete had left, Chip Woods getting out, coming to the stoop looking all about business, a folder sporting his company's logo under an arm, comparative market bullshit tucked inside. The realtor stuck on the winning smile, straightened the Dior jacket and waited for the door to open.

"Hey, Grey, my man, sure I got the date right."

"Yeah, yeah." Grey totally forgot he was coming this morning. "It's me, been kind of crazy." He adjusted the T-shirt over the sweat pants, saying, "Come on in, man."

Up came Chip's hand. A studied handshake. Firm and reassuring. Nice diamond ring. The cologne was woodsy, bergamot or something. Grey saw the bruise stamped on his face, decided not to ask.

Slipping off the Pradas, Chip stepped in, saying, "Heard about what happened, but wow . . ." meaning the bullet holes in the siding out front.

"Yeah, well, we party hearty, Chip. You know me."

"Should've seen it with the police tape, the window all boarded up," Dara said, coming into the hall, barefoot, doing up one of Grey's shirts, introducing herself, offering her hand.

"Least there's no chalk outline," Chip said, shaking her hand, thinking of Richie Winters, heard he got himself killed. No surprise there. Taking a seat at the kitchen table, he turned down a bowl of Rice Chex. He caught the wobbly table leg, hoping it didn't collapse while he was mid-pitch, all his shit in the folder sliding to the floor.

"Waiting on my insurance guy, not sure they cover drive-by shootings," Grey said.

Chip said he hoped so, too; either way, this place was going to need some major staging. He told Dara he might have a rental coming up for her, remembering she had called two days back, betting this punk girl could never make the rents up here.

She said they were past that, taking Grey's hand across the table. Getting the picture, Chip got down to cases, explaining current market conditions, talked about office tours and showings and open houses, how he liked to present offers. Finally, winding down, he put an x on the listing agreement, showing Grey where to sign, then where to initial on each page.

"And if you're looking to upsize . . ." Chip said, taking a listing from his folder, the listing belonging to a competitive broker, the Mortons switching agencies after Chip had the bad sense to rent their place on the golf course to gun-crazy thugs. Feeling guilty for it, Chip talked up the place, shot up worse than this one, saying it needed a bit of TLC but a restoration company was getting to work, be as good as new; threw in that the price was right. He didn't say he felt Whistler was turning into another Detroit, the gaming commission promising a five percent boost to the local economy when gambling came to town, nobody talking about the increase in crime; casinos having a way of drawing it like a magnet. And nothing but a small detachment of county Mounties to stop it. Said he knew a gal at RBC, worked magic with financing. Chip waited, looking hopeful.

Grey stopped him, saying, "We're going no-fixed-address, for a while anyway." With the sale, Grey would have enough money to last them like forever. Get himself out of the weed business. Open a little bar. Learn to surf. Thinking of Mexico again. Looking at Dara, he felt free of the ghosts.

"Well, you ever change your mind . . ." Chip said, flipping the folder closed on the listing agreement.

Grey nodded, looking at Dara. "Feels good to be getting out of here. Go some place that's got a beach."

"Place we can get naked," Dara said, loving the look on Chip's face.

Chip was grinning like she was kidding, pretty sure it had been three months since the wife let him into her bedroom, the woman not understanding him these days.

"Yeah well, you haven't met her yet, that's why," Dara said, dreading the thought of Grey meeting her mother. She took a porterhouse from the fridge and unwrapped it, Dara the vegetarian looking at it like it was gross, asking Goob how he wanted it. Goob looking up, a string of saliva making it to the floor.

"Stop worrying," Grey said, slipping on his high-tops in the hall, checking to make sure he had the tickets and joints and his water bottle. "Just cut it up for him."

"It's what I do, worry." Dara took a steak knife from the drawer, took the meat between thumb and index finger, laying it on the cutting board, looked at Goob standing there drooling, saying to him, "You sure you want it raw?" Then to Grey, "I'm serious, the woman's got a way . . ."

"Hey . . ." He pointed a finger, putting on the stern, saying, "We're having fun today. Listen to music, catch a buzz and some sun. No talking about your mother. Besides, we're just staying with her a few days."

"Long enough." She set the knife down, came over to

him and snapped her teeth at his pointing finger, catching it and holding on.

"Ow. Stop that."

"Uh-uhn." She shook her head, playing, kept her teeth around his finger until he lifted the black T and went for her ribs, tickling, making her let go.

"Hey, no fair."

He held up his finger, showing the crescent indents from her teeth. "Look what you did."

"Whiner," she said, going back to the piece of meat, slicing it in strips, Goob whimpering, shaking his head, saliva flying.

"You, too, stop whining."

Goob stopped, sat and kept drooling, his look asking what was taking so long.

"How about giving Mungo a rest?" she said, meaning the disc playing on the stereo.

He went in the living room, lifted up the tone arm, stopped when he heard brakes outside, the needle dropping back on the platter.

"Chip forget to give us a fridge magnet?" she said, dumping the meat strip's in Goob's dish, Grey checking out the window.

Lance stepped out of the SUV, another RCMP Tahoe, no bull bars on this one, the department promising to make good on his wrecked Laredo, written off in the line of duty.

Grey swung the door back, hopeful the cop had word on Tuff Dub, saying, "Detective Edwards. What a lovely surprise."

Dara came up behind him, holding the knife, asking Lance if he had a warrant, then saying, "Just kidding."

No word on Tuff Dubb, but he told them the two Indos that shot Jimmy had pled not guilty at their arraignment, both of them in neck braces, the case set to go in front of a Supreme Court judge and jury, the media swarming all over it. Grey and Dara read about it the papers, Lance chasing down the Accord, giving the bastards a taste of the bull bars, flipping them over a couple of times, doing it for Jimmy. Lance hailed as a hero. Askay with some cracked ribs, along with a concussion. Nav Pudi with bruised organs; the double Glock with enough prints on it to put both shooter and wheelman away for life.

Lance pulled Grey aside, told him about an anonymous tip the department got earlier, some guy driving an obscure back road near Port Mellon, came upon two bodies getting past ripe next to an old Jeep. Benny Rivers and Ivan Glinka, found shot to death; he didn't say they'd been partly eaten by wild animals, making the bodies hard to ID. But he did say he bet the two dozen casings found at the scene were fired from the same double Glock that shot up the van where Officer Harper went missing, killed Nick Rosco and put one in his partner, right where they were standing.

Grey asked what happened to Travis Rainey, Lance saying the guy got lucky, likely slipped the roadblocks, but with the manhunt they had going, they'd get him in the end.

The latent prints the techs found on the cement sacks — prints belonging to Pete James Melton and Jimmy "Airdog" Tan — were about to get lost in the shuffle. Lance betting it was Pete Melton that made the anonymous tip, telling them where to find Rivers and Glinka. Who knows, maybe they'd turn up Rick Harper in the same area. As far as Lance was concerned, him and Pete Melton were square. Two-bit pot growers weren't on Lance's radar anymore, promotions having a way of changing the landscape. They stepped back over to Dara, kneeling with Goober, the dog licking his chops.

"And your buddy Jimmy's okay? Gallo like the wine, right?" Dara said.

"Yeah. He's getting released tomorrow. Jimmy's happy about it, got no taste for hospital food. Told the nurse they ought to get a fryer." Lance held his hand to Goober, patted his head.

"Filling his cakehole full of Jell-O?" she said, wiping at her eyes.

"No kidding. Should have seen him shoveling it in. Whatever flavor red is." He told them Janice Beltram, the woman from the cheese tent, stopped by to see him, brought Jimmy a book of crosswords and some cream-of-something soup, keep up his strength.

The three of them were laughing. Go, Jimmy. Then Lance told them Jimmy put in for a transfer to Langley. "Going to stick him behind a desk, probably hand him an extra stripe for what he did."

"For taking one for the team?" she said.

"Something like that."

Dara said to wish him their best.

"I will," Lance said, looking at Chip's sign in the foot-high grass. "Put the place up for sale, huh?"

"Yeah. Moving someplace with less crime," Grey said.

Lance grinned and went around the back of the Tahoe,

pulling up the hatch. "It's never about the crime," he said. "It's about the quality of the police force."

"Right."

"Heading to Mountain High?"

"Wouldn't miss it," Dara said, "especially the flashmob."

"I'd offer you a lift, but figured you'd rather pedal." Lance reached in back and pulled out Grey's baby-blue BMX, setting the wheels down, holding it out for him.

Grey did a perfect kid-at-Christmas, mouthing *holy shit*, saying, "You found her." He took the handlebars, rolled it back and forth, checking it out. Not a scratch. Even had the pegs still on it.

"Boys up here did a follow-up with a warrant, took a closer look inside the lockers at the Ah-So-Easy, the storage place."

"Yeah?"

"One of the units was packed with everything from skis to Ski-Doos, stolen property destined for offshore. Turns out the owner's kid had a little export thing going on the side, breaking into chalets."

"The dope his, too?" Grey asked.

Lance grinned at him, like who you kidding, saying, "Pulled a couple of strings, got your bike cleared with the staff sergeant."

Grey swung his leg over the bar. "Thanks, man. Sure means a lot."

Dara went and hugged Lance. Didn't say a word, then stepped back. The last track on the B side of Mungo Jerry was playing through the open window. It was time to go.

Roy Scheider was back in his picture window across the street, his hand inside the robe. Lance thinking somebody ought to go bang on the guy's door, give him some shit. But hell, as of Monday, this wasn't his jurisdiction anymore.

ACKNOWLEDGMENTS

THANK YOU to Jack David and the great team at ECW Press, my fabulous editor Emily Schultz, copy editor Peter Norman, designer David Gee for another great cover, and my son, Alexander, for all his love and support and for giving this book that important first read.

At ECW Press, we want you to enjoy this book in whatever format you like, whenever you like. Leave your print book at home and take the eBook to go! Purchase the print edition and receive the eBook free. Just send an email to ebook@ecwpress.com and include:

Get the eBook free!*
*proof of purchase required

- the book title
- the name of the store where you purchased it
- your receipt number
- your preference of file type: PDF or ePub?

A real person will respond to your email with your eBook attached. And thanks for supporting an independently owned Canadian publisher with your purchase!

Published by ECW Press
665 Gerrard Street East
Toronto, Ontario, Canada M4M 1Y2
416-694-3348 / info@ecwpress.com

Cover design and illustration: David Gee
Marijuana bud photograph © deux/Corbis
Author photo: Andrea Kalteis

This is a work of fiction. Names, characters, places, and incidents either are the product of the author's imagination or are used fictitiously, and any resemblance to actual persons, living or dead, business establishments, events, or locales is entirely coincidental.

LIBRARY AND ARCHIVES CANADA CATALOGUING IN PUBLICATION

Kalteis, Dietrich, author
The deadbeat club / written by Dietrich Kalteis.

Issued in print and electronic formats.
ISBN 978-1-77041-152-4
also issued as: 978-1-77090-748-5 (pdf);
978-1-77090-749-2 (epub)

I. Title.

PS8621.A474D43 2015   C813'.6
C2015-902793-4   C2015-902794-2

The publication of *The Deadbeat Club* has been generously supported by the Canada Council for the Arts which last year invested $153 million to bring the arts to Canadians throughout the country, and by the Government of Canada through the Canada Book Fund. *Nous remercions le Conseil des arts du Canada de son soutien. L'an dernier, le Conseil a investi 153 millions de dollars pour mettre de l'art dans la vie des Canadiennes et des Canadiens de tout le pays. Ce livre est financé en partie par le gouvernement du Canada.* We also acknowledge the Ontario Arts Council (OAC), an agency of the Government of Ontario, which last year funded 1,709 individual artists and 1,078 organizations in 204 communities across Ontario, for a total of $52.1 million, and the contribution of the Government of Ontario through the Ontario Book Publishing Tax Credit and the Ontario Media Development Corporation.

Ontario — Ontario Media Development Corporation

ONTARIO ARTS COUNCIL / CONSEIL DES ARTS DE L'ONTARIO — an Ontario government agency / un organisme du gouvernement de l'Ontario

FSC — **MIX** Paper from responsible sources — FSC® C016245

Canada Council for the Arts / Conseil des Arts du Canada

Canada

PRINTED AND BOUND IN CANADA   PRINTING: FRIESENS 1 2 3 4 5